THE STANFORTH SECRETS

"Just as everyone said. This spot can't be observed from the house."

"True," said Chloe. "Is that of significance?"

He looked down at her with a smile that melted her bones. "It depends on how discreet you want to be," he said. Even his voice seemed to stroke her skin and set it quivering.

"Why?" she whispered, though she knew, and was frantically trying to decide what to do about it.

For answer, he took her in his arms and pulled her down to sit on the smooth grass. One arm around her, he cradled her face with his other hand. Reason lost. She stayed quiescent as his lips came to hers.

Her lips opened like a flower to the sun. It felt, thought Chloe, nothing like a first kiss. It felt as if they had been lovers all their lives.

Other Regency Romances from Avon Books

By Kasey Michaels
THE DUBIOUS MISS DALRYMPLE

By Loretta Chase
THE ENGLISH WITCH
ISABELLA
KNAVES' WAGER
THE VISCOUNT VAGABOND

Coming Soon

THE STOLEN BRIDE
by Jo Beverley

THE CHAOTIC MISS CRISPINO
by Kasey Michaels

THE SANDALWOOD PRINCESS
by Loretta Chase

THE STANFORTH SECRETS

JO BEVERLEY

AVON BOOKS ◆ NEW YORK

All the characters and events portrayed in this story are fictitious.

AVON BOOKS
A division of
The Hearst Corporation
1350 Avenue of the Americas
New York, New York 10019

First Avon Books Printing: September 1991

Writing is a solitary profession, but I have always found my fellow writers to be immensely supportive. I thank them all and wish to single out four here—

Audrey Jessup and Liz Palmer, my fellow regency writers, who make sure I stay genteel;
Vicki Cameron, who snipped any loose threads in my mystery plot;
Linda La Prade who put fire into my French.

Thank you.

FRANK HALLIWELL, undergroom at Delamere Hall in the county of Lancashire, rode into the stables and swung off his sturdy cob. He was a tall young man with unruly, straw-coloured hair and dimples when he smiled. He didn't smile often these days, however.

The stable boy took the horse away, and Frank went up to the house with the postbag he had collected from the village of Heysham. He entered the large greystone house by the kitchen door, wiping his boots carefully before stepping on Mrs. Pickering's tiled floor, even though that lady had far too soft a spot for a handsome lad to scold.

"Morning to you, Frank. Here, have an Eccles cake. Fresh and warm, just for you."

The cook was a buxom woman, with the smooth skin of a Lancashire lass despite her forty-odd years. She gave him a buss to flavour the pastry.

A slight smile eased the young man's expression. "Go on with you, Mrs. P. It's not me that pays the wages."

"No," said a wiry young footman sitting at the table polishing silver. He glanced at the groom with a smirk. "But it's in the family, so to speak."

An ugly scowl banished the humour from Frank's face, and it looked as if he would take a swipe at the footman. Instead, Frank dumped the leather postbag on top of the other man's work and stamped out.

"What did you have to say a thing like that for?" asked Mrs. Pickering.

As he removed his cuff-protectors and washed his hands, Matthew Riggles only said, "I have my reasons."

The cook turned back to her pastry-rolling, shaking her head. Troubled times at Delamere, troubled times. She'd come to work at the Hall as a girl, when the first viscount—and he'd only been a baronet then—had been newly married to a woman pretty as a picture and happy as a lark. Miss Sophronia Stacey, she had been, Toast of London. They'd called her Sweet Sophy.

A duke had wanted to marry her, or so it was said, but she'd chosen Sir Henry. There'd never been a sign she'd regretted it. Lady Delamere seemed as happy in this simple northern spot as travelling about Europe with her diplomat husband; happy to be anywhere as long as she was with her darling Henry.

See what times they were come to now, with the first viscount eight years in his grave, his sweet lady's wits gone wandering, and his two successors dead within one year.

Stirred to philosophy by her thoughts, Mrs. Pickering said to the footman, "Life's too short for quarrels, lad."

"Life's too short to let others spoil it," he retorted.

With that, he shrugged into his braided jacket, picked up the postbag, and went in search of the person regarded by all as the mistress of Delamere Hall.

He found her, as he expected, in the Sea Room, the saloon with three large windows overlooking Morecambe Bay.

Chloe, Lady Stanforth, a widow at only twenty-three, thanked Matthew with her usual warm smile, but did not immediately investigate the contents of the bag. Instead, she let her gaze return to the grassy headland outside the large windows and the Irish Sea beyond.

She had been raised in Leicestershire and educated in Gloucestershire. Before her elopement from the schoolroom she had never seen the sea. When her late husband, Stephen, had brought her to his home, the vista of Morecambe Bay, backed by the distant hills of the Furness Peninsular and the Lake District, had stunned her. Delamere Hall—a simple, modest manor—sat square and strong on the cliffs above the sandy bay, just outside the ancient village of Heysham. From many of its windows the tableau could be enjoyed through the seasons, and that was one of Chloe's greatest pleasures.

Changing moment by moment as the tide swept in to fill the bay or retreated to leave it as mud; as the distant shore shone clear in sunlight, fields and houses distinct, or became shrouded in mist so she could imagine the sea to go undisturbed all the way to America; as the vault of sky formed an arch of pure cerulean blue, or filled dramatically with the tumbling clouds of an approaching storm; this vista always enchanted.

Just now the tide was receding, and flocks of birds called as they picked over the exposed marine life. The blue October sky reflected in the deeper channels of water ruffling under a brisk autumn breeze. In pleasant weather Chloe often pulled on a pair of sturdy boots and walked far out across the pebbles and mud, investigating the tidal pools. This cool day, however, did not tempt her.

An observer would have found Chloe as entrancing a sight as the view beyond the windows, for she was that rarest of creatures, a natural beauty. Of medium height, her form was slender, but with nothing of frailty about it since she was by nature active. The only part of her which suggested weakness was her long neck, which appeared almost too delicate to hold her fine-boned head and mass of dark curls. She was even gifted with natural colour—shapely lips of a deep pink and a fine-grained skin which showed the roses in her healthy cheeks. The penalty, of course, was that embarrassment could not be concealed, but Chloe Stanforth could not be easily discomfited.

The most interestingly uncoloured part of Chloe's features was her eyes—a clear silver grey, they were saved from insipidity by a dark outer edge to the irises and thick dark lashes. They shone brilliantly whenever she was in spirits, which was often, and so were commonly spoken of as her finest feature.

These days, however, Chloe was not often in spirits. She

had been cooped up at Delamere since the summer of 1809, when she had come north for her annual stay. In September of that year she had been preparing for a return to her husband and the social life of the south, when she had received news of Stephen's death in a carriage accident. She remained at Delamere for her year of mourning, so recently over. Now, despite the appeal of the scenery, she wanted to escape and build a new life for herself. She didn't feel able to leave, however, until the new Lord Stanforth arrived to take responsibility for the Hall and all its dependents.

Justin Delamere, Stephen's cousin . . .

Sliding away from thought of Justin, Chloe turned her attention to the postbag and unfastened the clasp. At that moment the door opened, and an ancient lady tapped her way into the room with the help of a sturdy cane.

"Grandmama," Chloe smiled as she rose to escort the lady to her favourite straight-backed chair near the fire. "I might have guessed the postbag would bring you hot-foot."

"Hot-foot!" snorted the Dowager Duchess of Tyne as she eased her body into a position of comfort. "It's many a day since I've been even *warm*-foot, my dear. But I confess I do like to read my letters."

"And you always have some," remarked Chloe. "What devoted correspondents you have, Grandmama."

"The secret is to keep writing, gel. Then they must write back. Well. Open it up and see what we have."

Chloe obediently pulled out the handful of letters and began to sort through them in search of something for the impatient old lady. "There," she said at last. "And the frank suggests it's from Lady Mackering in Bristol."

"Saucy chit," said the Duchess as she snatched her letter.

"Lady Mackering?" queried Chloe with a twinkle. "Why, I would have thought her at least sixty."

The Dowager cackled. "Seventy-seven. She's a year older than I. What airs and grace she put on about that year when we were girls!" She broke the seal and began to read greedily.

Chloe sorted the remaining post more methodically. Three

missives were clearly accounts and she placed them to one side. One was addressed to Lord Stanforth, and this too she put apart. There had been three Lord Stanforths within the space of one year, and the current viscount was still abroad with his regiment. Anyone unaware of the confusion could hardly have urgent news to impart. The remainder of the post presented more of a problem. Chloe sighed.

Her grandmother looked up. "Are you maundering again, Chloe? Why don't you just open them all?"

Chloe shrugged. "It is so distasteful to be opening other ladies' correspondence. I don't know why people cannot learn to address them correctly. See, here is a letter from my old friend Emily Grantwich—we were at Miss Mallory's together, you know. It is clearly and correctly addressed to Chloe, Lady Stanforth. Here is one simply addressed to Lady Stanforth. You know Belinda is hurt whenever I open her letters, but it does look as if it's from Herr van Maes. He is doubtless hoping to wheedle a few more invitations to dine at the Hall."

"Let him wheedle," said the Duchess. "He springs for handsome gifts, I'll give him that."

Both ladies looked at the fine set of oil paintings which the Dutch antiquarian had presented to Chloe last Christmas. The four small landscapes represented the seasons with pictures of villagers around an apple tree.

"Yes," said Chloe. "Almost too handsome. I admire the pictures but they seem excessive payment for a few quiet dinners."

"Perhaps he was attempting an investment," said the Duchess with a smile. "It wouldn't be strange if he had an eye to more than your dinners, gel."

Chloe shook her head, accustomed to her grandmother's naughty tongue. "I never saw any sign of it. Anything younger than a half a millennium holds no interest for him at all. In fact, he probably just wanted to dispose of such modern pictures. Now, what should I do with these letters?"

"You could let Belinda handle all the business," said

the Duchess unsympathetically. "As the widow of the most recent viscount, it's her responsibility."

"Do you really think so?" said Chloe with a slight frown. "I am not sure . . ."

"God's sake, gel. Don't take me seriously! It's bad enough having that farmer's daughter around the place, ingratiating herself. She wouldn't know how to run a hedge-tavern, never mind a place like Delamere."

Chloe had to fight back a giggle. Daughter, wife, and mother of dukes, the Duchess had a low opinion of the local girl married by Stephen's successor, his Uncle George.

"Really, Grandmama, how can you say such things? Be fair. Belinda was educated at a respectable seminary. She does not disgrace herself, and I believe she genuinely likes to help. She's not without sense, you know, and if necessary she could learn to manage the Hall. With George dead, however, we all know there's no point. If her child had been a boy and inherited the title, I would have trained her, but with a daughter she will not reign here. As soon as Justin arrives he will doubtless marry, and then we will all be free of the burden."

"Ha," said the Duchess. "The sooner the better. Can't wait to see you upon the Town again. There won't be a man in London with his wits left."

"Grandmama!" said Chloe, blushing very prettily. "Among all the latest blossoms?"

"I haven't seen one to match you in a decade, my dear. You know I never condemned you for eloping from the schoolroom, but you deprived me of an anticipated delight—seeing you take Society by storm. I can't say it won't be better this way, though. You were a pretty little thing at seventeen, but your beauty has grown stronger over the past six years. Your character has matured too."

"Goodness, you'll give me an altogether too exalted opinion of myself. Besides," added Chloe thoughtfully, "I am not entirely sure I want to marry again."

"You trying to tell me you're still grief-stricken?" asked the Duchess skeptically.

Chloe's hands fluttered as if she would protest. "Oh, Grandmama, I did grieve for Stephen. Truly I did. But it was *for* him. He was so young and he loved life. I confess, though, I have not missed him so very much. We had grown apart. He continued to love a rackety sort of life which ceased to appeal to me once the novelty had worn off. And when we were together he was so infuriating. I could never depend on him for anything. We would make plans, then some idea would pop into his head and he would forget all about it. He was . . ."

"A charming, feckless half-wit," supplied the old lady bluntly. "So why don't you want to marry again?"

Chloe sighed. The Duchess might be nearly eighty but her wits were needle-sharp and there was no chance of deflecting her. "Stephen at least had sense enough to arrange matters so I am comfortably situated and have no need to marry. Having been rash the first time, I am determined to be cautious the second. If I meet a man who is sensible and dependable, I will consider remarriage."

The Duchess pulled a face at this, but beyond a "humph" she made no comment and returned to her letter. A few moments later an exclamation distracted her again.

"At last," said Chloe, looking up from a letter. "Grandmama. It's from Justin. He must be in England."

The new Lord Stanforth had been, until his succession, a major with the dragoons in Spain. Upon the untimely death of Stephen, the first viscount's son, the title had passed to George Delamere, his uncle. As George was childless, Justin, son of the first viscount's third brother, had been the heir presumptive. George, however, had promptly scandalised the County by marrying the young daughter of a local farmer, Belinda Massinger. Everyone had expected him to produce an heir of his own.

Perhaps this intent had been unwise in a man of his years and girth, for George only lived as Lord Stanforth for six months before succumbing to a seizure. That had been long enough, however, to get Belinda in the family way. The title of Lord Stanforth had been in abeyance from February until August, while everyone waited to see whether Belinda would give birth to the next viscount or to a daughter. The twenty-third of August 1810 had seen the arrival of little Dorinda—an outcome which caused considerable relief throughout the area. Since then the Hall had awaited the arrival of its new master.

Chloe broke the seal and unfolded the crisp sheet. She quickly scanned the strong, clear script. "He writes from London. He means to stay there, at Brookes, for a few days to take care of business and then come up. We can expect him any day, I suppose. What a relief it will be to turn this whole *ménage* over to him and escape."

Chloe put the letter down and gazed into the flames of the fire. "I love Delamere, Grandmama, but it just hasn't been the same this last year. It has been a house of mourning, of course," she mused, "but it is more than that. Things just haven't seemed right. . . . I will be glad to be away." She looked up, smiling, her fine eyes twinkling mischievously. "Perhaps I will go adventuring—Italy, Turkey, Africa. Would you come with me, Grandmama?"

"I wish my old bones were up to it, my dear," said the Duchess with a grin. Then she added, "You'll not find your sobersides-suitor by jaunting around the world."

"Oh," said Chloe, arrested. "I suppose I won't. I don't suppose I should enjoy such an existence anyway. It would be just the sort of thing Stephen would have done."

"Not if organized properly. I don't know what maggot you've got in your head to keep trying to tell the world you're a starchy one, Chloe. You're too much like me."

Chloe did not meet the shrewd gaze of the Duchess. "I'm delighted to be like you, Grandmama, and I do not wish to seem starchy, exactly. Surely, though, it does me no discredit to be seen as mature and responsible."

"None at all," said the old lady with a grin, "as long as you do not give up climbing trees."

Chloe turned red and looked at her grandmother in astonishment. "I . . . I . . ."

"That eyeglass you gave me has a sight more uses than

looking at the hills and watching shrimp boats. I saw you up that appletree not many weeks past.''

Chloe struggled for words. Eventually, she said, ''It was a great piece of foolishness. I caused a bad tear in my fawn muslin.''

''It's foolishness to be trying to make yourself into what you're not. Still worried about what the world says of you?''

Chloe looked down at the letter in her hands. ''I have grown accustomed. I will always be the scandalous Chloe Ashby, won't I? It does seem unfair, though, to have to live my life with a youthful indiscretion around my neck.''

''But you have the notion,'' suggested the Duchess shrewdly, ''that a respectable husband will wipe out the memory of your elopement?''

Chloe refused to admit it, at least openly. ''Oh, no. That is not my intent. I have learned to live with my mistakes. But, despite any natural tendencies you perceive in me, Grandmama, I have a positive thirst for dependability in a spouse. I will settle for nothing less.''

''Just as long as you don't confuse tedium with reliability, gel. Tell you one thing about dependable husbands, they tend to be around a lot. You wouldn't know what that was like—I doubt Stephen was by the fireside one night in a hundred—but if you have some earnest Ernest prosing on at you night after night, year after year, you'll soon find fecklessness an appealing quality.'' The old lady noted her words had gone home. ''Perhaps you'd better wait until you meet the new Lord Stanforth again before you make any plans,'' she added slyly.

''Justin?'' queried Chloe blankly. ''Why? Grandmama!'' she said in amazement. ''Marry another Dashing Delamere? Justin and Stephen were like two peas in a pod. I'll have you know Justin was the mastermind behind my elopement. The things he and Stephen used to get up to . . . Oh no. Another Delamere is *not* my idea of a comfortable husband at all.''

2

THE DRIZZLING DAMP of London in October suited his mood exactly, thought Justin Delamere, as he hurried to his appointment. It wasn't only the damp, which crept into his bones after years on the Peninsula, but there'd been a chill in his heart for the last year. He'd thought it was the war, and that selling out would ease the depression. He'd looked forward to picking up old friendships and rediscovering the *joie de vivre* of the old days. But laughing and joking, and bearing his end of a witty conversation, was more of a strain than he would ever have believed possible.

Of course it might have been different if Stephen had been here to greet him, instead of cold in his grave for over a year. How strange that after years of blood and death in one battle after another, it was Stephen's death back here in England, a simple carriage accident, which had struck the hardest.

He realised he had passed the Grosvenor Square mansion which was his destination and retraced his steps. As he did so, he assumed the lighthearted manner which was his cloak, his disguise. Everyone loved a soldier, but no one wanted a sad one. After all, he was a Dashing Delamere, wasn't he? He and his cousin Stephen had earned the nickname back in '04. Well-heeled and unrestrained, they had set Society on its ear, culminating in that elopement.

The young viscount shook his head as he mounted the

broad steps up to the gleaming mahogany double doors. He shuddered now at the things they had done six years ago.

A sharp rap on the knocker and the door was swung open by the footman. Justin gave up his drizzle-damp greatcoat, glanced in a huge wall mirror, and decided he'd pass muster. Six years of army discipline are not wiped away in a fortnight, no matter how many documents one signs. It felt strange to be out of uniform, but at least he'd been able to chivvy Weston into producing some clothes in a hurry. He was pleased by his fashionable dark blue jacket with large brass buttons, and the new-style pantaloons in a soft fawn which disappeared into gleaming Hessians. He hadn't been able to do anything, however, about his sun-darkened skin, which marked him out among the pale-faces of Society. He had refused to do more with his brown curls than have them trimmed.

He shrugged. Whatever had caused this summons to the house of the Secretary of State for War, his sartorial magnificence or lack of it was unlikely to be of importance.

He was expected and found himself swiftly in the presence of Lord Liverpool. With shock, he recognised the other man in the room as His Royal Highness, the Duke of York, Commander in Chief of the British Army until the recent scandal—the Duke's mistress, Mary Anne Clarke, had been caught dealing in commissions and promotions. After a parliamentary enquiry, the Duke had been forced to give up his post, much to the disgust of the serving soldiers who still regarded him as a true army man. He was a good soldier.

Justin addressed a profound bow to the Duke.

"No need for formality," said the portly man gruffly. "Here incognito, don't you know. Sit down, Stanforth. Sit down."

Justin took the seat indicated, wondering what on earth was happening to bring him to the notice of royalty. He had been sufficiently surprised to be summoned to speak with Lord Liverpool.

That gentleman addressed him. "You are doubtless wondering what is the purpose of this meeting, Stanforth. As you can see, it is of considerable importance. Though we are always sorry to lose a good officer, particularly at a time such as now when events in Portugal are coming to a head, I have to say that if you hadn't sold out on inheriting your uncle's title, you would have been ordered to do so. In fact, if the dunderheads who have been handling this matter had realised you were the heir presumptive, you'd have been ordered home before now."

"This matter, Sir?" queried Justin blankly.

Instead of answering, the Earl rose to serve wine. It was obviously not a business to be discussed before servants.

Justin searched his mind for an explanation. He had received a few letters from Chloe, his Cousin Stephen's widow, and correspondence from the family man-of-business, and yesterday he had spent the morning with the Delameres' London agent. None had indicated anything out of the ordinary.

Seated again, Lord Liverpool crossed his legs and spoke. "It is a somewhat complex matter, Stanforth. Over a year ago—in August of last year to be precise—patient work by an agent in Paris gained him access to a list of French spies residing in England, information which could surely save thousands of lives. The documents, the codes, and a letter were all ingeniously disguised and sent on their various ways. The codes, the letter, and one set of documents arrived in England by tortuous routes. They were each concealed in wax fruits—not hollow ones but solid with the papers a part of the whole. The letter, torn in pieces, had been made into cherries for a lady's hat. The others were an apple and a pear, much like this one."

He passed over a seemingly real pear, yellowing with ripeness. Justin handled it, marvelling at the skill with which it was made. Unlike many such pieces made solely for ornament, the weight and the texture of the skin were right. When he raised it to his nose, however, there was no aroma.

He wondered where the connection to himself was to be found, but his years in the army had taught him to wait for his commanders to come to the point.

He returned the artificial fruit to Lord Liverpool, who then continued. "One piece of the message never arrived, the vital second part of the list of names. From the letter we know the list had been sent by a highly trusted courier who goes by the name of d'Estrelles, a man entitled, in fact, to a more eminent name which was lost, along with large estates, during the Revolution. The letter itself is incomplete, one of the cherries having become dislodged, but it was clear d'Estrelles was to make his way via Bordeaux and Ireland. . . ."

Now Justin found himself in possession of the letter, carefully pasted onto a piece of board. It was composed of seven ragged-edged rectangles with one rectangle missing three-quarters down the right-hand side. The letter was in French and outlined the nature of the three packages, their disguises and proposed routes. It stressed that all the couriers had complete discretion in altering their itineraries. Fortunately, the missing rectangle did not greatly hinder the understanding of the message. The package sent via Bordeaux was *au forme de la pomme*—disguised as an apple. At that point the line ended in a jagged tear.

Amazing luck. One word sooner and they would never have known the disguise used.

"Was d'Estrelles caught?" Justin asked.

"We do not know," said the Earl. "The dispatch of the documents was discovered sooner than expected, and the ports were under surveillance. All the couriers had a great deal of trouble. We do know d'Estrelles made it from Bordeaux to Cork, but with a French warship at his heels. We can only conjecture the rest. He must have decided his chances of making it to England with his package were slight, so he decided on a bold stroke. He set himself up as a decoy, hired a small fishing boat to take him to Wales, and slipped anchor one night. He sent the package another way. He gave it to a sailor, presumably feeling he could trust the man, with instructions to go north to Dublin and take ship there. The man was told to deliver the package to Lord Stanforth at Heysham."

"Stephen?" queried Justin in amazement.

"No. Unfortunately d'Estrelles had been heavily involved in undercover work on the continent for years. He was sadly out of touch. He was sending the package to the first viscount, Stephen's father, who, as you know, had been involved in a number of matters of foreign affairs. He was a negotiator of the Peace of Amiens in '02 and d'Estrelles had been there, in a less official capacity. They doubtless became acquainted. In extremis, d'Estrelles would have remembered that Delamere Hall is situated on the coast, a short hop across the Irish Sea."

"Remember the first viscount. Remarkable man," stated the Duke. "He would have handled the matter right."

"Assuredly, Sir," responded Lord Liverpool.

"The papers were given to Stephen?" hazarded Justin with a puzzled frown.

"No," said the Earl bitterly. "He, we can be sure, was the one person who could not have been given them. We don't know to whom they were passed by the sailor, nor have they ever been seen."

"Some damned traitor destroyed them," barked the Duke with disgust.

"That is possible, Sir," said Lord Liverpool. "On the other hand, we have clear evidence that the French are still searching for them. We intercepted a message recently which fiercely enjoined an agent here in London to discover the papers and destroy them, for his own safety as well as the safety of others. Unfortunately, we could not discover for whom that directive was intended, though we destroyed yet another of their message-lines." He slammed his hand down on the arm of his chair. "We need that list! Even in my own office I cannot be sure who is to be trusted. The part of the list we received revealed some traitors we had never expected. . . ."

The Earl collected himself. "We must do everything in our power to gain those papers if they still exist. The chance is small, but we must try. Poor, brave d'Estrelles never made it to Wales. We can only assume the French blew him out of the water and thought the message had gone to the deep with him. . . ."

"Brave man, brave man," muttered the Duke.

"Brave indeed, and his ruse was successful. The sailor, by name of Samuel Wright, made his way unhindered to Dublin, and then took ship to the port of Lancaster, disembarking at Sunderland Point, close by to Heysham, as you doubtless know. Once in the village—he is well remembered there, for they don't get many strangers—he discovered Lord Stanforth was in London and sent off a message. He made no secret of the fact that he had a package for the viscount and settled down peacefully to wait, ambling around the village, talking to the fishermen. We can only deduce his instruction was to give his package to no one but the viscount, and to wait patiently for him to come."

"You say 'We can only deduce'," said Justin. "Why can Mr. Wright not speak for himself?"

"He is dead," said the Earl baldly. "Drowned in Morecambe Bay."

Two men dead, thought Justin with a chill. No, more. That ill-fated fishing boat used by d'Estrelles must have had a crew. "If a message was sent to Lord Stanforth, it must have gone to Stephen."

"Yes," said the Earl in a voice frosted with disapproval. Justin felt resigned. What had poor Stephen done? "The letter arrived at your cousin's house in Clarges Street. The sailor's message so bewildered him," he added icily, "that he showed it around all over London, asking what people made of it!"

There was a growl from the royal personage, and Justin struggled to keep a straight face. It wasn't funny, but it was so typical of Stephen.

"One of my young men, Cardew Holmes, happened to

hear of it and put two and two together. He nabbed your cousin and brought him to me. I sent the viscount to Lancashire to collect the message. Holmes was sent with him to keep him in order.'' There was a touch of disbelief in Lord Liverpool's voice as he commented, ''It took Holmes a whole twenty-four hours to persuade the young man to treat the matter with urgency—''

''Should have told me,'' growled the Duke. ''I'd have damned well put a squib up his backside!''

''I'm sure you would have, Sir. It occurred to none of us that he would not immediately perceive the importance . . .'' He broke off and shrugged. ''When he was brought to understand the situation, however, Lord Stanforth did set off with great enthusiasm. According to Holmes it was . . .''

''Hair-raising,'' supplied Justin with a sigh. ''Stephen always did drive faster than his skill allowed, and he would have loved the excuse of urgency. That was when . . .''

''That was when he was killed, yes. September second. Holmes merely suffered a broken leg, but your cousin broke his neck.'' A slight inclination of the head indicated sympathy not apparent in his voice.

A mutter from the royal Duke might have been ''Good riddance.'' Justin decided he really couldn't plant a facer on the son of the king just to defend poor Stephen's memory.

''What happened to the message?'' he asked. ''Presumably you sent someone else quam celerimae.''

''Of course we did. By this time, however, almost a week had gone by since your cousin had received the letter. The day before my man got there, the sailor paid his tab at the inn and left. The next day his body was washed up on the sands. The innkeeper said he'd earlier gone up to the Hall, but nobody there admits to having seen him.''

''So you think he passed his package on. To someone at the Hall? Who?''

Lord Liverpool regarded his thin fingers. ''It is hard, of course, to imagine anyone at Delamere Hall being in league with the French. . . .''

"Impossible, I would have thought," said Justin firmly. "Who was there at the time?"

"Lord Stanforth's—I mean Stephen's, of course—mother, the Dowager Lady Stanforth. She is something of an invalid, I am told, and does not go about very much."

"Her wits are wandering," said Justin bluntly, "and she never leaves the house unaccompanied."

Lord Liverpool gave a little cough. "Quite. Your uncle Mr. George Delamere was there. Upon your cousin's death, of course, he became Viscount Stanforth, so the sailor might have given him the package, except that, by the time he succeeded to the title, Mr. Wright was already dead. In addition, he is . . . er . . . generally held not to be the sort to become involved with intrigues."

"He was one of the stupidest men I've ever met," said Justin uncompromisingly. "Result of a childhood brain fever. It's to be hoped the sailor didn't give his precious cargo to him. Or is that the problem?"

"Would that we knew," said Lord Liverpool bitterly. "When my man got to the Hall, George Delamere denied any knowledge of the sailor or his business and flew into a rage if pressed. Everyone we have asked is in agreement that George Delamere could never have been a French agent, and what other reason could he have had for denying receipt of the package?"

Justin thought his Uncle George had never needed reasons for his strange starts, but couldn't imagine why he would deny receipt of the package. "What of the staff, then?" he asked.

The Earl shrugged. "The lower orders can be bought, as we all know, but all the staff at Delamere have lived there forever. Some families go back to the Domesday Book. As there was no plan to send the documents there, it is scarcely believable that one of the staff suddenly decided to become a traitor. Also, it is unlikely that Samuel Wright would have passed his package on to a servant."

"Perhaps then, he was persuaded to give his package to another local worthy. The parson perhaps, or the justice?"

"The Reverend Sotherby was absent all during this time. The justice is Sir Cedric Troughton, whose land runs alongside yours. He is a man of the old style, who lives on his land. Lancaster is as far as he travels. It is very difficult to imagine a reason for him to deal with the French."

"It seems to me you are out of suspects entirely," said Justin.

Lord Liverpool considered his long fingers. "There was one other inhabitant of the Hall. Your cousin's widow, Chloe, Lady Stanforth."

Justin looked up suddenly. "You suspect *Chloe?*" Astonishment was succeeded by anger. Beautiful, enchanting Chloe. It was bad enough what he and Stephen had done to her reputation six years ago, but this . . .

Lord Liverpool pursed his lips. "Suspect is a trifle strong, Stanforth, but there is, as you point out, a shortage of candidates. Chloe Stanforth was the only person in residence of Delamere Hall that night who had her wits about her. With her history of . . ."

Justin sat tight-lipped and refused, this time, to offer derogatory details about his family.

Royalty had no such qualms. "Eloped from the schoolroom at seventeen. Led a damned rackety existence with your cousin, jollying up with the scaff and raff. Who knows what bad influence she might be under?"

Justin decided again, with much more regret, that he couldn't bloody the man's nose, but that didn't mean he would allow Chloe to be abused.

"Chloe might be unconventional, Your Highness," he said firmly, "but, with respect, she's intelligent and loyal. She would never turn traitor. What possible motive could she have, Sir?"

"Lover," spat out the Duke. "Women'll do anything for a certain type of man."

Justin told himself bitterness over the behaviour of his pretty mistress was doubtless colouring the Duke's point of view.

Lord Liverpool cut in before Justin could voice the protest on his lips. "Remember, Stanforth, you haven't seen the young woman for three or four years. Ladies are flighty creatures, and I gather her marriage was not entirely happy. We do not suspect evil intent, but who knows into what foolishness she may have been led? Whoever is involved, we urgently need to gain possession of that list if it still exists."

Her marriage was not entirely happy. The marriage he had largely brought about. . . .

Justin dragged his mind back to the matter in hand, thought of the growing count of deaths in this affair, and frowned. "Do you think they are in danger at the Hall, Sir?"

"It is to be hoped not," said Lord Liverpool. "We have no sign of activity there, but it is hard to believe some Napoleonic agent didn't overhear your cousin blabbing about his letter. This is one reason we have not instigated a more open search of the area. After all, if the French become sure the package is in the Hall, they could well blow up the place, and the list would be lost forever."

And a score of good people, thought Justin, chilled.

"Smugglers!" snorted the Duke of York. "In Lancashire!"

Justin was bewildered and Lord Liverpool looked put out. "We sent a carefully selected troop of the Fifth Light into Heysham," he explained, "claiming rumour of smuggling. They conducted a pretty thorough search of the cottages and the area in general."

Justin wondered what the locals had thought of that. It was true there was a little contraband brought over from Ireland, but not enough trade to warrant a full-scale search. He supposed they all muttered about crazy southerners and went on with their business.

"What of the house?" he asked. "Has that been searched?"

If anything, Lord Liverpool looked even more uncomfortable. "We have introduced someone into the house who has had no success. Now you will be in an excellent position to take on the matter."

"But it's over a year ago, Sir. The trail will be stone cold."

"Do you think we don't know that? As long as your uncle was Lord Stanforth, however, we saw no benefit in enlisting *his* aid. Then, when he died and the succession was in doubt, there was no one to look to. As I said, we have done what we could. The local people there are a secretive lot. You may be able to find out more."

"Chloe would have been able to sort this out months ago," said Justin bluntly. "The estate manager says the local people adore her."

Lord Liverpool cleared his throat. "We really didn't think we could take that risk, Stanforth, and I believe it would be wiser to keep her in the dark a little longer."

"Consider that an order, Stanforth," snapped the Royal Duke. "I understand she's a pretty little witch, but keep your wits about you. No business for a woman anyway." This was accompanied by a glare at Lord Liverpool.

"Yes, Sir," said Justin coldly. "Could I ask whom you have sent to investigate from within the house?"

The Earl cleared his throat. "We . . . er . . . could hardly send a man after your uncle died and it was a house of women," he said a little uncomfortably. "It had to be someone with a reason for staying in the house, and someone we could trust." One bony finger came up to rub his noble nose. "We sent the Dowager Duchess of Tyne."

Justin stared. "Chloe's grandmother? Good Lord, Sir. She must be eighty!"

"Not quite, I believe, and still with good health and all her wits. She has an excellent reason for being there to support her granddaughter in her bereavement, and she and her family have always been staunch supporters of the Royal family. It is sad to relate, but the taint of the Stuarts still lingers in some of our oldest families, making their allegiance not totally trustworthy."

Justin gritted his teeth as he thought of the sons of these families spilling their blood in Spain, but he kept his counsel. If he had once been as wild and impulsive as Stephen, time and the war had taught him a great deal.

"Has the Dowager discovered anything?" he asked coolly.

"No. She too rejects any idea that Chloe Stanforth might know of the message, but then the young lady is her granddaughter and they are close, I believe. She will welcome your arrival, Lord Stanforth."

Gathering that this disturbing interview was over, Justin rose. "Very well, Your Highness, My Lord." He directed a bow to each in turn. "I don't hold out much hope but I will do my best. There have been a number of deaths in this affair. I am concerned for the residents of the Hall."

He was struck by a sudden thought. "Do you think Stephen was murdered too?" he asked sharply. "And what about Uncle George?"

"Don't let your imagination run away with you, Stanforth," said Lord Liverpool. "Cardew Holmes was with your cousin. It was simply a question of reckless driving. Poor Holmes took months to get his nerve back after that ride. Your uncle died of a seizure. He was nearing fifty and a tub of lard with a young wife. He was safe in his own home when it happened, with his old friend Humphrey Macy at his side, and all the Lady Stanforths nearby. Including," he added with an edge, "the intelligent and trustworthy Chloe."

"I promise to restrain my imagination, Sir," retorted Justin. "If I may be excused, Your Highness, My Lord, I find myself anxious to get up to Delamere as soon as possible."

"Of course, of course," said the Duke of York casually. "Glad to see you keen on the job, Stanforth. Vitally important to the nation. Keep us posted, eh? We need those lists. Can't let the Frogs have 'em back."

Justin made two more formal bows and escaped.

If it hadn't been for the presence of two of the most important men in the kingdom he would have dismissed the whole thing as a joke, or at least an insane alarm. There'd been enough examples of botched orders and incompetence in the army to teach a man to look at information many times over but . . .

He made his way quickly to Brookes, where he was staying, and sent orders for his curricle to be ready early the next day. He'd drive himself up to Lancashire, travelling light and leaving his man and baggage to follow along more slowly. Justin was looking forward to savouring the fertile English countryside again, even if in the foggy damp. His return to Delamere, however, was not going to be quite as he had expected. Murder, espionage . . .

He was sitting by the leaping fire in the lounge, sipping a glass of Madeira and turning over the strange situation in his mind, when a clear voice broke into his consciousness.

"God save the nation! A damned Delamere's turned up."

Justin turned to see a slender, beautiful young man with silky buttercup hair, mischievous clear blue eyes, and a wide smile.

"Randal?"

"Who else?" said Lord Randal Ashby, walking over to join his friend. "But what the hell? . . . Good God, I forgot," he said suddenly sober. "My dear fellow. Accept my condolences. It was a damned shame for Stephen to go off like that so young."

Justin rose and took his friend's offered hands. "I know and it hit me hard, but I've thought since he would have preferred it to old age. That could just be Peninsula thinking, though. We were always telling ourselves old age was an unpleasant prospect."

It occurred to him that was the sort of thing civilians didn't like to hear, but there was nothing but sensitive sympathy on Lord Randal Ashby's face. Both twenty-seven, they'd been at Eton and Oxford together, and Randal had taken part in many of the mad escapades they'd indulged in six years ago—he and Stephen, Randal and Verderan, Marlowe and Sterries—all of them supposedly studying at Oxford, but spending a good deal of their time elsewhere.

Perhaps following the same train of thought, Lord Randal said, "Hal Marlowe avoided old age at Cintra didn't he, and Grantly Sterries at Corunna? I understand it was a close thing for you there too, Justin.''

The viscount nodded. ''Leg. If I hadn't taken my mother's advice and taken along my own barber-surgeon, I'd have lost it. Rees was a treasure. I lent him to all my friends. There's no real medical care, Randal. . . .'' He recollected himself and looked up with a smile. ''I'm sorry. It must be the weather. Damned dismal.''

''I'll give you damned dismal,'' retorted Lord Randal sharply, ''if you think I'm too fragile a plant to hear the truth about the war. Anyone of sense knows things are bad at times. I tell you, though, I'd have been there alongside you if my father would allow it.''

Justin nodded understandingly. He knew all about the Duke of Tyne's poor health, his obsession with the succession, and Randal's older brother's disinclination to marry. ''Chelmly'll have to marry one day,'' Justin assured his friend.

''By then the war will be over,'' said Lord Randal glumly, then smiled apologetically. ''I'm sorry, Justin, but I hate wasting time here when I could be doing something.''

''I understand, and it is the most . . . I can't really describe it. Ordinary life seems very dull by comparison. Safer, more comfortable, but dull. I tell you though, Randal, and you're likely to be the only one I ever tell, even if I hadn't inherited Delamere and a pile of problems, I'd have sold out anyway. I'd just seen one too many gutted horse, one too many severed limb, one too many corpse.''

''You'd done your part,'' said Randal, meeting the other man's brown eyes. ''And what's this about problems? Is the estate encumbered?''

Justin realised he wasn't sure how much he could reveal. Probably nothing, even though he'd trust Randal with his life and, as a grandson of the Dowager Duchess of Tyne, he was perhaps officially approved. But then, he was also a cousin of the suspect Chloe.

''No. In fact, it's in surprisingly good heart for property

which passed through both Stephen's hands and Uncle George's. It's just in a bit of a muddle. I don't know if you followed the saga?''

"Of course. Poor Stephen died in September of last year and your fat Uncle George succeeded him. Knowing George, I assume the reason he didn't fritter away the whole fortune was he only lived till February and chose to spend that time at Delamere. Must have been the charms of his bucolic beauty, Belinda.''

Justin choked on his Madeira at the tone of his friend's voice. "Have you seen her then? Chloe has mentioned her in letters, but never with a description. I assume she must be a raving beauty to have got Uncle George to marry her.''

"Well," said Randal with amusement, "I don't know about that. Henry Staines says he saw them in Lancaster at Christmas and she's an ordinary sort of girl with gingerish hair. The County were a little put out at having to entertain her, I gather, though he did admit her manners to be acceptable and her accent only slight.''

Justin looked blank. "Why the hell did Uncle George marry her, I wonder? Oh well. Love is a strange business. What about you, Randal? Cupid's arrow found you yet? If you were to get married and set up your nursery, you'd be free to rush off to the wars eventually.''

Lord Randal looked down at his glass. "Rather a long-term project, ain't it? Actually, I don't think I'm the marrying kind. What of you? You're the last of the Stanforths. You'll have to do your duty.''

"I suppose so," said Justin casually. "But not for a while. First I must go up to Delamere and see how things are fixed.''

"Tell you what, Justin. How would it be if I came with you? Town's devilish dull. Verderan killed Brightly Carstock in August, good riddance. Ver's in Ireland to let the heat die down. David became Lord Wraybourne a few months back and he's off in deep mourning, being a proper Lord and Master. Besides, Grandmama may want to return to the Towers now, and I could escort her. Chloe too, if she wanted to come.''

Justin looked up quickly. ''Chloe will be welcome to consider Delamere her home. I was of the impression your family didn't accept her.''

''No. *Her* family ain't too hot for her, my Uncle William and my horrible Aunt Susan, that is. I know the Ashbys come either starched or saucy, but they're an extreme case of the starched, and Chloe's an extreme case of the saucy, along with yours truly. Chloe and I have always been good friends. That's the only reason I didn't blow Stephen's brains out for running off with her. Anyone who got her out of that house was doing her a favour, but I won't say I didn't reconsider a few times. There was no malice in him, but he made a damned poor husband, Justin.''

The viscount swirled the last of his wine in the crystal glass. ''I know. It probably wouldn't have come to anything, Randal—his mad passion for Chloe—if I hadn't lent a hand. You knew Stephen. He would have forgotten all about it in weeks. He appeared to be madly in love though, and she was, as you say, so out of place in that house. . . .'' He sighed. ''One of the reasons I bought my commission was so I didn't have to watch what I had wrought.''

Lord Randal's eyes sharpened a little, and a smile twitched his well-shaped lips. ''Well. Chloe has turned out to be a more balanced Ashby than you might expect. I look forward to seeing her again. Am I invited?''

Justin considered. He could see no harm in taking Randal along, and no plausible reason to refuse the request. The company would be welcome, and if matters turned nasty at Delamere, Justin could imagine no one he'd rather have at his side than Lord Randal Ashby.

3

WITH A SENSE of premonition, Chloe heard the sound of wheels and hooves on the coast road behind her. She allowed herself to hope, however, that they would sweep past and be on their way to the vicarage or Troughton House, anywhere but Delamere. After all, fate could not be so cruel as to have her meet Justin again for the first time in four years when she was covered in mud. Half an hour before, a silly young horse had unceremoniously dumped her onto the damp sands of Half-Moon Bay and then taken off for the stables.

There was a clear word of command, however, and the vehicle stopped. With resignation Chloe turned to confront not one but two smart equipages with grooms already at the horses' heads and two equally smart young gentlemen laughing at her as they leapt down from their seats. Hands on hips, Chloe glared at her Cousin Randal, looking beautiful as always, and her cousin-in-law, Justin, thinner, darker, tougher-looking, but still handsome. Still heart-tuggingly like her dead husband.

"Chloe?" Justin said in surprise. More surprise than just at seeing her trudging along the road. Had she perhaps changed too?

With some notion of showing him she was no longer a hoyden, she dropped a curtsey. "Welcome home, Lord Stanforth."

His brows went up and he grinned as he bowed. "Thank you, Lady Stanforth."

This appealed to Chloe's sense of the ridiculous and she burst out laughing. "I warn you there's a plenitude of Lady Stanforths these days. Two a penny, we are." Chloe wanted to use his name. Once he'd been Justin to her, but now she felt . . . shy? Surely not.

She turned quickly to her cousin, and Randal swept her up for a hearty kiss. "You're looking very fetching, Chloe. It must be the smears of mud which are the finishing touch."

"Regulation wear in Lancashire," she remarked and rubbed her dirty gloved finger down his elegant nose. "Can one of you take me up back to the Hall?"

As she was standing by his side, it should surely have been Randal who made the offer, and yet somehow she found herself handed up into Justin's curricle. She caught a glint of familiar amusement in her cousin's bright blue eyes. What was Randal up to now?

Justin took up the reins and sent his groom to ride behind the other vehicle. "I do hope you're going to tell me how you came to take a toss, Chloe. It must be an unheard-of event."

"Very nearly," she agreed as she arranged the skirts of her ruby-red habit and took control of her agitated nerves. "But everyone gets thrown now and again. I was on a young horse and woolgathering when a seagull chose to fly at us. That is the sum of it."

"Is the horse likely to be hereabouts? Perhaps Corrigan could find it."

"Oh, Mercury will be home by now, I'm sure, the discourteous beast."

"How is everything at the Hall?" Justin asked. "I find it difficult to think of it as my home, even though I spent many happy times here as a boy."

He spoke so casually, thought Chloe. As if it wasn't four years since they had last met, since that moment . . . They had never spoken of it, that flash of awareness, and so she couldn't be certain he had felt it as much as she. She had told herself over and over it had been imagined, and yet here she was, within moments of meeting him, her senses disordered.

It would not do. She had meant every word when she said she would not bind herself again to a Dashing Delamere.

She sternly controlled her thoughts and addressed the businesslike subject. "Everything is running smoothly. Scarthwait, who was Stephen's manager, has carried on, and he is very efficient. You'll find the land in good heart."

"I was a little surprised to find how well-to-do I am. After the estate had been through Stephen's hands, and then Uncle George's, I expected to inherit nothing but debts."

"That is unfair," said Chloe sharply. "Stephen may not have been organised, but he left everything to Scarthwait. And he was not terribly expensive. He didn't gamble, you know."

"Except with his life," said Justin quietly and drew the horses up again, waving Randal to pass them and go ahead. He turned to Chloe. "My wits and manners must have both gone begging. I'm very sorry, Chloe, for speaking like that. I wrote, after I had the news, but I'll say again how sorry I was to hear of Stephen's death. It has been a year, so I suppose the first pain must have faded but . . ."

"Oh please don't, Justin," said Chloe, looking away, for he was bringing tears to her eyes. "As you say, it is so long ago now. My mourning is past, and there's no point in going over the ground again."

He covered one of her hands with his for a moment. Chloe felt the warmth of it through two gloves, a warmth which swept through her. Her breath caught. Then he clicked the horses to a walk. They drove in silence a little way.

How would he feel if he knew her hypocrisy? That the tears had come from sadness at not feeling more bereft?

"How long have you been in England, Justin?" she asked, to break the silence. It was only then she realised she had used his name twice without the heavens falling in.

"Three weeks. I wrote as soon as I reached London."

"Yes, I received it," said Chloe, summoning up a

lighter tone. "With relief and prayers to the Lord, I assure you. I cannot wait to drop the responsibility for Delamere in your lap and flee to a more comfortable place. What with the Dowager wandering the place scaring the servants, and the problem of quite how to treat Belinda, particularly when there was a chance she would be the mother of the next viscount. . . . I have been disturbed in the night by ghosts, and have had to handle a stream of tenants complaining about the sudden influx of soldiers. Some imbecile in London sent them because of rumours of smugglers hereabout. Smugglers! In Lancashire! If it wasn't for Grandmama, I think I would have gone mad."

Justin had tried to interrupt at various points in this tirade but now he only said, with a frown, "Ghosts? Delamere Hall has never been haunted to my knowledge."

"Or to mine," said Chloe, her mood lightened by having released some of her annoyance. "But there have been strange noises in the night. Disturbances to furniture and particularly to the cellars. As the chimney of my room passes down by the storage rooms, I have been awakened sometimes by noises. It isn't only I who hear them, either. I usually find Grandmama, who is a light sleeper, there ahead of me. Twice the pantries were found in disarray and," she said forcefully, "I assure you we do not have rats."

He looked sharply at her, but his voice was casual as he said, "I didn't know ghosts were interested in turnips and potatoes."

"Nor did I. This one seems mainly interested in apples. Shades of Adam and Eve?"

"I think I would be more likely to look for a dishonest servant than a spirit," he suggested. "Are any of the servants new?"

"No," said Chloe. Then added, "Well, Matthew, the footman, has not been with us long. Delamere had been without a footman for a while, since Stephen was so rarely in residence and never entertained here. Uncle George hired him. I think Matthew was recommended by George's old friend, Humphrey Macy. Macy spent a lot of time at

Delamere after George inherited. I was very grateful for it. For one thing he has a normal share of sense, and George would listen to him.''

The road had swung away from the coast, and ran now between hedges. Soon it would pass the driveway to the Hall.

"And what sort is this Matthew?" said Justin. "Honest?"

"I think so, or I would have dismissed him. He seems to have settled in here very well, and I have no reason to think he sneaks around the pantries stealing fruit. For one thing, the staff are well fed at Delamere. Now, however,'' Chloe added with satisfaction, "it is entirely your problem, thank goodness, and you will do as you think best.''

She saw his lips twitch with amusement.

Chloe felt a surprising spurt of satisfaction to have made him smile. He was too solemn for a Dashing Delamere and there were shadows in those warm brown eyes. She remembered the Justin of six years before, bubbling with light-hearted enthusiasm for life, just like Stephen. In the short time before she left to make a new life for herself, it wouldn't hurt to brighten his spirits.

Justin swung the curricle between the gates of Delamere Hall and sighed.

"It must be strange for you," Chloe said softly, "coming here like this.''

"Yes it is. I can't accept yet that Stephen is dead. He was always so full of life. But then I sometimes feel a hundred years old. At least I've had this year to accustom myself, though it must have been an awkward time here. Was George's wife distressed to give birth to a girl?"

"Belinda is not given to drama but she was disappointed, I think. As mother of the viscount, she could have ruled at Delamere. She thinks little Dorinda gives her a right to live at the Hall, and I suppose she may be correct—Oh dear.''

The last two words were caused by a figure which had just stepped out from the rhododendrons into the middle of the drive—an elderly lady in the flowing skirts of the last century. Justin reined in his horse and glanced at Chloe.

"That's your Aunt Sophronia," she said quietly. "It must be one of her bad days. Wherever is her companion?"

Justin looked at the Dowager Lady Stanforth with astonishment, and she glowered at them.

"What are you doing that is evil?" she asked fiercely.

"My God," muttered Justin.

Chloe leapt down from the carriage. "Oh dear. Why don't you drive her up to the house?"

"While you walk?" he said in consternation, and then shrugged. "If you can persuade her up here."

The elderly lady greeted Chloe with a sharp, "Hussy!" and made as if to pull away from her hands. Then she recognised her daughter-in-law and her mood changed. She happily allowed herself to be hoisted up into the curricle. Justin looked over her head at Chloe.

"I feel terrible at leaving you here."

"You feel terrible at being alone with her," she replied quietly with a grin. "Don't worry. She's harmless. And no, I am not driving your team even if they are tied. It's no distance. When you get to the Hall, they'll take care of her."

He accepted his orders and drove on.

"A very pleasant gel," said the Dowager in the best manner of a Society Lady. "Niece of the Duke of Tyne, you know."

Justin looked at her and found that, apart from her clothes, she seemed completely normal. Many elderly ladies clung to the styles of their youth, not liking the high waists and straight skirts of fashion. He was shocked, however, at the deterioration in her since he had last been at Delamere. Aunt Sophronia looked to be well over sixty and yet he doubted she had reached fifty yet. He remembered when he had first visited Delamere at age ten. Then his aunt had been a plump and pretty woman with a merry sense of humour.

"Yes, I know," he said in reply to her comment, and got no response. He remembered the lady's hearing had been failing for years.

"How are you, Aunt Sophronia?" he shouted.

"Very well, thank you," she said. "But I am your mother, Stephen. Try to remember these things. I am sure I don't know where you have been recently but you are far too brown. I have a lotion. . . ." Her voice trailed off. After a bewildered pause, she said, *"Potpourri* is quite delightful."

Justin stared at the Dowager, wondering what response to make. As the lady was looking ahead and humming a little song to herself, he decided to make none. He had to confess, however, that the thought that he was now responsible for her terrified him more than enemy fire.

They arrived in front of the house and servants came forward. As soon as someone was at the horses' heads Justin went around to assist his aunt to the ground. "I'm not Stephen," he shouted, feeling more than a little foolish, "I'm Justin."

The Dowager looked at him. "I suppose you are," she said with a frown. Then she smiled sadly. "First Stephen, then George, now you. You see," she said, with a smile which hinted at the teasing beauty of her youth, "I do know what is going on. Do you want an apple?"

Justin looked at her with close attention.

"Why?" he said loudly, wishing he could whisper as seemed more appropriate. "Do you have one for me?"

She looked at him with well-bred astonishment. "Why would I have an apple with me? I haven't the teeth for one. But Stephen was coming here to pick apples, and George kept laughing whenever anyone asked for an apple. I don't think eating apples is particularly humorous, do you? George was dicked in the nob, though, and greedy. Even the Duchess is always asking for apples. Personally, I like a grape. Remind me to give you that lotion, dear. . . ."

With a fond tap on his cheek, the Dowager Lady Stanforth allowed herself to be led off by her anxious companion, leaving Justin staring after her.

He thought about driving back to pick up Chloe but saw

she was already in sight, walking at her usual brisk pace.
She had never been a dawdler.

Chloe had been hurrying directly towards the house.
She was later than expected and there would be matters to
be handled, especially with the advent of two young men
of fashion.

When she saw Justin still standing by his carriage, however, she slowed her pace. She didn't want to speak to him
again just yet. It wasn't only her grubby habit, but the
effect he was having on her. She tried to tell herself it was
just his resemblance to Stephen, but that wasn't so strong,
not now Justin had toughened. . . . Perhaps it was simply
that she'd grown unaccustomed to having gentlemen
around. Sir Cedric Troughton from nearby Troughton
House was the only regular caller, and there was no comparison between formal Sir Cedric and Justin Delamere.

When Chloe saw Justin turn to Randal and take him
into the Hall she speeded up again but changed course to
use the conservatory door. She could make her way to her
room from there without any chance of bumping into the
new Lord Stanforth.

How strange the words "Lord Stanforth" had become.
She had always associated them with her warm-hearted,
feckless butterfly of a husband. Then they had designated
fat, greedy, sneaky Uncle George. Now they described
Justin, an enigma to her.

She shook her head at her woolgathering and hurried up
to her room. A sharp tug on the bell-rope brought Agnes,
her maid, and soon Chloe could soak her bruises in a bath
and get rid of the sand and mud. When she was clean she
surveyed her wardrobe.

She was not long out of mourning and had not yet bothered to order new gowns. Her choice was between the
somber colours of half-mourning or her old clothes. Never
having been a slave of fashion, she cheerfully selected a
pink silk gown which was fully two years out of date. It
had always been her favourite, though, and if she couldn't

dress up for the arrival of two of the most handsome men
in England, what could be a cause for celebration?

From the fashion magazines Chloe knew the styles were
becoming more elaborate than when this gown had been
made in London. Perhaps, she thought, it could be refur-
bished by the addition of some lace or beads, but for all
its simplicity she was not dissatisfied with her appearance.
Her maid had dressed her dark curls high on her head and
threaded them with pink and white ribbons. Chloe had
chosen a pearl necklace and eardrops as her only ornament
other than her wedding and betrothal rings. It was a simple
ensemble, suitable for country dining, and yet she knew,
with satisfaction, that she wouldn't be ashamed to be seen
at the most fashionable affair.

She left her room and went first into the north wing, to
the Dowager Lady Stanforth's rooms, to check on that
lady's health. By the time Stephen's mother had become a
widow in '02, she had already been failing, given to spells
of forgetfulness and anxiety. Her beloved husband's death
from cholera had been a further blow to her mental sta-
bility, one from which she had never recovered. She had
been given a companion and a suite of rooms in the north
wing, over the conservatory. There was a veranda opening
off her *boudoir,* where she could sit in the sun. The Dowager was generally content to spend her time in her rooms
with her companion Miss Forbes, inhabiting whichever
strange version of reality occurred to her each day. Chloe
hoped the poor lady had not been too upset by her afternoon's adventure.

Miss Forbes admitted Chloe. She assured her that the
Dowager was feeling well and intended to go down to dinner.

Chloe's heart sank, but she made it a practice not to
interfere with her mother-in-law unless the lady's actions
seemed hazardous. This had, after all, been the Dowager's
home far longer than it had been hers. The oldest Lady
Stanforth was smiling happily, dressed in wide-skirted
green satin.

Chloe went to kiss her on the cheek. "How are you, Mama?"

"Very well, my dear," said the Dowager brightly. "Isn't it delightful to have young men in the house again?"

"Very."

"We should have a party."

Chloe thought this was a surprisingly good idea. It would be a way to introduce Justin to the local gentry.

"Don't you be naughty, though." The Dowager waggled a finger archly. "Remember Stephen."

Chloe had never decided how far the reality of the death of her only child had penetrated the Dowager's mind. She had spoken of it, even cried a little, but since then had often seemed to expect him to visit her, write to her.

"I will, Mama. I see you are ready to come down tonight."

"Oh yes. It would be so rude not to. How is the prince?"

Chloe ignored the latter question and looked for another topic. "How sweet a smell there is in here, Mama. It must be one of Belinda's blends of *potpourri.*"

"Yes," said the Dowager. "The Massinger girl is very willing, but forward. It is a while since she refreshed it, though. Perhaps you could cover it now as we will be going down. Then it will last better, you know."

The Dowager always referred to Belinda as the Massinger girl, or Miss Massinger, if she had to address her. Chloe could never decide whether this was snobbishness, or an inability to remember George's marriage. Belinda certainly did her best to be obliging to the older lady.

Chloe went obediently to the container which sat on the mantelpiece. "Why this is a different pot, Mama. How pretty."

"Yes it is, isn't it? The Massinger girl brought it." The Dowager wore the pleased smile of a young child. "Pretty."

The white china urn was in the Japanese style, delicately painted. It was straight-sided, with a silver wire grid set in the top, the wire wound together into ornate patterns. Inside, Chloe saw the dusky jewel colours of the dried blossoms. She smelled the delicious fragrance again before placing a lid over to preserve the aroma.

Making *potpourri,* and the collection of pots for its use, was Belinda's hobby. Chloe thought one day soon, before she left Delamere, she should have the young woman share some of her knowledge. This particular pot was the loveliest yet, and it was kind of Belinda to put it in the Dowager's room. As she turned it, however, Chloe thought it was not a very good design. The wires of the grid were set into the clay and clearly immovable. The mixture would have to be dribbled in. Time-consuming.

The Dowager's voice broke into her thoughts. "That girl brought me something for my lumbago too. Amy," she said to Miss Forbes, "show Stephen's wife that stuff."

Chloe went over to join the companion at a table crowded with jars and potions. Miss Forbes passed a wide-mouthed earthenware bottle to her, and she unclipped the cap to be assailed by the reek of camphor and turpentine.

"Ugh." She hastily capped it again. "If smell is any indication, it must be powerful enough. Does it work, Miss Forbes?"

"I rubbed it in and it seemed to ease the stiffness, but Sophronia doesn't like the smell. I'm sure it is effective, though. My mother used just such a mix for my grandfather."

Chloe looked at all the jars and bottles. The numbers seemed to be growing every day. "Surely all this cannot be necessary."

"Oh, it's more like a collection," said Miss Forbes comfortably. "Sophronia is very well most of the time, but she likes to talk of this and that problem, and Belinda always knows of a lotion or potion. Very kind of her really."

Chloe looked at the collection doubtfully. "I leave it to your judgment, Miss Forbes. Please be careful with anything to be ingested, though."

"Oh I am. And so is Belinda. She only ever gives such things as coltsfoot drops, or liquorice cough lozenges. Quite harmless."

"Do you think I should wear my red slippers, Mama?"

said the Dowager suddenly in a girlish voice. Chloe glanced at Miss Forbes, who clucked.

"Certainly not, dear," she said, as if speaking to a child. "Not with green."

"But I like my red slippers." The Dowager's lips began to pucker and Miss Forbes hurried over to hold her hand.

"You shall wear them tomorrow," said Miss Forbes firmly, and the Dowager sighed.

Then she smiled. "That's right. That's when Henry's coming to call," she said. "He may not be a duke but he is so distinguished."

Chloe again looked questioningly at the companion. It seemed as if her mother-in-law was sliding into one of her bad times. Miss Forbes stepped aside to talk with her.

"She will be better in company, you'll see, Lady Stephen. She's so looking forward to new faces. If she is any trouble at all, I will take her away."

"Only if absolutely necessary," said Chloe. "This is her home. We are so fortunate to have found you, Miss Forbes."

The little lady blushed. "Oh no. I consider myself the one blessed. A comfortable situation, and treated with such courtesy. And Sophronia can be a very pleasant companion at times, great fun. What will happen, though, now the new viscount is here?"

Chloe heard real anxiety in the woman's voice. It had never occurred to her before that Justin might want to change the Dowager's situation. She would just have to make sure he had no such idea.

"Nothing will change," she said firmly.

Miss Forbes relaxed. "Oh, that is such good news."

As she returned along the corridor, Chloe hoped she could make her words come true. She could not believe, however, that Justin would be harsh with the harmless old lady, or try to send her away from her home.

Chloe went back into the main part of the house and scratched at a door, to be admitted by a pretty young maid.

Chloe went over to drop a kiss on the cheek of her grandmother, who was sitting before a mirror, delicately applying rouge to her withered cheeks. Her dressing table was also crowded with jars and bottles, but this time they were all creams, perfumes, and cosmetics.

"Prettying yourself up for Justin?" Chloe teased as she perched on the padded bench beside the old lady.

The Duchess poked her with a bony finger. "Wait until you've fifty more years in your dish, gel. You'll take to the paint pots too so as not to look like a death mask. It's your colour, anyway, which sets me off."

Chloe looked at herself in the mirror and her eyes twinkled. "This pink does suit me marvellously well, doesn't it?"

The Duchess dropped the brush carelessly among the pots and turned to her granddaughter. "What are you about, Chloe? Fancy remaining Lady Stanforth now you've seen him again?"

Chloe hoped the extra colour she could feel warming her cheeks was not obvious. "Of course not. I told you. No more Dashing Delameres for me. I'm looking for sober respectability."

"Gone off, has he?" said the Duchess dryly. "He used to be a handsome rogue and I didn't hear he'd got scarred or anything, though it was touch and go with his leg at one time I understand."

"In '08. He was in England for a while to recuperate, but he stayed in Essex with his sister. Stephen went to see him and said he'd grown stuffy."

"Grown stuffy? He was mentioned in dispatches not long after he got back to his company. Anyway," the old lady added slyly, "I thought stuffy was what you wanted, my dear."

As her grandmother stood to have her black gown slipped over her head by the pretty maid—"I always wear black because at my age someone's always dying. One ugly face in a room is enough,"—Chloe considered the matter.

"After your words of wisdom, Grandmama, I'm not sure I want stuffy by my fireside for the rest of my life. Besides, it was Stephen who said Justin had sobered, and perhaps it was just pain and a brush with death, for he does not seem so very changed to me. No, I still seek dependability, and Justin is not so changed as all that. I'll lay odds he's still ripe for adventures. Why else would he bring Randal along?''

The Duchess's shrewd eyes took in her finery again. ''Then it's not Randal you're seeking to impress either, I suppose. Dependable ain't the word for him.''

Chloe tilted her head thoughtfully. ''I've never known him to let anyone down.''

''There's a lesson for you if you've wit to see it. I always said the two of you were dashed alike, but don't set your cap at him. I don't hold with cousins marrying, and you wouldn't suit.''

''Set my cap!'' exclaimed Chloe, feeling flustered. ''Grandmama, really. I'll have you know I have dressed so smartly merely to impress upon everyone that I'm a fully grown woman who has not totally lost her attractions.'' She ignored a disbelieving snort from the old lady and carried on, ''I assure you, however, that I think of Randal as a brother, and Dashing Justin Delamere is the last man I will marry.''

The old lady's shrewd eyes twinkled in her wrinkled face. ''I hope whoever you choose is, my dear, or you'll be regarded as a bit of a jinx. Come along then. Let's go and inspect the new Lord Stanforth. I can't wait to see what he makes of all the Ladies Stanforth he's inherited.''

4

CHLOE THOUGHT JUSTIN looked a little dazed at times and glancing around at the women in the room, she couldn't blame him.

There was something to be said for the fact the Dowager could still fit in the green gown, which must surely date from before Stephen's birth, but it would have been improved by the hoops it must originally have had. Their lack, and some loss of height over the years, meant the gown trailed around her in a very hazardous manner. Chloe wished she had noticed earlier. She made a mental note to have all the Dowager's clothes shortened. In a quiet word to Miss Forbes she reminded her to make sure the Dowager went nowhere near the fire.

At least the oldest Lady Stanforth had not attempted the high hair style of her youth, but had contented herself with a voluminous cap decorated with love knots of matching green ribbon.

By comparison, the Dowager Duchess of Tyne, in her smart black with discreet diamonds, looked positively decorous—if one ignored the rouged cheeks and tinted lips. After a startled look, Justin seemed able to do just that. He was slightly acquainted with the Duchess, as most aristocracy were with each other, and Chloe was pleased to see them both conversing in an unexceptional manner.

Belinda, Lady Stanforth, widow of George, was officially in half-mourning, but insisted in holding to deepest

40

black. Chloe was not sure of the reason, as the young woman made no pretence of grief. Perhaps Belinda thought black suited her, though it did not in fact enhance her rosy cheeks and gingerish curls. Perhaps she thought it gave her dignity, and established her place at the Hall. She could not be unaware of how peculiar most people thought it of George to have married her.

Justin treated her with perfect civility. "I am very pleased to meet you," he said. "As there is a confusing number of Lady Stanforths, I wonder if you would permit me to call you Belinda, or Aunt Belinda if you would prefer."

"Aunt Belinda, I think, Stanforth," said the young woman stiffly, younger than the man she was addressing. Her voice was quite well-bred, though it still held a trace of Lancashire. She lowered her eyes as she added, "I would not like any impression of familiarity between us, us being of an age and living in the same house, perhaps alone together when Chloe leaves."

Chloe stared. Was this nervousness, or was Belinda perhaps thinking she could remain Lady Stanforth? She had not thought the girl so foolish as to think Justin would marry her. She was aware of a spurt of outrage at the thought. She was also reminded of something.

"Justin. A letter came a few days ago from Humphrey Macy, Uncle George's friend, asking leave to visit. Knowing you would be arriving soon, I put it on one side for you."

"Humphrey Macy likes apples too," said the Dowager in her piercing voice, causing a slight hiatus in the conversation.

"Most people do, Aunt Sophy," said Justin after a moment, and Chloe admired his kindness to the older lady. "What would he want here?" he asked of Chloe.

"Well, he was here nearly all the time George was viscount, you know. He . . . er . . . well, to be straight about it, he says he wants to become better acquainted with Belinda."

Belinda coloured at this but did not appear unequivocally pleased. In fact, she looked a little alarmed, though her voice was calm. "He is a very pleasant gentleman, I'm sure. But old."

This was accompanied by a glance at Justin, and a rather more cautious flicker of the eyes towards the glittering Lord Randal. Chloe saw that young man's lips twitch, and resolved to have a word with him as soon as possible. It would not do for him to tease Belinda.

"No older than George," Chloe responded pointedly. "They were at Harrow together."

Belinda did not reply but her eyes shifted. She still looked worried, as she had since the mention of Humphrey Macy. She could be worried about her future, though George had provided handsomely for her and her daughter in his will. Perhaps, thought Chloe, Belinda believed they would use Macy as a means of forcing her out of Delamere. Chloe couldn't help experiencing a twinge of guilt because, in a way, that had been exactly her purpose. She did think, however, that providing Belinda with a good second marriage would be a kindly act.

"Would you object to Mr. Macy visiting, Aunt Belinda?" Justin asked.

Belinda hesitated, and that confirmed Chloe's suspicions.

With noble motives, Chloe pleaded the gentleman's case. "There is no hurry, of course, for you to make a second marriage, Belinda," she said. "And when you are ready, I am sure there will be no shortage of gentlemen wanting to offer for your hand. But the interest of a man like Mr. Macy is very flattering. He comes from an old family and is an intimate of the Prince of Wales. You would move in the highest circles."

In a betraying movement, Belinda's fingers rose to touch the frill at the high neck of her black gown. Then her hand was returned to its place in her lap. "No," she said at last, looking down and turning her wedding ring on her finger. "I wouldn't object. He probably wants to look at

Dorinda. I know George wanted him for godfather. Perhaps we should have the christening while he's here."

"That would be an excellent idea, Aunt," said Justin.

Chloe noted with admiration the clever way Belinda had divested Macy's visit of any amorous intent. Ah well, if Macy wasn't to her taste, there would be others. But likely not so eminent.

"Do you know," said Belinda, with a slightly flirtatious smile at Justin, "I think it would be better if you called me by my name. Aunt sounds monstrous strange."

The minx *does* have designs on him, Chloe thought.

"On the contrary," said Justin with an implacable smile, "it so neatly delineates our relationship, doesn't it?"

Belinda flushed and Chloe felt rather sorry for her. Her country wiles were no match for men like Justin. She hoped the girl had learned her lesson.

Perhaps not, for she retorted rather pertly, "And what then are you to call Chloe?"

"Chloe, I think," said Justin with a mischievous light in his eyes as he turned to her. "If that is acceptable, cousin?"

Faced with this confusion Chloe retorted, "You may call me whatever you wish."

Justin grinned, the wide grin which took her straight back six years, to a time of recklessness and blood-stirring excitement. She felt her pulse speed.

"May I?" he said. "How kind." He strolled towards her and placed a finger beneath her chin, the better to study her features. "Dulcinea, perhaps. Queen Mab? Gloriana? Brilliana? Did you know," he added lightly as he released her, "that Brilliana, Lady Harley, was so called because she was born in Brill?"

Chloe laughed out loud, her head light as if with champagne. "How disenchanting. What if she had been born in Flushing?"

Randal hooted with mirth.

"Or Dieppe?" suggested Justin.

"Rome?" offered Chloe.

"Brest?" shot back the viscount, and Chloe was amazed to feel herself blush.

Randal, damn him, burst out laughing again and was joined by the Duchess, while Belinda looked shocked in a mildly bewildered kind of way. Chloe, struggling against laughter herself, sought the words to put Justin severely in his place. . . . But for heaven's sake, this was his home. . . .

Fortunately, at that moment, dinner was announced and the small party, five ladies and two gentlemen, went in for the meal. Lord Stanforth took in the two older ladies, Lord Randal the two younger, and Miss Forbes trailed behind.

Chloe thought that, for such a strange group, the meal went surprisingly well. The Dowager Lady Stanforth was in one of her better states and, apart from her deafness, presented no problem. Meanwhile, the most recent Lady Stanforth was generally quiet, and Chloe was glad to see that Belinda's interest in the two young men did not bring her to act boldly. In fact, Chloe had to acknowledge that Belinda never behaved in a way to make one blush for her. If she were wise enough to leave this area, where no one would ever forget her origins, she would doubtless do quite well for herself. Chloe resolved, if Belinda was not interested in Mr. Macy's suit, to encourage her to live elsewhere once her mourning was done.

Most of the conversation was between the Duchess, Chloe, Justin, and Randal, and it was witty and flowing. Apart from the considerable social expertise of the participants, there was plenty of ground to cover. Justin was eager for *on-dits* of society, and everyone else was keen to hear his amusing stories of the lighter side of the war, and his personal recollections of such heroes as Wellington and Sir John Moore.

"Moore is responsible for the army we have today. It was an honour to serve under him," said Justin. "He understood that the men are more than cannon fodder, that they are capable of a great deal if encouraged. Do you know, Napoleon is reported to have said, 'Moore is the only general now fit to contend with me.' ''

"He must have rejoiced at his death," said the Duchess sourly.

Justin smiled slightly and shook his head. "More likely he wept for all the confrontations which would never occur. Napoleon Bonaparte is a strange man, but a genius. It will be a tragedy if England underestimates him."

"We're not likely to do that," said Chloe, "when he's squatting like a spider with Europe in its web. Everyone knows a soldier. Belinda, your brother is with the army, is he not?"

"Yes," said Belinda, a frown of concern on her face. "He is with the Eighth Foot. I wish the war was over."

"Don't we all, gel," said the Duchess.

"What of Sir Arthur Wellesley, or Viscount Wellington, as he is now?" asked Randal, who was obviously fascinated by tales of war. "Can he handle the Corsican?"

"He's brilliant," said Justin, a light in his eyes. "I was invalided after Corunna but made it back in time for Talavera. Fifty thousand against our twenty thousand. Only Wellington could have prevailed."

"He lost a quarter of the army," said the Duchess severely, "and has done mighty liitle since."

"The Spaniards won't pull together," defended Justin. "Venegas let the French reinforcements through at Talavera, and now they squabble among themselves instead of driving the French out. It's wise of Wellington to hold off and protect Portugal. Our forces are retreating behind the lines of Torres Vedras. If Massena wishes to follow him, he will do so through a wasteland."

Chloe noticed a faraway look in his eyes, and knew he was back with his men and his comrades. She was surprised at a twinge of jealousy in herself. Jealousy and anxiety. He had sold out, but when his affairs were in order, would he return to the war?

She was aware of her intention to pull him back to the

present, back to herself, when she said, "Lord Wellington believes that by holding Portugal, Britain will foil the French in Spain. Do you agree, Justin?"

"Yes, Napoleon will not rest until he controls Iberia," said Justin. "He cannot leave us in Portugal."

"Do you think you will go back?" she asked, hoping the question sounded inconsequential.

"No," said Justin quietly. "Unless Britain is in desperate straights, I will not fight again." Then, in a clear effort to change the subject, he said lightly, "Unless, as Randal implies, I will have to fight off the husband-hunting infantry of Almack's."

"Well, of course you will," said Chloe with a chuckle. "A hero from the war, a rich nobleman . . . You will be a prime target, I'm afraid. What a shame you sold out. If you could still wear your uniform they would swoon at your feet."

Justin looked dubious. "I think you mixed a metaphor there or something, Chloe. After all, any infantry that swoons at the sight of regimentals would be in a parlous state."

"No, no," she said mischievously. "War paint is all a question of context. What would the gentlemen in uniform do when faced by those beauties with their glossy curls and low, filmy gowns?"

"Stand to attention, I would think," he said dryly. The wicked glint in his eyes had warned her, but she still choked on her sip of wine.

Randal and the Duchess laughed and Chloe could not help but chuckle. She told herself she had no taste for these *risqué* conversations, so why did she feel inebriated on one glass of wine? Why did she know her eyes sparkled more brightly than the crystal lustres on the chandelier?

Later, as the company laughed at one of Randal's wry anecdotes, Chloe exclaimed, "Oh, this has been such a pleasant meal. I had forgotten how it could be. I cannot wait to rejoin Society. Grandmama has invited me to the Towers for Christmas and then I shall go south for the

Season. There are any number of friends I wish to visit on the way.''

"I hope you won't rush away too soon, Chloe," said Justin with a frown. "After all, I have a great deal to learn.''

"No, of course not. But before the end of the month I would think.''

"Why not stay here for Christmas?" he asked, and Chloe thought, guiltily, that it might be lonely and awkward for him here, with only Belinda and the Dowager. But she could not stay, must not stay.

"Oh, I don't think so, Justin," she said hastily. "It is kind of you, but I have promised Grandmama.''

A glance at that surprised lady begged for support.

'Well," said the Duchess. "I do want to be home before the hard weather, true enough.''

With that, Chloe rose to lead the ladies to the drawing-room and their tea. The Dowager Lady Stanforth was obviously tired and soon decided to seek her bed. Belinda sat by her embroidery frame to do some pretty work on the hem of a dress for her child.

'What was all that about, gel?" asked the Duchess quietly.

"All that?" queried Chloe.

"My rushing back home.''

"Well, I'm sure you do want to be at the Towers for Christmas, do you not?''

"A mere three months away," pointed out the old lady.

Chloe felt as beleaguered as Lord Wellington's retreating forces. "Now Justin is home," she said firmly, "it is time to leave.''

The Duchess sipped her tea and eyed her granddaughter. When she spoke, however, it was to say calmly, "As you will. Why don't you play the pianoforte, my dear. Some Bach perhaps.''

Obediently, Chloe went to the piano. As she opened the instrument, however, she remembered a past comment of her grandmother's that Bach tended to straighten tangled minds. She looked suspiciously at the old lady but the Duchess sat nodding and staring into the fire, as innocent as a lamb.

Chloe played Bach's fugue in E minor with clarity and precision. Her mind was as clear as a tidal pool, she told herself. She had the chance to start her life afresh, and she would not allow the undoubted Delamere charm to sway her once again.

The unwary might have thought the Duchess sleeping, but as soon as the gentlemen entered the room her head came up and her eyes scanned them, as bright as ever.

"Ha! About time," she declared. "We'll have a hand of whist. Find the cards, Chloe." She looked at Belinda. "You don't play, do you, gel?"

Belinda coloured at this but it was the only sign of discomposure. "In fact, I do, Your Grace," she said calmly. "George was used to say I play very well."

"Oh. Well, you are doubtless busy with your needle-work, are you not?" said the old lady anxiously, and then looked around at the others. "Damn it. It's not that I don't want to play with Belinda. I just don't want the fact there's five of us to put off the game. I'm partial to a game of whist, and I haven't had one for months. That useless Miss Forbes doesn't know a heart from a handshake."

Lord Randal came over to take the old lady's hand and kiss it. "Don't worry, my dear. You will have your game. I think I'm the one here who is least fond of cards, so I'll take Chloe's place at the piano."

This arrangement suited everyone. The Dowager, to make up for her rudeness, insisted on playing with Belinda as her partner. She was well pleased when it became clear the young woman was a very skillful player, with an amazing memory.

As Belinda calmly led out an unbeatable six of clubs, forcing a discard of his queen of hearts, Justin groaned, "Remind me, Aunt Belinda, never to play with you for high stakes."

The Duchess swept the cards up with a gleeful grin. "Ours again. Fine play, gel."

"Thank you, Your Grace." She turned to Justin with a rueful smile. "Please, Lord Stanforth, can I prevail upon you to call me Belinda? If I was foolish before, it was only nerves, you see. We will be a laughing stock with you calling me aunt."

Chloe glanced at Belinda thoughtfully. Clever.

While George had been alive, Belinda had been rather awkward in her manner, trying far too hard not to make mistakes. George himself did not help by being moody and petulant. For a while as a widow, Belinda had seemed to relax and become much more natural in her manner. Now, Chloe thought, Belinda had gained new poise. She was not displeased. The girl was now part of the family, and Chloe did not want to have to blush for her. On the other hand, she did not want Belinda to inveigle an offer out of Justin.

Justin was also eyeing Belinda thoughtfully. "You are right, of course. Why do we not settle for 'Cousin.' It would capture the spirit of our relationship."

Belinda nodded. "I would be pleased to call you Cousin Justin."

"And I to call you Cousin Belinda."

"Cousins everywhere," said the Dowager. She added with a sly smile, "Just remember, all of you. Cousins should never marry."

There was no reason for it, but at the word "marry," Chloe's eyes went to Justin's, and surely his just escaped being caught in the same reflex.

After a moment, his eyes returned deliberately to hers, filled with amusement. Chloe only then became aware of the melody Randal had suddenly began to play *con amore,* a popular ballad called "Now You Are Near."

Chloe blushed as she remembered the words: "Sweet, sweet the thought of you, my dear, But sweeter still the day now you are near. . . ."

She glared at her cousin and, with an unrepentant grin,

he slid off into a wordless tune. Chloe hastily dealt the cards for the next hand.

The game broke up when Belinda was obliged to go up to her child, whom she nursed herself, and the Dowager admitted to needing her bed. Randal ceased his playing.

"I had no idea you played so well, Randal," said Chloe, with an edge in her voice as she leaned against the piano.

"It's a soothing occupation," he replied innocently, "but not one to which I'm willing to apply myself. You play considerably better than I."

"But not so eloquently," Chloe said, moving to stand beside him. "Keep your meddling fingers out of my business, coz," she said pointedly and he laughed.

Justin had come over to join them and she turned to him. "I know this is your house, Justin, but I have to ask if there is anything you need."

He took no offence at her words, but he seemed to eye her pose strangely. She realised she was resting one hand on her cousin's firm shoulder, and removed it.

"I'm only too pleased," Justin said, "to leave the running of Delamere to you for a little while, if you will be so kind, Chloe. Tomorrow is soon enough even to think of taking up the reins."

"You won't find it so hard. Scarthwait has it all in hand and can be trusted."

"Still, it's not my way to leave matters in the hands of employees without an understanding of what they are about."

Chloe looked at him with a touch of surprise. This was quite the opposite of Stephen's approach to property. "Well," she said. "I'm sure Scarthwait will be delighted. If you're eager to take up your tasks there are a number of items of business and correspondence on the desk in the office."

With that Chloe went up to her bedroom, and the two young men looked at each other.

"An interesting inheritance," remarked Lord Randal, long fingers idly picking out a tune.

More so than you think, thought Justin, trying to decide whether he should clear the house of all the ladies during these dangerous times. It might, however, be a sign to the enemy.

He put those thoughts aside for later and said, "How about a game of billiards, Randal. Or shall we take brandy to the office and see what horrors await me there?"

Lord Randal laughed. "Oh no you don't. If you want someone to hold your hand while you grapple with balance sheets and crop records, wait until tomorrow and I'm sure Chloe will oblige. For now, I'll take billiards and beat you hollow. I'm sure you're out of practice, my boy."

This proved only too true; but, as they had taken the brandy decanter to the billiard room with them, they soon forgot to keep careful score. By the time Chloe heard their laughing voices in the corridor as they made their way to bed, neither had the slightest notion of who had won the games.

Chloe had lain awake in bed for two hours by then, seeking her normal, peaceful sleep. She was not in the nature of deceiving herself, thus she had to accept that Justin had an effect on her which was quite out of the ordinary. She thought back, so many years it seemed, to the time of her elopement.

Two handsome young blades, men of fashion, visiting in the area and turning the heads of all the young ladies. Even her older sister Cassandra had blushed when Stephen bowed to her in the village, and Cassandra was the most proper of young ladies. At the same time, however, Cassandra had passed on to Chloe their parents' warning about the young Delameres, who were known to be wild in their ways.

Chloe, riding out alone one day, as she was not allowed to, had come across the Dashing Delameres racing their horses, joined the race, and beat them hollow. The next thing she knew, one of them was asking her father's permission to woo her and being told he must wait at least a year, until he was twenty-one and she had left Miss Mallory's.

Her father's reply had seemed so unreasonable. Chloe and Stephen were in love, or thought they were. She now recognised that she had been at least partly in love with escape, with racing free in the wind, but at the time she had not been able to distinguish those feelings from love. When Stephen suggested they elope, she scarcely hesitated. He was, after all, no fortune hunter. He was an eligible *parti*, and her parents' objections were ridiculous.

Chloe rolled over in bed and beat the pillow in an attempt to force it to cradle her head in comfort. What crazy children they had been, even Justin—though he had been a year older than Stephen, twenty-one. He had travelled with them all the way to Scotland, organising the trip perfectly. Not such a child. It was he who said it was déclassé to go to Gretna, when anywhere in Scotland would do. As a consequence, she had at least been decorously married in a church in Edinburgh, not over an anvil in a hovel.

A memory, long suppressed, rose up of her wedding night when Justin had disappeared, leaving Stephen and Chloe alone for the first time. She had felt abandoned. She had told herself at the time it was merely the strangeness of the moment which had brought on that feeling, and yet there was the other time . . .

Chloe resolutely turned her mind. Justin was not the man for her and he would be horrified by the betrayal of his cousin it represented. If she decided she wanted another husband, Chloe would seek one far removed in type and geography from the Dashing Delameres.

5

CHLOE AWOKE THE next morning feeling poorly rested and unsettled in her mind. She tried to plan her departure from Delamere, but made little progress. She told herself a brisk ride would clear the cobwebs.

She pulled on her dressing gown, rang for her breakfast, then took her accustomed seat at the small table by the window. Her bedroom, like the Sea Room, gave a view of the bay.

She had longed so much to escape Delamere, but now there was sadness in her. What a contrary person she must be.

She had meant to leave once George married Belinda, but the young woman had asked her to stay a while to put her in the way of things at Delamere. Being in deep mourning at that time, Chloe felt no particular desire to go elsewhere and had agreed. Her parents would have thought it their duty to offer her a home, but would also have expected her to submit to their direction. Her only other choice would have been to set up her establishment in some spa or quiet town.

When George died after only a few months' tenure, there had been no question of her abandoning Belinda and the Dowager, not just for their sakes but for Justin's if he should inherit. There was no knowing what would happen without an experienced person in charge.

Now Chloe was free to go and yet . . .

It was fortunate that her maid arrived with her tea and

toast before Chloe could think herself into a decline. She ate her breakfast, watching a few tardy fishing boats catch the tide.

Despite the distraction of the scenery, her mind still tended to slip into disturbing pathways, so she took a sheet of paper and began to plan a small dinner for the local notables. If she carried through with her intention to leave Delamere in the near future, it would only be fair to introduce Justin to his neighbours before she left. She set the date for Thursday. Short notice, but it would do for an informal gathering. She was nagged by a desire to be away, a sense of danger to her plans if she stayed.

Chloe looked over the list carefully. Though Delamere was not a particularly large house, the viscount was undoubtedly the social leader of the area. Anyone incorrectly left off this list would take offence. Satisfied, she quickly wrote out the invitations and sealed them. As long as Justin approved, she would have them off straight away.

Agnes returned and helped Chloe dress in her habit. Breakfast and positive plans had brightened Chloe's spirits. The sun was shining and the wind had dropped. It was time to show Mercury, the horse who had thrown her, who was in charge.

In the entrance hall she encountered Belinda, holding a flower basket, followed by the nursery maid carrying a well-bundled-up Dorinda. Chloe looked at the babe, marvelling at the big blue eyes which stared up at her. If only she had borne a child. . . . Perhaps she should marry, after all.

"She is so beautiful, Belinda."

"Yes," said the young woman complacently, "and healthy. We Massingers breed well. My mother bore eight and lost only one."

"A good inheritance. I'm sure the clean sea air helps."

"It could be. The Prince of Wales is taken with his Brighthelmstone, they say. I try to take Dorinda into the fresh air every day. Today I am checking the roses. If there are any blooms suitable for display should I cut them?"

"Perhaps not," said Chloe. "If Justin approves, I intend to hold a dinner on Thursday for our neighbours. If there are blooms left, it would be pleasant to have them in a centrepiece then."

Belinda nodded and went on her way, but Chloe had noticed her tensing. An event with the local gentry would be a trial to her. Chloe shrugged. If Belinda chose not to attend, that was up to her but it would be completely improper for Chloe to exclude her from the evening.

Chloe popped her head into the breakfast parlour. Both Justin and Randal were there. She asked Justin about the dinner.

"I suppose I must," he said with resignation. "Need it be so soon, though?"

"As soon as I have you established," Chloe said lightly, "I can be on with my life. Now, I am for riding. Do you want to come?"

"I feel I should devote myself to duty," said Justin with a grimace. Again, Chloe thought how unlike Stephen he had become. "I'll spend the morning looking at the neglected correspondence. Can I not persuade you to assist me?"

For a moment, Chloe felt an absurd temptation to say yes. "Definitely not," she said, with perhaps a little too much fervour. "You'll manage very well, I'm sure," she hurried on, "and Scarthwait can always be found if you need him. This afternoon I will be at your disposal, but this morning is far too fine to stay indoors. Randal? I believe we have a couple of horses would do you if you wish to accompany me."

"With pleasure," said that young man, rising. "If I stay here, Justin'll try to drag me into his affairs, and there's nothing I'd like less."

Chloe was relieved to make her escape before she fell into folly. She hadn't, however, been able to ignore a bleak look on Justin's face. She felt as if she had abandoned him. She hardened her foolish heart.

As they walked down to the stables Chloe asked, "What

on earth would you do, Randal, if Chelmly were to die
and you became the heir?"

"Put a period to my existence?" he suggested. "My
dislike of managing things is only one of many reasons I
wish to God my brother would marry and get himself a
nursery full of boys."

"Surely you can find someone to suit him. After all,
there is no shortage of ladies willing to marry the handsome heir to a dukedom."

"None at all," said Randal with a laugh. "It's Chelmly
who jibs. Heaven knows what he's looking for, but he ain't
found it yet."

They arrived at the stables and Chloe gave Garford, the
head groom, the invitations.

"I'll send the lad with them, if that's all right, ma'am,"
said the man. "He'll enjoy a jaunt on a day like this and
he's reliable."

"Very well. Mercury for me, Garford, and Dorset, I
think, for Lord Randal."

While Garford saddled the grey, Frank, the undergroom, led out a rangy chestnut gelding for Randal's approval.

"He'll do," said Randal, eyeing the young man, who
was decidedly surly.

With a scowl, the groom took the horse off to be har-
nessed.

"Pleasant individual, I'm sure," remarked Randal.

"Oh, don't mind Frank," said Chloe, feeding an apple
to Mercury. "He's a good worker—been with us since he
was a boy, and his father worked on the home farm. But
he's some kind of connection of Belinda's, and he's been
in a strange mood ever since she married George. It must
have put his nose out of joint. Fortunately she doesn't ride
and they rarely have to deal directly."

Lord Randal looked at the sturdy, handsome young man.
"Odd setup. I'm surprised he doesn't find work elsewhere."

Chloe looked at him. "Find work elsewhere? Randal,

really. These people have been here forever. They consider going to Lancaster a mighty enterprise. When I found a kitchen maid an excellent position as undercook in Carnforth, it took me weeks to convince her to take it up."

At that moment a fine Irish setter bounded into the stable yard and up to Chloe.

"Hello, Pepperpot," she said, pulling its ears as it gambolled around her. "Want to run too?"

The dog clearly expressed its assent, then went over to inspect the newcomer. Randal allowed the dog to check him out and was soon accepted. "A fine dog," he said.

"Yes, Stephen gave him to me but he's not a town dog, of course. He deserves to get more hunting than he does here, especially now. Perhaps Justin will keep him, and take him out now and then."

A few moments later, Randal's mount was brought forward by the still surly Frank. Randal checked the straps and girth before dismissing the man, then tossed Chloe into the saddle of the grey before swinging up onto the bay.

As soon as they were out the gate, Chloe said, "What were you about? Frank knows his job and I'm afraid you offended him."

"Be damned to that," said Lord Randal. "If a discontented servant wants to play tricks, it will not be at my expense."

Chloe laughed. "As if he would. It's the sort of thing *you* would do, you mean."

"Take care you don't provoke me, wench," said Randal. "I promise you, if I ever find myself working as undergroom in an establishment of which you are the lady, I'll play you every trick in the book."

They trotted along the coast road and down a path onto the sweeping sands of Half-Moon Bay, then they gave their horses their heads, even going down to splash along the shallows where the sea was beginning to recede. Turning, Chloe could look back at the reddish cliff with the Hall atop it, slightly obscured from this angle by a windbreak of high bushes.

When he pulled up, Randal exclaimed, "This is marvelous fun! I never realised how good it was to ride the sands."

"Isn't it?" said Chloe, her eyes shining like the sun-flecked sea and her colour heightened by exertion.

She saw Randal stop and stare. "God, Chloe. You must be the most beautiful woman in England."

Chloe was taken aback. "Don't be silly. I do well enough—"

"Well enough! You'll have the pick of the eligibles, now you're on the hunt again."

"On the hunt!" Chloe echoed. "I do wish everyone would stop harping on my next marriage. I have very high standards. Only a handsome, intelligent gentleman not too advanced in years, who is to be relied on in all matters of importance, would be even worthy of my consideration. Unless you know such a one, do not mention the matter again."

Randal bowed slightly. "There is myself."

Chloe looked at him in amazement. "Randal, is that an offer?"

"God no!" he said in alarm, which made her break out laughing. "Don't scare me to death, Chloe. I merely point out that such as you describe are not rare. Justin would fit the bill too."

"Just get that bee out of your head, cousin," said Chloe firmly, "or I'll accept your next flippant offer and make your life a misery."

She turned Mercury's head sharply and set him to the trot again, but Randal soon caught up, completely undeterred.

"In what way does Justin fall short? Think how convenient, too. You wouldn't even have to change your stationery."

Chloe began to wish her favourite cousin hadn't come

up to Delamere after all. If he took the notion to interfere, he was capable of anything.

She changed the subject. "Where's Pepperpot gone?"

They looked around. Finally, Randal spotted the dog at the base of the sandy cliff upon which Delamere stood. Pepperpot was pointing as he had been trained to do, clearly indicating something of interest among the rocks there.

"Race you!" called out Chloe and was off.

They thundered over the dark brown sands towards the setter.

"What've you found, boy?" asked Chloe. "A dead fish? A gull?"

Randal was already off his horse and handed his reins to her. "I'll just make sure it isn't a wounded animal."

The headland was twenty feet or so high at this point, and where it met the sand there were many rocks and boulders. Some were half as tall as a man and, piled together in places, they formed caverns. Having gained their attention, the dog dashed ahead, but it took Lord Randal a little longer to negotiate the rocks.

"Hold on, you damned hound . . . Good God!"

There was silence. Chloe wished she could abandon the horses to follow her cousin, but Mercury in particular was not to be trusted. Then Randal reappeared from behind a clump of boulders.

"It's the groom, Frank," he said soberly. "I'm very much afraid he's dead, Chloe."

"Dead." Chloe was stunned. "But how? It's scarce an hour . . ."

"Yes. It looks as if he fell off the cliff. There are any number of injuries, but I'm fairly certain it's a broken neck that's finished him."

Chloe looked at the reins in her hands with impatience. "Come and hold the horses so I may look, Randal."

He came forward but said, "Nonsense. He's dead. There's nothing to do here. I'll stay. You ride back to the

Hall for help. Who's the local Justice? He should probably
be informed.''

"Sir Cedric Troughton," said Chloe automatically, offended by this high-handedness. "I don't see what right
you have to give me orders, Randal."

Randal looked up at her. "You've become damned uppity, my girl. I can hardly ride off and leave you to guard
the corpse, and there's no point in your viewing the remains. So do as you're told."

Chloe pulled Mercury's head around and rode angrily
off. Fury at Randal's manner pushed aside even the thought
of Frank's death. Among Stephen's many faults was the
virtue, as far as she was concerned, that he had never tried
to rule her. Since fleeing from her home at seventeen she
had been her own mistress. Randal had just made her
aware of how readily that could change. Remarriage would
have many disadvantages.

As soon as she arrived in the stableyard she told Garford
what had occurred. He was much shocked and hurried off
to summon the assistance of the two gardeners. Soon a
small party with a pony cart set off to fetch the body.

Meanwhile, Chloe went directly to Justin in the office
and found him going through a stack of files.

"Hello, Chloe." He rose at the sight of her agitation.
"What is it?"

"Frank—he's your undergroom. He's fallen off the cliff
and killed himself."

Justin came forward and put an arm around her. It felt
wonderful.

"Bear up, my dear. Did you find the body? Where's
Randal?"

That revived her recent grievance, and she pulled herself away. "Will you not treat me like a vapourish female.
I didn't even see the body. Randal found him and he's
stayed there. He sent me to get help. He said you should
go, so I suppose you must. What right he has to come all
dukely over us I'm sure I don't know. Now I suppose I

should follow orders and go and get Cedric, as he's the Justice.''

Chloe finally ran out of breath and Justin took her back into his arms. "Randal only did as he ought, you know. Does he suspect foul play?''

Chloe was so involved in trying to handle being in Justin's arms, no matter how impersonally, that his words took a moment to register.

"Foul play? Whoever would want to hurt Frank?''

"It does seem unlikely," said Justin, rubbing Chloe's back till she felt like purring. "It was just Randal sending for the Justice . . .''

Justin seemed to pull his thoughts together, stopped his stroking, and put Chloe away from him a little. "If you don't mind, Chloe, would you go for Sir Cedric? Are you up to it? If, as I gather, the head groom has gone off to get the body, there's no one else.''

"Of course I don't mind," said Chloe, moving completely away from him. "But it's nonsense to think of anyone having a hand in Frank's death. Nothing of that kind ever happens here. The nearest thing to murder we've had in years was when Jenny Moorcock hit Sam Sharp over the head with a tankard and he didn't get his wits back for days. They were both drunk, though, and it's an old quarrel.''

"Perhaps, if there has been foul play, it is something similar. A quarrel and no real harm intended. Would he have had any reason to be on the headland, though?''

"None that I can think of," Chloe said with a frown. "I must go.''

She had been thinking over Randal's words, and though they still stung, she had to admit that in the world's view, he had a point. After two steps she turned back. "I'm relieved you're here to handle this, Justin. I have to say, however, that I've been mistress here ever since my marriage, and I fear I may try to rule the roast. Randal says I've grown uppity, and he's doubtless right. Tell me if I overstep myself.''

His smile was singularly sweet. Stephen had also been gifted with such a smile, but she had discovered there was nothing behind it, that he would bestow it as readily upon an innkeeper, a dowager, or a wife. For some reason, Chloe had the feeling that with Justin it was different.

"Of course," he said, "but I don't expect it."

"Then you don't know me," said Chloe saucily. "I have a very managing disposition."

He walked forward and took her hand, still covered in her York tan glove. If, as it seemed, he had taken the notion to kiss that hand, it was of course sensible of him to peel the glove back a little so his lips could brush her skin. Her breath quivered and their eyes met for the first time, she thought, in their lives.

After what seemed like years he said, "No, perhaps I don't know you, Chloe."

He slowly smoothed the leather over her wrist once more. Chloe's breath caught, and she retrieved her hand a little awkwardly as Justin walked back to straighten the papers on the desk.

"You must do exactly as you wish, my dear," he said.

Chloe searched her mind for rational words and found none. Quite simply, she fled.

Despite the urgency of the occasion, Justin stood in thought for some time after she had gone. He tried to make himself consider his duties. Was this event in any way connected with the missing papers? He couldn't imagine how, but another violent death following so quickly upon his arrival was highly suspicious.

Was anyone else in danger?

Instead of tackling these questions, however, his mind was filled with the sensation of having Chloe in his arms for the first time. Her name seemed to pound in his brain, like the beat of a drum.

Chloe. Chloe. Chloe.

With a movement almost violent, he kicked the coals of the fire into flame, then went to join Randal on the beach.

* * *

Cantering the mile to Troughton House, Chloe tried to make sense of her feelings. The shock of a death and Randal's high-handedness, topped off by Justin's sudden tenderness, seemed to have rendered her incapable of rational thought. Was she insane to think Justin still felt that special awareness which had troubled them four years ago? If he did, what on earth would come of it? She had no wish to repeat the pattern of her marriage. Justin and Stephen had been very alike. She had thought she loved Stephen once and found only a hollow shell. Why should she think this time it would be any different?

She did not need to ride all the way to the Grange, for she came across Sir Cedric leaning against a gate talking to one of his tenants. His untethered horse grazed nearby and raised its head curiously as she approached. Sir Cedric came over as soon as he saw her. At her news, he mounted to ride back with her to the scene of the accident.

Sir Cedric, in his thirties, had been Chloe's only regular male visitor during the last year, and she knew he would one day propose to her if she gave him the opportunity. She hoped it would not come to that. She had told herself over the past year that it was her desire to escape the associations of this locality which held her back, but there was another reason as well. Sir Cedric was boring.

He was an intelligent, well-circumstanced gentleman of thirty-five, and immensely dependable. It was somehow typical that he was not only available when required, but on the road and waiting. He was even quite handsome, with a healthy trim body, regular if undefined, features and neatly cut soft brown hair. Chloe did not have to see him beside Randal and Justin, however, to know he would fade in their company. There was so little animation about him, and no spontaneity. Chloe remembered her grandmother's words. The thought of fifty years of evenings spent by the fireside with Sir Cedric made her shudder.

He glanced at her and said, "You look upset, my dear.

Why don't you go back to the house. This is no business for a lady.''

Chloe ignored his suggestion and urged Mercury to a little more speed. She had determined to go to the beach to show the men she wasn't to be shunted aside, but when she arrived at the path she saw the body was already in the cart and coming towards them.

Sir Cedric halted beside her. "That's right. No need for you to come down, my dear," he said kindly. "I suggest some hot sweet tea and a rest in your room. In times of stress, my sister is a great believer in Dr. Linmer's Nerve Pills and always has a supply on hand. She will be only too pleased to send some over if you request it." He patted her hand. "How fortunate this happened when Lord Stanforth was here to take the burden from you."

Chloe smiled tightly and agreed. After he had ridden ahead to the beach, however, she walked her horse and waited. She saw Sir Cedric stop the cart and pull back the cloth to look at the corpse, then continue down to where Randal and Justin waited. The cart rolled on, up to the road.

Garford gave a salute. "Nasty business, Your Ladyship. Reckon we'd best take him to his Aunt Katy's place."

Chloe looked at the shape beneath the cloth—so recently a man and now no longer. Frank Halliwell had lived above the stables, but Chloe recollected now that he had been raised by his mother's sister, a spinster who kept goats and chickens for her livelihood.

"Very well. I will go ahead to break the news," she said.

She picked the undergardener to accompany Garford in the cart and sent Budsworth, the gardener, back to his tasks. Then she trotted inland to Katy Stack's smallholding.

Chloe found the well-padded, middle-aged woman digging up potatoes in her plot, her strong movements showing that her bulk contained a lot of muscle. She looked up and stopped to lean on her spade.

" 'Day to you, Milady.' "

Chloe slid off the horse and tethered him to the fence. "I'm afraid I come with sad news, Miss Stack."

The woman's face became blank, almost stupid—the universal reaction of the local people to any hint of trouble. "Frank, I reckon. What's he gone and done?"

Chloe walked up the path towards the older woman. "I'm afraid there's been an accident, Miss Stack. He fell off the Head. He's dead."

There was a moment of silence. Then, with a sharp, almost vicious movement, the older woman drove her spade into the earth so that it stood there straight, and wiped her rough hands on her apron. "You'd best come in the house, Milady."

"Thank you. They're bringing the body here, Miss Stack. I hope that is all right."

"Where else? I'm the only family he has hereabouts. His mam and dad died of fever when he were nobut a lad." She led the way into the kitchen of the small cottage. The room was clean and pleasantly decorated with flowers and bright pieces of embroidery. Chloe looked at plain Miss Stack with surprise.

"This is a very pleasant room, Miss Stack," she said.

"I like it," said the woman flatly. "Reckon we'd best have some tea," she added. There was a blackened kettle sitting on a grid over one corner of the fire. She pushed it further over the heat. Immediately, steam began to wisp out of the lid. "Sit you down, Milady."

Chloe chose one of the plain chairs by the pine table. Miss Stack washed her hands in a bowl of water before taking a seat opposite.

"How'd it happen then?"

"We're not quite sure, Miss Stack, but he appears to have fallen from the headland near the house. It would have been very quick."

"Aye." The woman looked at her rough, strong hands. "He were a good lad, Frank. A worker. He were saving to start his own livery in Lancaster. Had big ideas. Still had hopes, I reckon, of Lady Belinda.'' This last was said with a sarcastic edge which told Chloe the woman was aware Belinda had no right to be so called.

"Frank loved Belinda?" she queried in surprise.

"Aye. They were close as you like not that long ago. None of us'd been surprised if they'd have wed, even though her la-di-da mother wanted better for her. But then she up and married Mr. George.''

The woman heaved herself up to attend to the boiling kettle. "Don't do, that sort of thing. Folks should keep to their own. But Nellie Massinger's always had notions. Sending Belinda to that school in Lancaster, and the boys to the grammar school. Now that Belinda's My Lady, Nellie's took the notion to send the youngest to university down south.''

The pot was tinware, but Miss Stack opened a cupboard and took out two fine china cups and saucers. It was into these she poured the strong tea. She added milk and sugar and brought them to the table, placing alongside them an earthenware plate of lardy-cake.

Chloe took a small piece of cake and complimented her hostess. It was very good. Her chief appetite, however, was for information about Belinda and Frank.

"Once Belinda became the widowed Lady Stanforth, however," she said, "and had a jointure, she could look a great deal higher than Frank, I'm afraid.''

"I know that and you know that, but there were no telling Frank. He seemed to think she'd come round, seemed to think he could talk her round. He were an handsome lad, fair enough. Happen he thought that'd turn trick, but I told him, Belinda'll be looking for more than a bonny face now. Young'uns never listen.''

Chloe would have liked to learn more, but the cart could be heard in the lane. Miss Stack drank down the rest of her tea and rose to her feet. She took off her apron for the solemn moment and went to meet the men, directing them to bring the body into her small parlour and lay it on the floor there. She and Chloe observed the process, then Miss Stack placed a penny on each eyelid to hold it shut.

Frank did not look so very different, Chloe thought. He was dirty and bruised but if his neck was broken, the men had managed to lay him down so it was straight. He looked totally irrevocably dead, however. In such a brief time, the spirit had left the flesh.

She glanced at the older woman, wondering how she must feel. This man had been like a son to her. The total absence of expression was perhaps more telling than any tears. Stony-faced, Katy Stack laid a hand for a moment on the young man's bruised cheek, then draped the sheet back over the corpse.

"I'd best go see the vicar," she said as they left the room.

"I could do that for you if you wish, Miss Stack," said Chloe. "As Frank worked for the Hall, we would wish to bear the cost of his burial, if you would allow it." It seemed such an inadequate gesture of support.

Katy Stack nodded. Her face was still blank but Chloe saw there was moistness in her eyes. "Kind of you, Milady. I'd rather not leave him alone, you see."

"I understand." Chloe laid a hand for a moment on the woman's work-worn ones. "I'll make the arrangements, Miss Stack, and if there's anything you need, send someone to the Hall."

After conducting her business with the Reverend Sotherby—and receiving his acceptance of her invitation to the dinner party, which had completely slipped her mind— Chloe took the opportunity to walk through the graveyard to her husband's resting place. It was not a practice which had much meaning for her. She could remember him in his house, connect him with his horses and his acres, but not with this rectangle of earth and carved monument. The sight of Frank's body had brought back memories of Stephen's death, however. He too had gone suddenly from life into death.

The small Heysham church of St. Peter's was very old, dating back to before the Norman Conquest, and there were more historic connections. High on the headland was a ruined structure said to be a chapel built by St. Patrick. In the churchyard stood a curious Viking memorial, a hogback burial stone. It was a grey stone, the shape and size of a large pig's back, covered with carvings of people and animals. It supposedly marked the grave of a Viking warrior called Thorold, who died in the tenth century. It had been dug up only ten years before and attracted a steady stream of antiquarians, the latest being the Dutchman, Herr van Maes.

The whole churchyard was an ancient place, and Chloe always felt as if the spirits of a thousand generations hovered comfortably about. She could not blame them. Set on the headland in view of the rolling sea, this graveyard was a place to contemplate the hand of God.

Standing by Stephen's grave, looking out across the bay, she braced herself against the brisk salt wind. One day Justin would lie here, she supposed, with what Lady Stanforth beside him? The thought caused her discomfort. She could not, must not, think this way of Justin. His choice of wife was nothing to do with her. She must not again be trapped by the Delamere charm, experience a few moments of delight during a lifetime of exasperation and disappointment.

A small voice told her Justin was not as like Stephen as she thought. Then she remembered the tales Stephen had told of their adventures. She had always known her husband could never have been the instigator of the most ingenious and inventive mayhem to their credit. On their elopement journey, had Justin not foolishly challenged a carter to a wrestling match and, having beaten him, continued to take on all comers until a blacksmith had nearly broken his back? Such bravado was probably admirable in a soldier, but not in a husband.

As she rode slowly back to the Hall, Chloe was very aware that the sooner she left Delamere, the better.

6

WHEN THE INHABITANTS of Delamere Hall sat down to a cold luncheon, Sir Cedric joined them. The gentlemen were at first inclined to avoid discussion of the death but Chloe, and more forcefully, the Duchess, soon dissuaded them from being so delicate. Justin and Randal accepted this with resignation, but Sir Cedric was shocked. Chloe had noticed in the past that his notions of the behaviour suitable for a Dowager Duchess did not mesh with reality.

On this occasion he was bold enough to remonstrate. "I think, Your Grace, that Lady Stanforth"—he indicated Belinda—"cannot like to talk of it. She was . . . er . . . related to the dead man."

Chloe thought it was true that Belinda looked pale and not as composed as usual, which wasn't surprising if Frank had once been her sweetheart. When the young woman spoke, however, it was to say quietly, "I suppose we all know one another hereabouts, and Frank's mother was my father's cousin. But his death doesn't distress me any more than another man's would. I would like to know what you think occurred."

So, thought Chloe, Belinda does not intend to acknowledge any closer relationship than that. She didn't blame the girl.

The Dowager Lady Stanforth, who had drifted down to luncheon in yet another old-fashioned gown, spoke up piercingly. "A young maid was once blown off the Head in a storm."

"I have heard of such cases, Aunt," said Justin kindly. "But today there was no more than a brisk breeze."

"Do we know where he fell from?" asked Chloe.

"Yes. There are marks," replied Justin. "The drop isn't sheer, as you know, and it's obvious he tried to find purchase as he slid. It was quite close to the house, but over to the north a little and out of sight. If you and Randal had been looking towards the Head you would doubtless have seen him. It is doubtful anyone else did."

"Was there anyone else there with him?" asked the Duchess sharply.

"There is no way to tell from the ground, which is firm and dry. None of the staff is admitting to it. Was anyone here out of the house this morning, apart from Chloe and Randal?"

There was an uncomfortable silence, broken by Belinda. "Are you suggesting someone *caused* Frank to fall? Why would you think such a thing?"

Justin answered her. "It is certainly difficult to understand, but then he had no business in that part of the grounds. After Chloe and Randal rode out he was sent to the storage shed for a bag of oats. He was not seen again. The Head isn't dangerous. It's difficult to imagine him walking off the edge in a fit of absentmindedness."

"A young maid was once blown off the Head in a storm," said the Dowager pleasantly. Everyone smiled awkwardly and ignored her.

"Well," said Belinda stolidly. "I was out in the rose garden and I saw nothing untoward."

Chloe remembered seeing her leave the house. Frank had been alive then.

"The rose garden is to the south of the house. Is that not correct?" Sir Cedric asked. "It lies between the stables and the place where the young man fell?"

Belinda cut a piece of cheese. "I'm not sure where it is you say he fell, but the rose garden is on the southwest.

The most direct route to the seaside of the house from the stables would take a person that way.''

"And when did you go there?"

"Between nine and ten. I spoke to Chloe as I left the house."

Chloe corroborated this and added the fact that the maid and baby were with Belinda, just in case Cedric took the notion to consider George's wife a suspect. She guessed that, in addition to her grief, Belinda was nervous lest her relationship with the groom be exposed. Having been in such a situation herself, Chloe sympathised with anyone threatened by scandal. As a duke's granddaughter, Chloe had been able to face down Society but had still been scarred. Belinda would be destroyed.

Sir Cedric's interest in Belinda was obviously waning, but he asked, "And how long did you stay in the rose garden, Lady George?"

Belinda shrugged. "I can't be sure. I didn't have a thought as to time. After I'd gathered the petals from the blown roses, I walked further along the seaside of the house and down through the herb garden to pick a few other plants I needed. I was gathering supplies for my *potpourri*, you see. I spoke to Budsworth, the gardener. There had been no alarm raised then."

Justin broke in. "And how long was it before Chloe returned to the house with the news?"

"I don't know," said Belinda simply. "I had to go up to feed Dorinda. I heard nothing until my maid told me, just before lunch."

Justin looked around. "Frank would have gone by the rose garden and along the sea side of the house, or by the longer route around the front and through the kitchen garden to get to where he fell. As it happened, both were occupied. He must have proceeded to the Head after Belinda left the rose garden, but why would he go there remains a mystery."

"Unless he intended deliberately to do away with himself," said Sir Cedric solemnly. "That seems to be the most likely explanation. Nobody in the house had any apparent reason to wish him harm, and it seems clear nobody on the staff felt great enmity towards the young man. He was quite popular, particularly with the females. Everyone admits he had been in low spirits recently. There is no need to make a scandal of this, however. For my part, I am willing to accept this was just an unfortunate accident.''

Chloe thought it was kind of Cedric not to put the label of suicide on the death, but wondered at his exposition. Did he not realise Frank had been in low spirits because he was a servant in a house of which his equal was now mistress?

Furthermore, Chloe wondered, was Cedric really taking the word of the staff for truth? She knew they would keep their secrets from the gentry if they wished. No enmity towards Frank? She had caught a reference to him and Matthew, though she had thought it over a woman. If Frank had still been hopeful of Belinda, that did not seem likely. Chloe couldn't see Matthew setting his sights on one of the Ladies Stanforth, no matter how unexalted her birth.

She was dismayed to think, however, that she had spoken to the groom so soon before his death and been unaware of the forces converging upon him, whether they had been internal or external. . . . She dragged her attention back to the desultory decision-making.

Justin was agreeing to go along with a declaration of accidental death. Both he and Sir Cedric looked at Lord Randal, who had taken no part in the discussion.

"Nothing to do with me," Randal said casually. "Even if there was something fishy, I'll lay odds you'd never get to the bottom of it if you tried."

Chloe waited to be consulted but, happily in accord, the gentlemen rose and the baronet took his leave. Justin and Randal went off together. The Dowager and Miss Forbes rose and wandered away. Belinda said she had to go to Dorinda. Thus, Chloe and the Duchess were left to finish their cups of tea.

The Duchess looked at Chloe's scowl.

"And what's nibbling at you, my dear?"

"Men," said Chloe, darkly. "They have it all settled to their satisfaction, and not a word to us. Do they think we have no brains?"

The Duchess chuckled. "If you don't take care, my gel, you'll turn into a radical like that Wollstonecraft woman. Men do men's work and women do women's. Pity you never had children. You'd find you had enough to keep you busy without wanting men's tasks."

Chloe flushed. "Am I so unreasonable, Grandmama? I do not want to run the estate now Justin is back, but I do not relish being treated as if I were of no account. I know the people here better than any of them. Yet, they even asked *Randal* for his opinion!"

The Duchess shrugged. "You could work on them and bring them around, but what's the point? Save it for your husband. He's the one you'll need to impress with your abilities. The more I think of it though, Chloe, the less I like this notion of you marrying earnest Ernest. I ask you, who's more likely to let you run wild and poke your fingers in everywhere, someone like Randal or someone like Sir Cedric?"

Chloe refused to answer, though she silently gave the Duchess that point.

"What you need, gel, is another feckless man who'll go off and leave you in charge. Or, if you don't like that, marry a naval man. He can be depended upon to be absent nine months of the year."

Chloe knew this was not what she wanted, though she chose not to investigate her feelings too closely. She put her cup down decisively. "I'm more than half convinced not to marry at all. Having achieved that rare state for a woman—independence—would I not be foolish to give it up? Perhaps it's time we left Delamere, Grandmama. It's clear I am not needed, and I would like a change of scene."

The Duchess looked shrewdly at her granddaughter, then slowly took a number of sips of tea.

"Well, Grandmama?" asked Chloe impatiently.

"Just thinking," said the old lady. "You don't make rash plans when you're my age. Next week's a full moon. I prefer to travel when the moon's full even though I've no intention of carrying on after dark. Accidents can happen, and at least one can press on by moonlight."

"Next week, then," said Chloe with a sigh. Seven days seemed an age with Justin an ever-present temptation to foolishness.

"Don't look so fretful. You can't run away before your dinner party, and you'll need a few days to put Justin in the picture. He may have taken over things here, as is proper, but there must be a lot he don't know. Then there's Randal. He'll escort us to the Towers, but he's only just got here and deserves a few days with his friend. If the weather's fine, we could leave next Tuesday." With that, the Duchess pushed herself out of the chair and picked up her stick.

"Well," she said. "If we're to be rushing off, I'd best go talk to my maid. Get things in order."

Chloe sat alone. Rushing off, indeed. She wanted to be gone now, today. With Stephen, that had been the way of things. Form a notion, carry it out. No hesitation, no planning. Was she in fact more like Stephen than she had ever supposed?

If so, all the more reason not to marry again. Stephen had made a poor husband, but he'd have made a worse wife. Chloe shrugged and turned her mind to the more interesting speculation—had Frank been pushed off the Head, and if so, by whom?

There was one person in the house who knew a great deal about Frank Halliwell.

Chloe went to the suite of rooms used by Belinda—a bedroom, a *boudoir,* and a room used as a nursery for the baby. At Chloe's scratch, she was admitted by Belinda herself.

"Yes?" Aromas of rose and lavender, mint and citrus wove out of the doorway and gave Chloe her excuse for coming here.

"I was wondering," said Chloe, improvising, "if you would show me how you make *potpourri*, Belinda. Yours is delightful. I know it's an accomplishment which every lady should have, but I was never an attentive student and, running off with Stephen so young, I missed some of my lessons."

"I suppose you did," said Belinda as she let Chloe in.

Was there a trace of reluctance in her manner? It was hard to tell with Belinda, and her stolidness might be a concealment for grief, as with Katy Stack. Chloe wondered if she should not bother the younger woman at this time, but Belinda seemed composed as she walked over to a small table on which rested a bowl full of fresh rose petals.

"My mother taught me. Did yours not?"

Chloe smiled a little bleakly. "My mother taught us nothing but prayers and manners. I do believe we studied *potpourri* at Miss Mallory's, but I didn't pay attention and mine went mouldy."

"Well, it does take care," said Belinda with a sliding glance which Chloe could only interpret as being superior.

It came as a surprise to her that perhaps Belinda shared the world's view and saw her as a silly, unreliable chit. But how could she think so, after Chloe had run Delamere for years? Then she realised Belinda was probably unaware of much of the work of running a big house, thinking the servants could do it all without guidance.

Such speculating wasn't what Chloe had come here for, however. She went over to Belinda's work table and ran her fingers through the fresh petals, savouring the perfume.

"Do you only use rose?"

"Some do," said Belinda, moving the bowl out of reach as if Chloe's touch could contaminate it. "Some like to mix all kinds of blossoms, herbs, and citrus."

She opened a cupboard to show a number of jars on a shelf. They were plain white china, each about a pint in size. She took one down and opened it.

"Smell this. It has coriander and orange in it."

Chloe tested the aroma. It was delightful, not perfumed so much as tangy. "Lovely!"

Belinda took down another. "This has some pine in it."

By the time they had sniffed at all the jars, Chloe's nose was feeling ticklish and she was overwhelmed by perfumes, but she continued to be appreciative. Belinda made her mixtures with an artist's gift for aroma and beauty. The same could be said of her extensive collection of jars in glass and porcelain. They were of many shapes and sizes, and all had lids to preserve the perfume.

"I saw the lovely pot you put in the Dowager's room. You are very kind to her."

"Poor lady," said Belinda comfortably. "She's easy to please."

"Well, she is delighted with it. I couldn't help noticing it would be a little difficult to fill, though. All these have either a removable mesh, or a top which lifts off entirely. . . ."

Belinda smiled. "It's so pretty, though. Worth the trouble."

"Yes," said Chloe, idly lifting one of the plain storage pots which stood upon the table.

As she opened the lid, Belinda said, "It's empty."

Indeed it was, but Chloe had already raised the pot to her nose. "It still has a sweet aroma, though," she said, "and potent, to be sure. Let me see. I smell the roses, but there is another dominant fragrance. Honeysuckle."

She looked up at Belinda to see an intriguing expression on that lady's face, which almost could be alarm.

"Is something the matter, Belinda?"

In a blink the stolid gaze had returned, but Belinda turned away. "Not really. I just remembered I forgot to collect honeysuckle this year."

Belinda then quickly began a lecture on the making of

the fragrant mixes. "The main thing is to dry the petals thoroughly," she said, "unless you want to make a damp mix, in which case you need salt . . ."

Chloe tried to look attentive, but she was wondering about honeysuckle. She was also seeking a way to bring the discussion around to the subject of Frank, the real reason she had come to Belinda's rooms.

"It's quite simple," Belinda concluded, then added, somewhat pointedly, "if you have the patience."

"Yes, I see it is," said Chloe. "I really must try it." She abandoned the search for a subtle approach. "What a shame you had left the rose garden before Frank passed through, Belinda, or you might have saved him."

Belinda turned away again and began to spread the rose petals out to dry. "I can't see me being able to stop a great fellow like Frank from flinging himself off the Head."

"Well no. But presumably, he wouldn't have done it if you and the baby had been there."

"Perhaps. Perhaps not." Belinda ceased her work and looked at Chloe. "I see you've heard he was sweet on me," she said. "It's true. I'd told him and told him there was no hope, but he wasn't a man to take no for an answer. I think finally I'd made him see it was hopeless, though. It wouldn't be fair to Dorinda, now would it, to give her a stepfather such as Frank Halliwell?" Belinda lifted a handful of petals, then let them drift back down into the bowl. "If he flung himself off the Head," she said quietly, "it was probably because of me. I know that. But there's nothing I could have done about it, now was there?"

Was the question a plea? Chloe did not know and had no wisdom to offer. She and Belinda had little in common.

Thanking the girl for her lesson, Chloe took her leave and went to her favourite refuge, the Sea Room, to sit on the window seat and consider the conversation.

The idea had crept into her head that it was possible Belinda pushed Frank off the Head to conceal their relationship, but the genuine feeling in the younger woman's voice made that unlikely. Besides which, Belinda had been out with Dorinda and the maid. Concealing a past illicit relationship was a feeble kind of motive for murder anyway, Chloe thought, then reconsidered. *She* might not kill anyone for such a reason, but people took lives for trivial motives every day. To Belinda, in her precarious social position, Frank might have seemed a terrible threat. . . .

Justin came upon Chloe there, deep in thought. He sat down beside her and took her hand.

"Chloe? What is it? Are you troubled by what happened this morning?"

It took willpower to do so, but Chloe removed her hand. "Yes, I am a little. After all, a young man died. Just now, though, I was thinking about Belinda. I did form a notion she might have had a hand in his death. Is that not absurd?" She then recounted her conversations with Katy Stack and Belinda.

"You're correct, I think," said Justin. "Even if he had been her lover, Frank presented little real threat to Belinda. How would he, a groom, spread poisonous rumours to the people who really matter?"

Hesitantly, Chloe voiced her other suspicion. "What if Dorinda is not George's child?"

"Frank's?" queried Justin, unsurprised. "It's a distinct possibility. It could have been a problem if she had borne a boy, but as it is . . . It's unlikely Belinda would kill to prevent an accusation so impossible to prove. The child was born a full nine months after the wedding, which is all that counts."

"A struggle?" said Chloe. Then she shook her head. "Oh, this is terrible. Just because I don't particularly like Belinda—and I am sure that is outright snobbery—I am trying to make her a murderess! it's not as if she even had the opportunity. It is hardly likely that Rosie would keep silent about her mistress pushing the groom off a cliff. And after all," added Chloe with a cool look, "you men are quite convinced it was suicide."

Justin grinned wryly. "Not so much that, my dear. Randal put it more exactly. We decided, after looking into the matter, that there was no chance of sorting it out, and we might as well let the matter lie."

"Oh," said Chloe with a raised brow. "Is that how you keep the world spinning smoothly?"

Justin grinned. "I don't know how the civilians do it but it's pretty much the way the war is run. No point stirring matters that'll stay down if allowed to."

"But someone could have come upon Frank after Belinda had gone around the side of the house. If he was killed, don't we have to do something about it?"

Justin took her hand again, gently playing with her fingers. Chloe let him retain it this time. In seven days, she'd be gone.

"It depends on why he was killed," Justin said thoughtfully. "In other words, will the killer strike again?"

"Strike again?" she echoed faintly, more alarmed by the effect he was having on her than his words.

He made her alarm the excuse to take her other hand. "Have I upset you?" he said gently. "I'm sorry. Perhaps this is, as Sir Cedric says, no matter for a lady."

"Sir Cedric would say that," Chloe remarked, her consciousness centred on her hands, and his hands. Did she look as flustered as she felt?

There was an intensity in Justin's eyes as he looked at her. "I had the feeling, when talking to him, that he sees himself as a suitor, my dear."

"I suppose he is," she admitted a little breathlessly. "He *is* the only marriageable man in these parts."

Justin smiled slightly. "Not any more."

Chloe had been able to handle Randal with scarcely a moment's thought, but now she found herself in a panic. She pulled her fingers from Justin's and stood, looking away from him. "Randal noted much the same thing this morning," she said with an attempt at banter, "and then absolutely denied he had any interest in my hand. Are you also toying with a lady's affections?"

He had risen with her. Now he turned her to face him again. "Does the lady have affections?" he queried. A slight smile mirrored the lightness of his tone, but his brown eyes were serious and made tantalising promises.

Chloe collected herself. "I am tolerably well-disposed towards the world," she said, meeting his gaze boldly.

He stroked her cheek with a finger and grinned. "Far too broad-cast a style for me, my dear. I would want a lady to be particular in her affections."

"Well," said Chloe, moving out of his hold before she lost every shred of common sense. "I would lay odds Belinda would be most particular—if you've a steady foot on a cliff, that is."

He laughed and shook his head. "Still a vixen, aren't you?" Then, to her alarm, he sobered. "Be careful, Chloe. There's just the smallest possibility there is someone hereabouts who is . . . unhinged."

With that he went on his way, leaving her adrift. Was he going to woo her? What on earth was she to do? Her brain knew marriage to Justin would be foolish, but she was not at all sure her brain could control her wayward heart.

Later, Chloe wondered, with shock, whether his final words had indicated suspicions of her mother-in-law. Chloe had to confess she wouldn't be surprised to find the Dowager had pushed Frank off the cliff, if she'd taken it into her head he was evil. Fortunately, Miss Forbes was able to attest that the Dowager had been in her company all day. Feeling rather ridiculous, Chloe also checked on the Duchess and found she had still been in her bed breakfasting when Frank had died.

At that point, Chloe had to face the implications. Justin and Sir Cedric had already established that none of the staff could have been on the Head with Frank. The only person at Delamere who could possibly have pushed Frank off the cliff was Justin himself.

* * *

It was with this disturbing thought in mind that, later in the day, Chloe knocked at the door of the office and was told to enter.

Justin looked up with every evidence of delight when he saw her. Chloe told herself that was because he was sick to death of the piles of notes and ledgers which surrounded him.

"How are you managing?" she asked. She was already dressed for dinner. She had not examined too closely her motives in choosing yet another becoming gown, this time of a clear, turquoise blue.

"All the better for seeing you," he said with obvious sincerity as he rose. "You look like the summer sky, my dear."

Chloe knew she was blushing. She should have spent less time wondering about Frank's death, and more deciding what she was to do about an amorous Justin. "That's blue for you," she said prosaically. "What would you say if I was wearing yellow?"

"That you look like a field of daffodils up Yealand way? That seems a little trite, though. Give me notice and I'll work at it."

Chloe picked up a battered quill and fiddled with it. "Practicing for when you go hunting a bride, Justin?" She looked up to see a glint of humour in his eyes.

"Are you suggesting I need practice?"

Justin was looking at her like a man studying a text. Chloe had never been aware until this moment how little experience she had with serious flirtation. Married out of the schoolroom, and mured up at Delamere since becoming a widow, she had no idea how to behave when a man was serious in his intent.

Was Justin serious in his intent? What should she do? She decided to behave as she had when she was safely married.

She cast him a teasing glance. "Practice? Probably a little. After all, you're a rough soldier, aren't you?"

He grinned. "Am I? I thought the tailors had disguised me better."

"I wouldn't let it concern you overmuch," she continued. "Your handsome face will speak for you if you become tongue-tied."

He walked slowly around the desk until he stood close in front of her. Chloe could feel her heart pounding as the smile fled from her face.

"And what does my handsome face say?"

Betrayed into honesty, and perhaps with the notion of breaking the intimacy of the moment, Chloe said softly, "It speaks of sadness and unspeakable things."

The laughter fled from him, and after a startled moment he turned sharply away. "I'm sorry."

"Oh no," Chloe exclaimed. "It is I who should be sorry. I don't know why I said such a thing."

He turned back, sober but calm. "As always, you speak the truth. When we first met, you were still a child, younger even than you thought. You still believed in honesty and made no attempt to dissemble. We were all children then, but Stephen and I were not so innocent as you. You have learnt some sophistication, Chloe, but do not learn too much. We all have need of honest souls."

Chloe raised her chin. "Then why did you turn away?"

He shrugged. "Do we all not flinch under the knife?" He looked at the dancing flames in the fireplace. "War leaves its scars, my dear. I recommend, when you choose another husband, that you not choose a soldier."

Chloe swallowed and summoned up a smile. "You will have to take that up with the Duchess. She recommends a soldier, or a naval man. She thinks I'd do better with an absentee Lord and Master."

A trace of humour lightened his expression. "It would be a damned waste."

It was as if a power had been born in the room, leapt between then, drew her . . . Then Chloe remembered, with relief, her main reason for coming to the study. Any suspicion of Justin seemed ridiculous but still must be pursued.

"It would be a damned waste, as you put it, for my

husband to be around all the time," she said. "For then I would never have the opportunity to employ my management skills. Do you find everything in order?"

Seemingly at ease, passion fled, he strolled over to stand beside her. She could sense him there, like the heat of a fire.

"I thought it was your hand," he remarked, "making all those notes on Scarthwait's records. You have worked hard, my dear. Should I pay you a salary?"

Chloe moved away a few steps. "Stephen provided for me handsomely, thank you, and I would have died of boredom without occupation. Besides which, I find I cannot tolerate seeing things in disorder. Have you really looked through all these?" she asked, indicating a pile of papers. If he had, he surely must have spent the morning hard at work.

He made no attempt to pursue her. "Yes. I haven't finecombed them, but I am willing to trust you and Scarthwait on the whole. I am merely trying to familiarise myself with the estate."

Chloe spotted one thin ledger in the pile he had not yet touched. "Did you see the figures on the goats we started as an experiment?" she asked. "I think it is going famously."

"Goats?" he frowned.

"Yes. Over at Hest Bank. Oh, I'm sorry. It will be in the grey stock book over there. You will come to it shortly."

If he had only pretended to go through that pile of documents, surely he might have pretended to have seen something on the goats. Chloe felt relief, but did not want to give him time to think about her question, and perhaps perceive her ruse. She turned the subject to a letter atop a small pile of papers.

"Have you decided what to do about Humphrey Macy?"

"No. I don't think I know the man. Tell me about him."

"He was an old friend of Uncle George's, though what they had in common was hard to tell, unless it was the

Prince of Wales. Macy is one of the Carlton House set, and Uncle George was too when he had the funds. I suspect it was one of those friendships where the smart one has a slow-top hanging on who can be depended upon to always laugh at his jokes.''

"Macy's a smart one, is he?''

"I would say so, though anyone would look clever next to Uncle George. Macy would be a good match for Belinda, though. He's a real top-of-the-trees. He has a comfortable amount of money as one of the Oxfordshire Macys, and a government position. Customs, I think. It certainly can't be arduous, for he is to be found everywhere, and he spent months up here when George succeeded.''

"So I heard. Why was that, do you think?''

Chloe frowned slightly. "To keep George company, I suppose, but I never did decide why Uncle George stayed at Delamere. He'd come down in August, obviously rusticating. I expected as soon as he was the viscount and the estate probated, he'd be back to London. I was quite concerned. It seemed likely some Captain Sharp would relieve him of the fortune and Delamere in short order.''

"I must confess, I was pretty well resigned to that notion myself.''

"Perhaps it was the weather. He stayed a while for the legalities, of course, and then he married Belinda. By that time it was Christmas. I suppose it didn't seem a good season to be travelling the length of England. Uncle George liked his comforts. Macy acted the good friend and come up to bear him company. They spent their time drinking, gossiping, and rolling dice. I'm not surprised Uncle George wanted Macy to stay, alone as he was in a house of women, but I think it very noble of Macy to agree. He did seem to be genuinely fond of George, though. He was truly upset when he died. In shock, trembling.''

The viscount seemed lost in thought.

"Justin?''

He shook himself out of his deliberations. "Macy. I can

put him off if you wish, but I can see no reason to forbid him to visit. And, I confess, if he can win the hand and heart of the fair Belinda, that would be one less problem in my life.''

"Yes, but I doubt she'll have him. He would be a fine catch. He's well-connected, comfortably off, and in a reasonable state of repair for one his age. Now, however, I think she's got notions, as Katy Stack would say. If she doesn't entrap you, she'll be off to try her luck in one of the fashionable towns.''

Justin laughed. "I assure you, Chloe, I am completely safe from Belinda. Perhaps you should warn Randal, however."

Chloe frowned at his levity. "I'll warn Randal, all right. I'll warn him not to tease her. It's just possible she'll take him seriously, and I don't think she deserves to be hurt. Do you need to ask me any questions about the estate just now, Justin? Today has been a bit disorganised, but tomorrow I will spend some time with you if you wish.''

There was a distinctly mischievous light in his eyes as he said, "What gallant man could refuse such an offer?''

"Time poring over dusty ledgers, milk yields, crop rotations, and cottage repairs, Lord Stanforth!''

"The mere thought of your presence turns even the slaughtering records into poetry, Lady Stanforth.'' He made an extravagant bow.

Chloe tried to frown but burst out laughing. "Love among the compost piles? Really, Justin.''

She thought he might come to her then, but he didn't.

"No,'' he said seriously. "You are definitely worthy of a bed of rose petals, my dear.''

Chloe could not mistake the hint of passion in his eyes. Discretion being the better part of valour, she left.

After she had gone, Justin stared at the door with more attention than that piece of oak warranted. In fact, he was seeing Chloe. She was so easily alarmed, so quick to retreat. The temptation to pressure her was enormous, but he knew it would be a mistake. He knew also he should be focusing his attention on the missing papers.

A few simple questions had established that no apples were left in stock from the previous autumn. Moreover, there were no ornamental apples in the house. The dining room had one bowl of wax fruit, sometimes used as a centrepiece, but Mrs. Pickering had told him that the two apples belonging there had been found cut into pieces last Christmas. She credited George with that meaningless destruction but Justin wondered. Who could have been searching Delamere then? The only outsider in residence at the time was Humphrey Macy.

Macy could have been sent to Delamere as a government agent. If so, Justin should have been informed. He quickly wrote to Lord Liverpool for clarification. He sealed the letter, franked it, and placed it ready for the next day's post.

If George had received the package, it would seem he hid the apple very well, or took the papers from it. Would he do that? With George, one never knew. Justin had spent part of the morning in a cursory search of the study, which seemed the most likely place for papers to be concealed. He had found nothing.

The whole matter would be much simpler if he could enlist the assistance of everyone in the house. That was against orders, however, and there was the distinct possibility that someone here was working for Napoleon. More imperatively, any hint that the British believed the lists to be inside Delamere could easily lead to its callous destruction.

He realised he had only minutes to prepare for dinner and quickly tidied his work. He had been constantly distracted by Chloe. Her hand was obvious everywhere among these papers; there even seemed to be traces of her soft, flowery perfume here. Love among the compost piles . . .

Anywhere. Anywhere with you, my darling.

7

THE FOLLOWING DAY brought pouring rain and confined everyone to the house. There had been quick acceptances from all the parties invited to dine on Thursday, and Chloe spent the first part of her day in conference with Mrs. Pickering, who was delighted at the thought of entertaining. A suitable menu was soon agreed on as Chloe had no intention of debating the merits of veal over pork, and tench over barbel. She requested, however, a Walpole pudding. It was the only food she could remember Justin expressing a preference for, on that long ago journey to Scotland. Next, Chloe took Matthew to the cellars and chose a number of wines for him to prepare. She smiled to see the young man nearly burst with pride at being made a temporary butler.

By midmorning, Chloe thought the plans to be well in hand and returned to the main part of the house, where she was surprised to see Belinda coming down the stairs in a heavy cloak.

"Do you intend to go out, Belinda?" she asked. "You'll be drenched."

"Just as far as the herb garden. I need some thyme."

Chloe couldn't help but regard this as peculiar. Belinda, who was normally rather stolid, seemed almost disturbed. Was it grief? Or guilt? For some reason, these niggling suspicions of Belinda would not be quieted by logic.

"Surely it can wait, Belinda," Chloe said. "The ground

is a sea of mud. By this afternoon or tomorrow, it will have cleared. You know the weather hereabouts.''

''Better than you,'' snapped Belinda, then collected herself. ''You're right, though. I wanted to get something finished but it will wait.'' With that she turned and went back up stairs.

Chloe was thoughtful as she went into the Sea Room. The sluicing rain obscured the view, so she went to sit by the fire. She couldn't help leaping to the obvious conclusion. Belinda pushed Frank off the cliff and had remembered some clue which needed to be retrieved. What could it be? Surely a clue would be washed away in this torrential rain? Perhaps that is what Belinda had decided, and that was why she had returned to her rooms.

But Belinda *couldn't* have pushed Frank off the cliff. She had not been alone. . . .

Chloe was interrupted at that moment by Justin, who came in with a sheaf of papers in his hands. He was without his jacket, and his hair looked as if he had pushed his fingers through it repeatedly.

Chloe held back a smile.

''Is there any reason, Chloe,'' he demanded with asperity, ''that we have stored in the files long letters from an Italian nun?''

''Yes, of course,'' she said, as he came to sit across the fire from her. ''Do you not read Italian?''

''Very little,'' he replied. ''What with Latin and Spanish, I can piece together some of it. But the woman writes a damnably ornate hand.''

''I think Donna Ilena's calligraphy rather beautiful,'' said Chloe, taking one of the letters and admiring the flourishing italic. ''And she isn't a nun, you know. She's a Venetian lady of high birth. I rather suspect she was once your uncle's lover.''

''Uncle Henry?''

''Well, hardly George.''

''I always thought he was devoted to Aunt Sophronia.''

Chloe looked pensively into the dancing flames. ''I'm

sure he was, but as her illness progressed and she no longer travelled with him, perhaps . . . I might be wrong in my assumptions.'' She smiled at him. ''Whatever the truth of that, I am sure Donna Ilena loved your uncle. It is like a harmony in the letters, though they deal only with a convent there of which they both are patrons.''

He looked at her a moment before answering and she felt he might have addressed a quite different subject. Then he frowned. ''Why was my uncle a patron of a convent? He wasn't even Catholic.''

''He kept a journal,'' said Chloe, flustered. Why was it that they could not be together for a moment, even talking of purely business matters, without her nerves trembling. . . . ''You should read it one day,'' she continued hurriedly. ''He was in Venice shortly before he died, and this particular convent, which cares for orphans, came to his attention. Perhaps Donna Ilena brought it to his attention—it doesn't say. He was very much one for giving charity to clearly defined objects. All his projects continued under Stephen and George. It is for you to say what happens now.''

Again a pause and he looked at her. Then a sudden movement, as he dragged his mind back to business. ''And the lady still writes?''

''Yes,'' she said, speaking a little too fast. ''She tells of the work they do there, the little success stories. The letters are often delayed, but they arrive eventually. They are quite charming. You will have to brush up on your Italian.''

''Si, *mi amori*,'' he said with a lazy smile.

''*Amore mio*,'' she corrected.

''Am I?'' he asked, delighted. Chloe felt her skin tingle as it coloured.

Hastily, she said, ''You can hardly cut the poor orphans off without a penny, Justin.''

He sighed. ''I suppose not. How does the money get to them?''

''Your uncle set up a trust in Italy, through bankers

there. The interest is paid to the Little Sisters of the Angels."

"Painless charity," he murmured. "And doubtless the sisters pray for my uncle's soul, as well."

"Doubtless. Perhaps this charity was a kind of insurance. Many people up here still have lingering sympathy for the Romish faith, and you come of an old Lancashire family."

He looked at her with interest. "Have you studied the family history?" he asked.

She shrugged. "Lacking Hookham's . . ."

"Were we for Hanover or Stuart in the last century?"

Chloe looked at him in surprise. A somewhat abrupt interest in history. "Well, the second baronet, your great-uncle, kept his head well down in '45. Back in '15, though, the first baronet showed distinct leanings towards the Stuarts and the Church of Rome. He'd married a staunch Protestant, however, and I think she kept him loyal. You should read *her* journals. A strong and rather terrifying woman. She was still alive in '45 and I wouldn't be surprised if she was responsible for your great-uncle's discretion."

"What of you?" he asked. "Do you not have a soft spot for romantic Bonnie Prince Charlie? So many young ladies do."

Outrage jerked Chloe up straight. "I beg your pardon!"

Justin leaned slightly back and eyed her warily. "No?"

Chloe leapt to her feet, eyes flashing, and jabbed a finger hard at his waistcoat. "Justin Delamere, if I were a man, I'd call you out! The Ashbys were loyal to the Stuarts in the Civil War, but that ended when James II tried to bring back popishness. Anne created the earldom and George I, the dukedom. The Ashbys stand to a man—or woman—behind the throne."

Forced back in his chair, Justin threw wide his hands, laughing. "I surrender. I apologise."

Chloe retreated slightly, still fuming, but then she saw him laughing, brown eyes sparkling with merriment, skin flushed. He looked so young. He looked as he had when they first met.

He stood slowly and placed his papers on a small table there. Chloe retreated a step. Hand outstretched, he moved towards her, sober now, but with a different light in his eyes.

"No," Chloe said.

"No?"

She couldn't explain. It was too dangerous even to try to make sense of her tangled feelings.

After a moment he sighed and his hand fell. "As you will. I do need help in understanding all of the paperwork, though. Scarthwait spent an hour with me this morning, but most of the accounting seems to be yours, and I'm sure you would be best able to explain it."

The last thing Chloe wanted was to be closeted with him for hours, and yet she could not escape the necessity. It would be seen as ridiculous to insist upon a chaperone. On whom could she call? The Duchess? Randal? They'd both die laughing.

At least she must have time to gain control of her mind.

"I have a few household tasks to see to," she muttered. "Perhaps in an hour?"

"Very well."

He stood for a moment, looking at her. Then his eyes wandered to the Dutch paintings over the mantel, as if he sought inspiration there among the dancing villagers. Chloe wished he would go. She also wished he would sweep her into his arms and seduce her from all her doubts. She saw his gaze sharpen, as if focussing on the pictures for the first time.

"That is a fine set," he said. "I don't remember it. Did Stephen buy it?"

"No, of course not," said Chloe. "He had little interest in art. It was a gift from Herr van Maes. He's a Dutch antiquarian who has been in the area for some time, studying the hogback stone and other ancient pieces. You will meet him on Thursday at dinner."

"A handsome gift," he said. "Given recently?"

"At Christmas."

Chloe wondered at his interest, which seemed excessive. Then she thought it was possible he was jealous. She glanced at Justin again. He did look very serious. Jealousy was such an unpleasant emotion. Why did she feel a tiny thrill at the thought that it was eating him?

He seemed to drag his mind back to the matter in hand. "Try to help me as soon as possible, Chloe," he said with a smile which looked a little forced. "I am drowning in indecipherable figures."

"An hour," she said, and he left.

Chloe looked at the pictures. Had Justin been jealous? She shook her head. If she did not intend to have him, it was despicable to want him to suffer on her behalf. Chloe resolved to give him no encouragement, then pushed the incident to the back of her mind.

What task should she busy herself in now to make good her excuse? With relief, she remembered a complaint from the laundress about the quality of the washing soda, and hurried off to the steamy little room with its boilers and dolly tubs.

The sight of Rosie, the nursery maid, chatting as she folded the baby's napkins, distracted her from soda, and resurrected her lingering suspicions about Belinda. Here was someone who could throw light on Belinda's actions round about the time of Frank's death. Just how effectively had Cedric questioned the girl?

Rosie dropped a curtsey. Chloe tried a subtle method of questioning.

"When you went out yesterday with Lady George, do you know how long you were gone, Rosie?"

"No, ma'am." The girl looked thoroughly bewildered.

"Lady George went to the rose garden first?"

"Yes, ma'am."

"Then to the herb garden?"

"Yes, ma'am."

It was always difficult to prize information out of the staff. Chloe tried for more details.

"What did Lady George do in the herb garden, Rosie?"

"I don't know, ma'am."

Chloe repressed an urge to shake the maid, who was doubtless only trying to be honest. "You may not know the names of the plants, Rosie, but were they leaves, flowers, or roots? And how much did she collect? If we knew how much was picked we could estimate the time."

The girl was anxious now, twisting at her apron. "But I don't know, ma'am!"

"Rosie, I am not expecting a botanical lesson . . ." Chloe broke off at the glazed look on the girl's face and rephrased her statement. "I am not expecting you to know all about herbs. Did Lady George just pick a few sprigs or fill a basket?"

"But I don't know, ma'am. I weren't there."

Chloe stared. "What?"

"I brought Miss Dorinda back into the house. I had her changed and ready when Lady George came in to feed her."

"Oh, I see," said Chloe. "And did that take very long?"

"No, ma'am."

"Thank you, Rosie."

Chloe retreated to the Sea Room to consider. Probably Cedric had asked the same questions as she had begun with. Asking where Belinda was and assuming Rosie was with her. So Belinda, between leaving the rose garden and speaking to Budsworth in the herb garden, had been alone. She could have been with Frank.

There still was no motive for her to harm him or none that suggested itself, but something had jerked Belinda out of her normal placidity. Chloe remembered the day before when Belinda had almost become alarmed. Chloe had been sniffing at the empty pot, she recalled, and Belinda had said something about honeysuckle.

After a minute or two, Chloe shook her head. It made

no sense at all. If Belinda had met Frank, and if she had pushed him off the cliff, there still was no connection with honeysuckle. If there was any chance the young woman was a murderess, however, Chloe could not turn a blind eye. She was determined to pursue it, partly because she still regarded Delamere as her responsibility, and partly because she would teach the men not to ignore her abilities.

She found that as she was thinking, her eyes had been drawn again and again to the Dutch pictures above the fire. What was it about them?

They were in the wrong order!

Instead of being spring, summer, autumn, and winter, winter now came first. When had that happened? As with most familiar objects, she had scarcely been aware of the pictures for weeks. At the same time, something about them had niggled at her since she entered the room. She remembered discussing them with Justin earlier. Surely she would have noticed then if they had been rearranged.

She shook her head. She was fretting over trifles. One of the maids had doubtless had them down during cleaning and hung them differently. She went over and began to rearrange them. It was as she was hanging autumn that her finger caught in the back. She turned it. The backing had been neatly slit. She poked inside, but there was nothing.

She looked at the other pictures and discovered each had a slit in the backing, but smaller and less obtrusive. Had the cuts, perhaps, always been there? She could hardly imagine Herr van Maes giving her the pictures without repairing the damage. How inexplicably peculiar.

Chloe hung the last two pictures and then sat contemplating them. What possible reason could there be for such an act? Was she wrong to have this feeling constantly that things were not right at Delamere? Apart from Frank's death, which could well have been a freak accident, she really had nothing to go on. The feeling, however, would not be banished.

She wondered if the Dowager could be the explanation for the strange happenings—the disturbed stores, the slits in the pictures. But Stephen's mother was rarely unaccompanied and totally lacked guile.

Randal came into the room. "Are you cast into the dismals too?" he asked. "Grandmama says the weather has brought out her rheumatics."

"Oh, poor dear. Has she everything she needs? Belinda has a whole *repertoire* of receipts for anything which ails you."

"She is well at the moment. She says you want to leave on Tuesday."

"Yes. That should be time enough for Justin to settle in, and we should be on our way before the winter sets in."

"It's only October, Chloe. Why the hurry?"

Chloe looked up. "I've been here nearly two years, Randal. I've forgotten there's a world beyond Lancaster."

He dropped elegantly into a chair. "There is, and it's as boring as ever, and it ain't going anywhere. It seems a bit heartless to abandon Justin here with bucolic Belinda."

"Perhaps Humphrey Macy will solve that problem."

"He's coming, is he?"

Something in his tone alerted Chloe. "Don't you like him?"

Randal shrugged. "He's hardly a crony of mine but he's *bon ton*. Seen everywhere and pleasant enough. A bit fulsome, don't you think?"

"I suppose so, but that doubtless comes of toadying to the Prince of Wales all the time."

"Disrespectful chit," remarked Randal. "The Macys are an old Whig family, so it's almost his duty, but I'm sure he fits in at Carlton House like a plum in a basket of hothouse fruit."

Chloe chuckled. "With the Prince as a pineapple?"

Randal shouted with laughter. "God yes! And Lady Jersey a plump, juicy peach."

"What of Lady Hertford then?"

His blue eyes twinkled. "Undoubtedly a prune, and strangely out of place."

"As out of place as Macy here," Chloe commented idly. "Ah well. It was kind of him to keep George company, and it must indicate devotion if he is coming north again to woo Belinda. You think he's well-to-do, Randal?"

"He puts on a good show, but then half of Society is all tinsel and glitter over a hollow core. I've never seen him gamble deep, but he'd have to at Carlton House. Why so concerned?"

"If he's tied to the wrong connections," said Chloe, "we don't want Belinda to marry him."

"Don't we?"

Chloe fixed him with her sternest look. "No. Altruistically speaking, I don't see any reason why Belinda shouldn't make a comfortable second marriage. In more practical terms, if she's well-established, she won't hang around Justin's neck. After all, Dorinda is a cousin of Justin's, and of mine in a way."

Randal shrugged. "Just as long as you don't expect me to marry her."

"Of course I don't. And don't encourage her, either. I know she's casting eyes at you, just like every woman who crosses your path. Freeze her out, if you want, but don't raise her hopes."

Randal sighed. "Trapped here in boredom and she denies me the only available sport."

Chloe stood. "I'm sure you can find some pastime—"

Suddenly, she was spun down on Randal's lap. "An offer?" he queried wickedly.

Chloe struggled, but not very hard. She was laughing too much. "Don't be daft, as they say round here. Randal, let go." He was far too strong so she relaxed.

"That's better," he approved. "I'll let you go if you promise me some other amusement."

Chloe found she was enjoying her position. There was nothing particular to Randal about the pleasure, other than the fact he was the only man she could imagine feeling so comfortable with. It was just that it had been a long time since she had been held by a man.

"What amusement did you have in mind?" she asked, as she leant her head on his shoulder.

"You're the hostess."

"Nonsense," she retorted lazily. "Justin's your host. Go and discuss it with him."

"No need," said Randal.

Something in his voice made Chloe look up. She felt herself go red as she saw Justin staring at them with astonishment and, perhaps, anger. She leapt up before she realised this must give the whole scene an even more improper appearance.

"Pistols at twenty paces, Justin?" drawled Randal, laughter in his eyes. 'If not exactly amusement, it would enliven a dull morning."

Justin's expression was unreadable. "Unless Chloe is claiming molestation, I see no need for that. She is her own mistress."

"Of course he wasn't molesting me," said Chloe, flustered. Then she saw this did not quite give the impression she wanted. "You know Randal . . ."

"Of course I know Randal," said Justin coldly. "If you can spare the time, Chloe, I really do need your assistance with estate matters." He stood by the door in a way which made the suggestion an implacable command.

"Of course," said Chloe, knowing she was a flustered red. She followed him out of the room, aware of Randal's amusement, feeling very like a naughty schoolgirl.

Damn all men.

The atmosphere in the study was chilly as they went through all the current business of the Delamere estate with Chloe filling in the background. By the time luncheon was announced, she was heartily glad to escape, but Justin stopped her as she made her way to the door.

"I'm sorry if I reacted badly earlier," he said. "I can't

help but think of you as a lady under my protection, but you are not really that.''

"It doesn't matter,'' she replied, glancing at him and seeing no trace of anger or condemnation in his face. "I just felt rather silly, to be caught like that.''

"Not very discreet, to be sure. Chloe, I am not sure that Randal—''

"Heavens, Justin,'' Chloe broke in. "Never think that Randal and I were . . . We were just being foolish, playing a game.''

A smile twitched his lips. "Were you? Be careful, my dear. You can still get burned at that game, and Randal is, I think, somewhat inflammatory.''

Chloe put her hands on her hips. "Justin Delamere, we were not even playing *that* game . . . Oh, what a ridiculous conversation this is. As far as I'm concerned, Randal is about as inflammatory as a bucket of cold water.''

It was as if a cloud passed. He grinned. "You must be the only woman in England to feel that way. I must quote that to him when he's feeling full of himself.'' After a short silence he added, "Do you really mean to leave on Tuesday?''

Chloe nodded and looked away. "It's time.''

"It may seem like ages to you, my dear, but I have only just arrived.''

"You don't need me here any more, Justin.''

"Don't I?''

Chloe knew in that moment that she could stay. At a word Justin would offer her his hand, and perhaps his heart. Reactions warred within her and she turned away. He came up behind her and placed warm hands on her shoulders.

"Tell me what you are thinking,'' he said softly.

Chloe shook her head. She could not put her feelings into words even if she would. Was he moved by convenience, nostalgia, or could it be love? If it was love, would it make any difference? Stephen had loved her once, after a fashion.

His hand moved up to the bare skin of her neck and played in the soft curls there. Chloe sighed and leaned back against him. His arms slipped round and she rested there.

They had never touched like this before. They had been close, almost intimate in their knowledge of each other, and yet they had rarely touched. For she had been Stephen's.

They did not speak. They did not move. Still, they communicated. Chloe knew she was offered here a feast she hungered for and yet . . . and yet, she wasn't sure if it was real or not. If it was real, that perhaps terrified her most of all. She never had to surrender to Stephen as she would have to surrender to Justin.

"This has its virtues, my dear," he said, "but I can think of more promising positions. If I sit with you in my lap, will you be as quiescent as you were with Randal?"

Chloe pulled out of his arms and moved two quick steps away. "No."

She had expected a protest but when she turned to look at him, he was smiling broadly. "Why do you look so pleased with yourself?" she asked.

"When you are in my arms, Chloe, I do not want you to be quiescent."

"Justin—"

He stopped her with a raised hand. "Please don't run away on Tuesday."

"I must."

He sighed. "I had intended to stay here for a while, but I suppose I will have to follow you."

Chloe blinked. "You can't do that!"

"Is there a law against it?"

"I'll be going to the Towers."

"Do you think Randal won't invite me?" he asked.

"I'll tell him not to," said Chloe imperiously. Justin just raised a brow.

Chloe left abruptly, before he could say more. She ran

Randal to ground in the billiard room, potting balls with cool efficiency.

"Come to offer me a game?" he asked, leaning picturesquely on his cue.

"No," she said. "Randal, if Justin asks to be invited to the Towers when we leave here, can you not do so?"

He looked at her. "Be a bit uncivil, wouldn't I?"

"Your reputation will stand the strain, I'm sure," she retorted.

He idly chalked the button. "A man don't have so many friends he can afford to offend them."

"Are you saying you won't oblige me?" Chloe asked in amazement.

"Basically, yes."

"Why not?"

"Why should I?"

Faced with this, Chloe turned away. "Randal. He's . . . he's *wooing* me."

"Always thought he was a knowing one."

Chloe turned back. "Randal. He's a Delamere!"

"So are you."

"Not for long."

"Anyway, a saucy Ashby throwing up the dirt at a Delamere is like the pot calling the kettle black. I think you and Justin would suit very well." He turned and casually made a cannon, then moved round to the white ball and potted the black.

As he replaced the black on its spot he said, "What is it that bothers you so, Chloe?"

Forced to put it into words, Chloe hesitated. "I want a quiet life, Randal."

"You wouldn't like it. If you married Stodgy Cedric you'd be climbing the walls within a year. You'd probably run off with an adventurer."

"I have to get away from here before I make any decisions."

Randal look at her and shook his head. "All this rusticating has dulled your wits, my girl."

"And what is that supposed to mean?"

He laid down his cue and walked over to her, coolly elegant, and probably the most devastatingly attractive man in England. He took her hand and raised it to his lips, slowly. His lips brushed over her fingers softly, and then back again.

"Randal—"

"Hush."

He drew her into his arms. She felt his hands on her back and tilted her head up automatically, perhaps to protest. What was he about? If he had suddenly decided to pay serious court to her, it would be most embarrassing, but there was only wicked amusement in his clear blue eyes as one of his hands slid up to play in her dusky curls.

"What are you thinking, my dear?" he asked.

"That you have run mad," she said, just a little breathlessly. He was, after all, amazingly attractive, and she wasn't dead yet.

He lowered his head and his lips skimmed softly down over her forehead and nose, to hover over her own.

Chloe struggled slightly, but his arms tightened and she couldn't escape. "Randal!"

Very softly, he whispered, his warm breath mingling with hers. "What is worrying you, my dear? Be honest."

Then she knew. She looked up into his eyes, which demanded the truth. "Justin might come in again," she whispered.

He dropped a quick kiss on her lips and released her.

"The time for decisions is past, Chloe," he commented dryly.

Chloe took refuge in anger. "You conceited oaf! Do you think a woman can resist you only if she is in love with someone else?"

He leaned back against the billiard table, grinning insolently. "That seems to be the case so far."

Chloe made a little growl of exasperation and looked around for something with which to attack him. Finding nothing, she said, "I think I *will* set Justin onto you with pistols."

"I wouldn't if I were you. We visited Manton's and I'm by far the better shot. Give up, Chloe. You and Justin are in love. It's clear as a pikestaff to an observer. It's my opinion you've been in love since you first met, and you only married Stephen by mistake."

Chloe felt shock lance through her. Tears rose in her eyes. She brushed them angrily away as his expression turned from humour to concern.

"Sometimes, Randal, I could hate you," she declared as she ran out of the room.

Chloe took luncheon in her own room, only picking at the food. Randal had forced open a door into an area of feeling she had hoped buried forever. Young and heedless, she had never thought, on that long journey to Scotland, about the two men as different from one another. She had known she was going to marry Stephen, she had wanted to marry Stephen, but she had thought they would always be together, the three of them.

It was on her wedding night that reality intruded. It had not been an unpleasant business, all in all, for Stephen was a kindly lover, but she had missed Justin. Over the next few days, she had been bothered by the times he had gone off to leave them together. On the return south he had frequently ridden beside the carriage instead of within, and she had wished he wouldn't.

After the young couple, facing scandal boldly, had established themselves in Town, Justin had disappeared and his absence had been a void in her life. Soon she heard he had bought a commission. She followed the adventures of his regiment closely, scrutinised every casualty list. They had met briefly on only two occasions after that, and on the last one . . .

They had been in the small library of Stephen's house in Clarges Street, all three of them. Justin was in uniform, and looked splendid. Chloe remembered thinking that, and noticing how Stephen looked pale and puffy around the eyes by comparison.

She and Justin had hardly spoken to each other, and yet she was conscious of him at all times. When he passed her a glass of wine their fingers did not touch, and yet there had been a sensation, a vibration, between them. She had stared up at him, startled. His eyes held an arrested look.

Then Stephen left the room to fetch some object. She and Justin had sat in silence. She finally looked at him, and found him studying her. They had said something then, she did not know what.

She *did* remember suddenly being aware of his body beneath the uniform, of the long strong muscles of his legs, the tendons of his sun-browned hands, the breadth of his shoulders. It had come to her that in lovemaking with Justin she would feel more than the mild contentment she experienced with Stephen.

She had leapt to her feet in alarm, and he had risen too, concerned. Stephen returned at that moment. She had made an excuse and escaped.

She and Justin had never met again until he came to Delamere as Lord Stanforth. She had buried the memory of the occasion, of the betrayal she had committed in her mind, deep down.

To leap joyously now into Justin's arms, over Stephen's grave, was unthinkable. Did he not feel it? Perhaps he had not been as guilty as she. Perhaps he had not, in the secrecy of the night, toyed with the idea of Stephen ceasing to exist, so the other possibility could become reality.

Even now, the thought of it overwhelmed her with guilt. She covered her face with her hands. Thank God she could at least say that the news of Stephen's death had filled her with nothing but grief for him. Any other reaction, no matter how involuntary, would have been intolerable.

She picked up the miniature of her husband which stood upon her bedside table. Smiling and handsome, he looked out on life with merry anticipation. Chloe found herself comparing Stephen's features with Justin's harsher ones. His expression with Justin's bleaker one. She remembered that moment in the Sea Room when he had regained a youthful, carefree look.

She put the portrait down. Could she not summon a trace of sorrow for a life cut short so early? How could anything good grow out of such poisoned ground?

A scratch on the door brought a welcome interruption. Chloe hurried to open it and found her grandmother's maid.

"The Duchess asks if you would join her, My Lady."

Chloe glanced in the mirror to check that her disturbed mind was not evidenced in her appearance, and then followed the maid. The Duchess would have heard she had not gone down to luncheon. The old lady was still in bed but looked well, not in pain.

"How are you, Grandmama?" Chloe asked as she bent to kiss a withered cheek.

"Pretty fair, my dear."

"Randal said you had the rheumatics."

"Well, I would have if I tried to get about in this weather." The old woman studied Chloe. "You don't look so wonderful yourself. Got the rheumatics too?"

Chloe smiled wanly. "Just blue-deviled."

"Randal said he'd been a damned fool, and it appears he was right," said the Duchess.

Chloe felt herself flush. How much had Randal told their grandmother?

"Have you been in love with Justin all these years?" the Duchess demanded.

"No!"

"The truth, please."

Chloe looked at the stern face. It was not as if she'd been able to help it. "A little perhaps," she confessed.

"Niminy piminy. That's not got you blue-deviled. Did you love Justin more than Stephen?"

How could anyone ask such a question? Chloe turned

away and found she was twisting her fingers. "Grand-mama, what can it matter? Stephen's dead now."

"And if you didn't love him as much as you love Justin—I've seen it too, gel—you're doubtless feeling like a regular ghoul. Let me say this. If you have been regretting your choice and making the best of it, I respect you more. Once for keeping your marriage vows, and twice for having better taste than I gave you credit for."

"Grandmama!" Chloe protested.

"It's the truth. What are you going to do about it now you have a second chance? Not many of us are given those in life."

Chloe looked up sharply. "I never had a first chance. Don't put all the blame on me. Justin never indicated the slightest wish to marry me."

The old woman looked at her thoughtfully, then shrugged. "Ah well, It will work out. Things tend to. Randal'll learn not to be quite so meddlesome too. It's time his heart was touched. I worry about that boy. Far too good looking. Now, who do you think pushed Frank off the cliff?"

Chloe gaped. It was such a sudden change of subject and her mind had been completely on her own affairs. "Belinda," she blurted out, "but I'm not sure why."

"That's what I thought," said the old woman. "That maid of hers wasn't with her all the time, was she?"

"How did you know?" Chloe asked in amazement.

The old woman chuckled. "Could claim magical powers, couldn't I? Fact is, I heard the infant squalling as it was carried in, and then Belinda coming up later. She's next door."

"Why didn't you say anything earlier?"

"Why should I? The snobs around here would enjoy tearing her to pieces if they had the chance. If she quarreled with her lover and pushed him, God will be her judge. I just wish I was sure . . ."

"How did you know Frank and Belinda were lovers?"

"That spyglass. I've seen them meet a time or two.

They were generally arguing, but arguing like lovers do, if you know what I mean.''

"Sometimes I think you know everything, Grandmama.''

"Old age has to have some benefits," remarked the Duchess. "I certainly know things you don't know. Things you ought to know.''

"You do?" queried Chloe, feeling the conversation had got away from her.

"Send Justin up to me," said the Duchess, autocratically.

Chloe stared at her grandmother. "Don't you dare talk to Justin about me," she warned.

"I'll dare what I want, gel," the Duchess snapped back. Then her tone softened. "But I won't do *that*, I promise. Now, do as you're told.''

Chloe stood and dropped a saucy curtsey. "Yes, Your Grace.''

The old lady grinned. "I've no patience at the moment for please and thank you. Off you go.''

Chloe only realised as she went down the staircase that she had no particular desire to speak with Justin just now. She was thinking of ringing for Matthew when Justin walked into the hall from the study and stopped warily.

"Grandmama wishes to see you," Chloe said coolly, to disguise the jumping of her nerves.

He looked a trifle apprehensive. "Why?''

"I have no idea. She's being very mysterious.''

As he walked up the stairs, however, she watched him and felt an extraordinary desire to touch him. Was it impossible? How could she tell? She needed to get away from Delamere—and away from Justin—before she would ever know her heart.

Damn the rain. They were trapped in the house together.

8

AFTER HER GRANDMOTHER'S words, Chloe waited for someone to tell her those things she did not know, though what they could be she could not imagine. The dreary day plodded through, however, without revelations. To be sure, to avoid unfortunate encounters she threw herself into an orgy of housekeeping, but she could have been summoned if needed.

Most of her time was spent with Margaret, the upstairs maid, washing and polishing the china and glass for the dinner. Eventually over a hundred pieces of china were spotless, and a like number of glasses gleamed. She picked out two candelabra, and vases for flowers, wine coolers and serving dishes, carving tools and knife rests. Eventually, however, there was nothing more to be done, and Margaret was needed for other tasks.

Chloe then called Mrs. Pickering from the kitchen to go over the pantry and cellar. As they kept neither butler nor housekeeper at Delamere, the two women had shared these responsibilities but the cook was clearly put out at being summoned to the task at short notice.

"We will not mind a simple dinner," Chloe said by way of apology, "and it is an ideal day for such work. I would like to be sure everything is in order before I leave."

This obviously gave the woman something else to be concerned about. "I do hope you will have a word with his lordship, My Lady, about hiring a housekeeper. I won't be able to do everything."

"Of course I will, Mrs. Pickering."

The preserves, Mrs. Pickering's pride, were splendid—row after row of jars and pots full of summer fruit. In another section were the dried fruits and pickles. Chloe gave only a cursory glance to the bins of grains, for she herself had supervised their scouring out before the new harvest was brought in.

The vegetable cellar was in order as well, cool and well arranged. Chloe looked thoughtfully at the racks of apples. For a while last year there had seemed to be a flurry of interest in apples. There had been that strange message from Stephen, to expect him up as he was to come and pick apples.

Then those soldiers had scoured the whole bay shore, supposedly looking for evidence of smuggling, and yet she had received a number of complaints about them disturbing the stores and even stealing—and always apples. And there was the Dowager, who was inclined to suddenly make strange statements about apples. Chloe had noticed that, though her mother-in-law was clearly not right in the head, she often picked on a relevant matter for her madness.

"Is something wrong, My Lady?" asked the cook in concern. "The apples are set up right, and a good crop this year. We've russets and pearmains, rennets and pippins. . . ."

"No everything looks well in hand," said Chloe quickly. "And no further disturbances round here?"

"None at all, My Lady. The last time was in June or thereabouts and I never did fathom it out. I'm sure it wasn't the staff, but I'm as sure no one broke in."

"And always the apples," Chloe mused.

"Except the last time. Then the potatoes were disturbed as well."

"The potatoes," said Chloe in surprise. "I didn't know that."

"Well, it had got to be such a regular thing we scarcely

paid any heed at all. That silly Rosie insists it were a
ghost. Into apples and potatoes, I ask you.''

"It had obviously got its *pommes* confused with its
pommes de terre,'' said Chloe lightly.

The cook looked at her blankly. "In French,'' explained Chloe, feeling her joke had fallen rather flat, "apples are *pommes*, and potatoes are *pommes de terre*, apples
of the earth.''

"Oh, French,'' said the cook, clearly of the opinion
that that would explain any insanity. "Well I tell you sure,
My Lady, if we were to have a ghost at Delamere it would
be a good honest English spectre.''

With that, the cook returned to her kitchen, clearly feeling she had delivered a blow against Napoleon.

Chloe returned to the main part of the house wondering
what occupation she could find now to keep her out of the
way of the inhabitants, particularly the gentlemen. She
discovered, however, they were engaged in the billiard
room and felt at liberty to retreat to the Sea Room to write
letters.

Sitting as she was by the window, she could see the rain
begin to slacken and the first sunshine glimmer through
the clouds. Then the rain ceased. Like a blessing, a rainbow arched over the bay. Within minutes, it seemed, the
bleak scene was transformed into fairyland.

Chloe found herself sitting in contemplation of the vista,
letter forgotten. The rainbow reminded her of Stephen, as
charming and bright, and as insubstantial. That made her
think of Justin, whom she would never think of as a
rainbow, who was clearly not like Stephen at all.

What element did Justin resemble? Perhaps the sea—
deep, sometimes pure pleasure, and at other times dangerous power. What a strange way to think of him, who
had always been a perfect gentleman.

To distract herself she tried to think of an element for
Randal. A sunbeam? No—lightning, perhaps. . . .

What was she going to do about Justin? As her grandmother said, she had been given a second chance. With

newfound honesty, she could admit her marriage to Stephen had not been a success. It had not been a disaster, but neither of them had found the companion they expected. He had found her too conventional. She had been dismayed by the company he kept. She knew she must have more if she married again. In Justin she sensed that possibility, but it was too new, too surprising, to be trusted.

Like the sun-washed bay, however, her mood had changed. The problem no longer seemed so bleak. She would go on her way, and if Justin chose to pursue her, so be it. The choice in the end was still hers. There were many worse things in life, she thought with a smile, than being pursued by a devoted suitor who might well be the man of her dreams.

She sang softly to herself as she went up to dress for dinner, and laughed when she found herself humming the tune Randal had played that first night:

Sweet, sweet the thought of you, my dear,
But sweeter still the day now you are near.
Though, in the past, cruel fate has made us part,
The miles have never drawn you from my heart.

Unfortunately, when she rejoined the company for the meal, no one else seemed to share her light spirits. The Dowager, thank goodness, had chosen to stay in her rooms with Miss Forbes to accompany her. Stephen's mother always picked up on atmosphere, and this one would have surely brought on one of her bad spells.

Belinda was pale and abstracted, inclined to startle at the slightest thing. Most unlike herself. Randal and Justin appeared to have quarreled and apparently were not on speaking terms. Randal was unusually sober and wary of Chloe. Justin treated her with distant formality. And the Duchess was sulking. Chloe knew all the signs—the old lady was snappish and rude, looking for someone to tear to shreds.

Chloe set out, as a good hostess, to thaw the company. After attempting a number of different topics for conversation, with only Randal offering much in the way of support, she gave up and began a monologue on the state of the household supplies.

"I think, Justin, you will find nothing wanting over the winter."

"I'm sure the staff are pleased they will not starve," he responded coolly, and Chloe took the message. He still intended to pursue her. Her unruly heart sent up a little cheer.

"I'm sure you are also pleased to know," she said, "that whatever was disturbing the stores seems to have ceased."

"Perhaps it was just a person with a passion for apples," said Justin with a strange look at the Duchess, who narrowed her eyes, but then looked down to tackle her partridge.

"And potatoes," said Chloe.

With the worthy intention of lightening the atmosphere, she repeated her comment about *pommes* and *pommes de terre*, confident that here at least she had an educated audience. Randal smiled, it was true, but the Duchess ignored the comment as if she had suddenly gone deaf. Justin looked thunderstruck.

After a few seconds, the moment passed.

Then, as if woken from a stupor, Justin began to hold up his end of the conversation. He abandoned whatever had come between him and Randal, and that young man, of course, immediately responded. They quipped and chatted in best Society style, and Chloe could relax her efforts.

She remembered the Duchess's words earlier in the day. There definitely were things going on which she did not understand, and which might have a connection with Frank's death. Justin had taken the matter very seriously when she broke the news. He had virtually assumed foul play. Just now, he had reacted to her words about the storage rooms like a hound at the scent. The two things, however, had no apparent connection. Even if Frank had been pilfering apples, that could not possibly lead to his death.

She looked around the table. Did everyone else know whatever there was to know? Not Belinda, surely, though she might well have secrets of her own. Randal? If she found Randal had been made privy to secrets about Delamere which had been withheld from her, she would have someone's guts for garters. And how could Justin, who had been in Portugal at the time, know who had been poking around in the storage rooms of Delamere?

When the ladies withdrew to the drawing-room, Belinda excused herself and went to her rooms. Chloe determined to pump the Duchess. As she handed the old lady her cup of tea, sweet and well laced with brandy as she liked it, Chloe went straight to the point.

"Are you going to tell me what secrets you and Justin are sharing? You and Justin," she repeated. "It's ridiculous. Two days ago you were the remotest of acquaintances."

"True enough," said the old lady.

Chloe was not about to give up. "So why are you harbouring secrets together?"

"I'm not harbouring anything. I want to tell you, but I've been given my orders," said the old lady bitterly. "Silly fat fool."

"Justin?" Chloe queried in amazement.

"Don't be a nodcock. There's not a spare ounce of flesh on him. No, I mean York."

"The Duke of York?" Chloe stared at the old lady. "What, pray, has he to do with us?"

The old lady pursed her lips. "I am not at liberty to say."

Chloe knew she was thwarted. The Duchess might put on the airs of a spoiled child at times, but she remained a shrewd, intelligent woman. If she had determined not to speak, it would be so. Chloe could have screamed with frustration. What possible connection could there be between apples or potatoes, the Duke of York, and Frank Halliwell's passion for Belinda?

At the Duchess's request, Chloe went to play the piano. As her fingers made their way through familiar tunes, she chased unlikely scenarios around in her head: Belinda had somehow caught the eye of the royal personage, and Justin had been ordered to dispose of Frank to clear the way; there was a national shortage of apples, and Belinda and Frank had intended to steal the crop to sell in the high-priced London market; a French spy was poisoning potatoes and feeding them to the British troops on the Peninsula; Justin had lost his dearest friend to this plot and traced the evildoer to Delamere.

The Duchess abruptly announced her good-night. Chloe realised it was late and the gentlemen had not come to join them. Cowards. She, however, had no intention of seeking them out and went off quietly to her own bed.

9

THE NEXT MORNING, when the maid brought Chloe breakfast, she also brought news from Mrs. Pickering that there had been further disturbances in the storage rooms. Chloe felt resigned rather than shocked. She recognised that there was something about the disturbed stores which was important. She ate quickly and hurried down to the kitchen, where the cook was supervising the preparation of toast and the making of coffee.

"I don't know, My Lady. Speak of the devil, they say. There we were yesterday just saying it had all stopped, and the kitchen boy went to get some potatoes and found dirt all over the floor. It's clear as day someone's had all the taties on the floor, then put them back, but didn't sweep up after themselves."

Chloe went to inspect, but found Mrs. Pickering had already had the stone floor swept clean. The room looked exactly as it had yesterday. She peered around her as if the whitewashed walls would tell their secrets, all to no avail. She was eaten up with frustrated curiosity.

What she needed, she thought, was the sea breeze to blow the cobwebs from her mind. With this intent she began to climb the back stairs, which led from the kitchen area up to the higher floors. Quite clearly on the plain wood were traces of dirt.

Chloe rubbed some between her fingers. Packed earth, such as would cling to stored potatoes. Not damp now or when it was deposited, so not from someone's dirty out-

114

door shoes. Could it have been here for days? No. These stairs were regularly used and, knowing Mrs. Pickering, regularly swept.

Someone had come down from upstairs and meddled in the storage rooms, then returned this way. The only people to sleep upstairs were the ladies and gentlemen of the house, and the maids. Mrs. Pickering had a comfortable room off the kitchen, and Matthew had a smaller one in the same area. The kitchen boy slept over the stables with the grooms.

Chloe kept a careful eye open as she climbed the stairs. When she opened the baize-covered door into the bedroom corridor, she saw a trace of dirt upon the carpet. This time it was very little, but she felt sure it was the same earth. The indication was that the intruder had been someone from this floor—Belinda, Randal, Justin, the Duchess, or herself. Then she added the Dowager and Miss Forbes.

Chloe walked the corridor, looking particularly at the spot before the opening of each door, but she found no further traces to guide her.

As she peered at his threshold, Justin's door opened and he almost walked into her.

"Chloe!" His abstracted gaze turned to pleased surprise. "Is it possible you were coming to visit me?"

"Of course not," she said, ready to sink with embarrassment. "I . . . er . . . I thought I saw some wear in the carpet here."

He looked down at the rich pile of Axminster, then up at her with a raised brow.

"It must have been the effect of the light," said Chloe.

"And I always thought this corridor rather gloomy," he murmured.

"Easier, surely, to make a mistake," she retorted.

"Quite so," he said. "I have thought this corridor needs light. There should be windows. What little light there is near the staircase is quite lost at the ends of the corridor, beyond the bends."

Chloe knew what he meant. Justin's room, the master suite, sat opposite the head of the wide, curving staircase, and received light from the lower hall. The corridor, however, bent around the stairwell in both directions and the ends were gloomy.

"It was when the wings were built, forty years ago," she explained. "According to the records, there used to be windows at either end. I don't see what can be done about it now."

"Unless we rip it down and build again," he said casually. "It seems to be the fashion."

Chloe didn't reply. That "we" echoed in her mind.

He caught her hand. "It is Frank's funeral this morning," he said, "and I suppose I should go. I'll drag Randal along for support. This afternoon, though, I would like you to show me around the grounds and the home farm. Put me in the way of things. If we have time, we could also ride around the tenants and down to the village."

Chloe looked at him. He had planned a day in her company, cunning man. There was no reason, however, to refuse, and she really didn't think she wished to.

"Perhaps Randal would like to accompany us in our explorations," she suggested mischievously.

"I doubt it," he replied.

Just to tease, she put forward another objection. "The ground will still be muddy, and there is a chance of more rain."

"You will doubtless wish to put on your boots. If it rains, we will seek shelter. Anyone in Lancashire who stays home for fear of rain will lead a very dull life."

"I may have made other plans for the day," she persisted. "After all, we have a dinner party this evening."

Once more, the "we" seemed to hang in the air between them. She saw a smile twitch on his lips.

"It is you who insists on rushing off on Tuesday, Chloe."

This was only true and fair, so Chloe agreed. Justin grinned and went off to entrap Randal into attending a funeral. Once his back was turned, Chloe allowed a little smile of her own to show. This could prove to be an interesting day.

In addition to the obvious attractions of the project, these trips would be as good a time as any to discover the secrets she should know. She had not been above using her attractions to twist men around her finger in the past. There were problems, however. On the one hand, she was not sure Justin was amenable to such wiles. On the other, she didn't know if she could handle his reaction if she had any degree of success.

She continued thoughtfully down the corridor, and met Belinda emerging from her room, basket in hand, obviously off on another foraging trip through the fast-fading garden. Chloe wondered how Belinda felt on this, the day of her lover's funeral. Chloe decided Belinda might like company and gave up her notion of riding.

"You are going into the garden, Belinda," she said. "Would you mind if I were to accompany you? You could teach me a great deal."

No particular expression crossed the younger woman's face, but an overlong hesitation made Chloe think she was unwelcome. All at once, her previous suspicions of Belinda and her strange attempt to go out in the rain the day before came back to Chloe.

"I'm not in the mood for teaching," said Belinda curtly.

"I will watch you then," said Chloe with cheery persistence. "Perhaps we could pick some roses for a centrepiece. I'll just fetch a shawl."

As she expected, when she returned in a moment, with bonnet and shawl, Belinda had gone. By hurtling downstairs like a hoyden and nipping through the kitchen corridor, Chloe managed to catch up with the youngest Lady Stanforth as she entered the rose garden.

A flash of anger in the girl's eyes strengthened all Chloe's suspicions. Belinda made no comment, however, and simply went along, gathering the few good blooms

left. She occasionally asked Chloe's advice on a choice,
but otherwise ignored her presence.

Then they moved on to the herb garden. Belinda snipped
a leaf here, gathered a seedhead there. Chloe trailed like
a shadow, watching her every move. There could surely
be no connection between Frank's death and rosemary,
basil, chamomile, and comfrey. But then there had been
that business of the honeysuckle.

"Is the comfrey for your *potpourri?*" she asked, for
something to say.

"Hardly," said Belinda shortly. "I also gather herbs for
medicinal purposes. I will make the Duchess one of my
restorative infusions. If my mother has a supply of prickly
ash, I will be able to make up an excellent rheumatic oint-
ment."

Chloe remembered that, today being Thursday, Belinda
would be away all afternoon at her parents' farm. That
relieved her mind, for there would have been no purpose
to following the young woman about all morning, only to
leave her unobserved during Chloe's time with Justin.

Should she allow Belinda, however, to dose her grandmother? She knew Belinda had provided linctus mixtures
and ointments to various members of the household to
good effect, but . . . Chloe *must* persuade Justin to tell
her what was going on in Delamere before somebody else
was hurt.

They came upon Budsworth clearing the last of the run-
ner beans. Tom, his assistant, had been a friend of Frank's,
he said, and given permission to attend the funeral.

To Chloe's surprise, the otherwise taciturn Belinda
started a long conversation with the man. They discussed
the placing of all kinds of plants, winter protection, and
vegetable storage. Chloe could not decide which part of
the discussion was of importance to Belinda, but knew
something must be. She was not garrulous by nature and
generally avoided interaction with servants because of her
awkward situation.

Merely in order to enter the conversation, Chloe asked,

"How many more vegetables are there to be dug before winter, Budsworth?"

"Well, there's those that need frost, like the sprouts and the leeks. Otherwise, ma'am, only the late potatoes, carrots, and turnips. Then we'll set to bedding down the flowers."

"Let us pray, then, for good weather. Rain such as we had yesterday must make the earth heavy."

"That it does, ma'am, but I fear there's more to come," he said, looking up at the sky, which the local people seemed to read like a book.

Before any comment could be made, the distant tolling of a bell floated to them. They all became still. Budsworth took off his battered cap.

"That'll be Frank, God rest him."

"Amen," said Chloe. She glanced at the silent Belinda, surprising a look of bleak desolation on her face, a look that was immediately replaced by stony indifference. Chloe ached for the young woman, who could not properly grieve for her lover, perhaps the father of her child.

"Belinda, why do we not go inside for a cup of tea," she said quickly.

She thought Belinda would refuse, but then she seemed to sigh as she agreed.

Once settled in the Sea Room, Chloe poured the tea and added plenty of sugar, then passed it to the younger Lady Stanforth.

"Do not be ashamed to be sad, Belinda," she said softly. "I sorrow for a life cut short, and Frank was no more than a servant to me. He was your friend."

"Ay," said Belinda, lapsing into the local dialect. "Happen."

"He was a fine-looking man and a good worker."

"Ay." Then Belinda seemed to recollect herself, and her speech regained its usual educated tone. "He would have made something of himself, I'm sure. He was very ambitious."

"His aunt said he wanted to open a livery in Lancaster."

"Yes, he spoke of it. He needed money, though." She looked at Chloe. "Many people are ambitious, but few can find the way out of their places."

Which you have done, thought Chloe, and put yourself out of Frank's reach. She longed to ask, was it worth it? Her purpose at the moment, however, was not to pry, but to ease the other woman's pain.

"I'm sure Frank would have done. Hard work brings its own reward."

Belinda's lip curled. "It's a strange thing then, that it's the rich who are so idle," she said sharply, "and the poorest of the poor who drudge from morn 'til night." Then she put her cup down and abruptly stood. "I'm sorry. You're right in what you're thinking. My heart aches for Frank, for what might have been were the world a very different place. But I don't regret a single thing I've done. Not one. My daughter will live the life of a lady."

With that she walked out, and Chloe did not follow. She knew Belinda would almost certainly spend the time before luncheon with Dorinda, but even if that wasn't the case, she had lost the taste for spying on her. If Belinda had pushed Frank off the cliff to protect the place she had won for herself among the aristocracy, who was Chloe to hound her? She who, despite her overstrict parents, had been given every advantage of wealth and station all her life, could look as high as she wished for a husband. Vengeance is mine, saith the Lord, and Belinda would carry pain all her life for the loss of Frank, no matter how it had come about.

Nevertheless, Chloe was pleased to see Belinda, the baby, and Rosie drive off after lunch in the carriage. Chloe need feel no anxiety at all about her activities during the afternoon and could enjoy her time with Justin with an easy mind.

* * *

They walked out into the rain-washed, sun-gilded landscape, and Chloe felt the tangy sea breeze playing in her curls. In silent accord they detoured down towards the sea to watch the white-tipped waves, the white horses, dancing to the beach. Not so far away—ten miles or so but seeming closer—the hills and hamlets of the farther shore were picked out clearly by the sun.

"It all feels so clean," said Justin softly. "In Portugal, even the sun seemed heavy and hot, except on the coast, and there the wind could scour the skin."

Chloe turned, moved by the feeling in him, and laid a hand on his arm. "You are home now. I'm glad you seem to like Delamere. It needs a loving master."

He smiled down at her. "And a loving mistress?"

Chloe looked away. "That too, I suppose." She hurried on. "Stephen thought it too far from London. He lived in Clarges Street virtually all year round, only leaving to visit friends or popular watering places in the hottest months. And for hunting and shooting, of course. . . ."

"And you?" he asked.

Chloe felt there was an implication she had neglected her husband. "I spent the Seasons with him there," she defended. "And I sometimes visited friends with him. Someone had to spend time here too."

"I'm not accusing you of neglect, my dear. It's rather the other way around. Did he feel no need to accommodate your wishes?"

Chloe did not want to discuss her marriage. She turned to walk away, but he caught her by the arms. "I need to know how it was with you, Chloe."

"I do not intend to discuss my marriage with you, Justin."

A calling gull swooped past the cliff to land on a rock near the water's edge. Justin spoke at last. "Stephen stands between us, doesn't he?"

"Do you deny him that right?" Chloe demanded, her anger stemming from her own guilt, not his. "Will you just walk in and take everything that was his?"

He turned her and looked down with a puzzled look into her troubled eyes. "He's dead, Chloe. I am his heir."

"To me too?" she asked sharply.

"Of course not, but if you imagine Stephen would mind us marrying, you did not know him very well."

Chloe looked down. "He was always generous."

"I don't want to rush you, Chloe, but I have no intention of losing you through default. If you don't go away in a few days, it will doubtless all work out."

But he *was* rushing her. Chloe couldn't sort out her warring guilt and desire. She moved out of his grasp. "But I am going in a few days, so let us make our tour of the estate as planned."

To avoid further personal discussion, Chloe set a brisk pace through the gardens, both ornamental and kitchen, trying to keep her eyes open for anything out of the ordinary which might have been Belinda's object, but in fact achingly aware of Justin by her side.

Chloe had hoped a businesslike tone would break the feeling of intimacy between them, but it did not. They spoke only of practical matters, yet every moment seemed to draw them closer together. They constantly found shared interests and tastes. Chloe was delighted to find him willing to discuss the business of the estate with her as an equal, and relieved to have someone with whom she could share her concerns.

She pointed out the herb garden. "Even in the one year, Belinda has done wonders here. It is her particular area of interest."

"Perhaps she's a witch," Justin said lightly. "I wonder if she has any love potions."

Chloe looked swiftly up at him. "You had better hope not," she said coolly, "or she'll doubtless slip one in your brandy."

She then marched on to the vegetable plots. They spoke briefly with Budsworth and his assistant, who were turning over the carrot bed, and then took the long path down to the home farm.

Justin freely admitted he had little practical experience of farming. He had grown up mainly in London, as his father had been a hardworking member of Parliament. The small country place kept by Mr. John Delamere had been a villa, not an estate, and kept no stock larger than chickens. As Justin listened with care to the wisdom of Ramsdale, the tenant farmer, Chloe felt some of the intensity lessen and she relaxed. She was content to walk behind the two men, only entering the conversation to point out some comparison of which Ramsdale might be unaware.

Unfortunately for the state of mind she desired, it also gave her opportunity to study Justin at her leisure. What made a man so perfect in a woman's eyes? He was not as elegant as Randal and yet his proportions seemed exact to her. His slightly wider shoulders and more heavily muscled legs were exactly what they should be. She could imagine them . . .

She stopped herself before she went too far, and turned her attention immediately to the pigs in the sty, unknowingly awaiting the slaughtering day. She felt some sympathy with them. She too seemed increasingly helpless before her fate.

Justin turned and found her studying them. "Are you a devotee of swine?" he asked. "I confess I find them appealing only in the roast form."

"Oh do hush," Chloe said, biting her lip. "It's horrible to speak of their death in front of them."

Justin laughed. "Oh Chloe, you are a delight. A wonderful mixture of common sense and whimsy, strength and delicacy."

He held out his hand and she could not help but put hers in it. It seemed he would speak, but he just tugged her along to an examination of the Clydesdales, coming in from a work session.

Chloe and Justin returned to the house slowly, arm in arm, and though hardly anything had been said of their relationship, Chloe knew a point of significance had been passed. This simple sharing of practical things was the reality of life, and in it they had been together.

It was true what Justin had said. Stephen would never have minded her turning to his cousin once he had gone. Perhaps in time she could sort out her feelings, and accept what Justin had to offer without guilt and without reservations.

As they walked towards the stables, however, she remembered her need to pry information from her companion.

"Justin," she said. "Something is going on at Delamere, something more even than Frank's death, though there may be a connection. I need to know what it is."

"Why do you think there are things you don't know?"

"Grandmother as good as said so, for one thing."

He looked slightly rueful. "She doubtless did."

"And she mentioned the Duke of York. Justin, it makes no sense."

He smiled slightly as he plucked a wild rose from the hedgerow and lightly brushed her cheek with it. Chloe knew her colour would be rising to challenge the blush on the bloom and sought to remember her purpose.

"Tonight," he said softly, a glint of mischief in his eyes.

"Tonight?" repeated Chloe, perilously close to a squeak.

She saw his eyes darken and, for a wickedly delightful moment, she thought he would crush her to him in a passionate kiss. Then his eyelids lowered and he tucked the rose through the buttonhole of her jacket, his touch causing her to tremble.

"Tonight, after our guests have all gone," he said, "I'll explain everything. Or at least, everything I know."

Chloe swallowed ridiculous disappointment. "About time," she snapped. "You have made me wait too long as it is."

"You're probably right," he said, and his glance gave the statement quite a different meaning. Chloe could feel her heart begin a rapid patter, a large part of it nerves. She couldn't let him seduce her, no matter how desirable her body anticipated that to be. She must make this lifetime decision with care and a cool head.

He was not, however, making that resolve easy for her to maintain. He took her hand as they walked to the stables. That contact, so much more intimate than the customary arm in arm, sparkled on Chloe's consciousness like sunlight on the sea. She struggled to pay attention to his words.

"I'll give you the bare bones now, Chloe, because I want you to help me talk to people as we go around. Last autumn some valuable government papers were lost. A sailor brought them to Heysham, and Stephen was on his way up to collect them for the government when he was killed."

"Stephen!" This was sufficiently startling to focus her wits. Had her husband been a more responsible man than she thought?

"When we go to the village," Justin continued, "I want to see if anyone knows anything about that sailor."

After a short silence, Chloe stared at him. "Is that all you're going to tell me? Why were these papers brought to Heysham? Does this have anything to do with the disturbed stores and Frank's death? Do we have a spy loose here, attacking people?"

"I don't know," he said, boosting her into the saddle. "That's one of the things I'm trying to find out, but the highest priority is to locate those papers if they still exist."

His words were businesslike, his actions courteous, but he took her hand and again peeled her glove back to press warm lips against the skin of her inner wrist. There was nothing cool about his eyes either. They smouldered with passion. Had he also entertained wanton thoughts during that walk?

He turned sharply and swung onto his own horse. By the time he'd guided the beast over to her, he was in control again. Perhaps it was the shortage of time which made him set a sharp pace, but Chloe didn't think so. She could not resist a satisfied smile, knowing she could stir him to insanity just as he seemed able to deprive her of her wits.

They stopped frequently to greet workers in the fields, a woman at a cottage gate, Dr. Williams in his gig; in open country they cantered. There was not time for intimate conversation, a circumstance for which Chloe was intensely grateful.

After an hour they stopped for a mug of mulled ale at the inn in Heysham village. The innkeeper was gratified to be formally introduced to the new viscount.

"There have been a lot of changes this last year," said Justin. He had the way, Chloe saw, of being at ease with his people without losing the dignity of his position.

"That there have, Your Lordship. And some funny goings-on."

"Yes?"

"Well, all those soldiers out searching for smugglers for a start. A right lot they were, into everything, and not above a bit of stealing." Searching for missing papers, Chloe suddenly realised. Why had no one come to her about all this?

"Anything else?" Justin asked casually.

"We've had a surprising lot of people staying hereabouts this year. Almost like ten years ago when they dug up that stone in the churchyard and there were always historians and the like coming to examine it. Now, there's only the Dutchman that's boarding with Mrs. Holyoak. But there was a poet who said he needed to study the sea, and a man who collected shells. A Mr. Caulfield said he was seeking the sea air to recover from a lung disease and a Professor Rigley claimed to be looking for old dead creatures in the cliffs, if you'll believe that. Good for business, of course, but mighty strange."

"It's a very pleasant spot, Mr. Satterley. You mustn't be surprised if it becomes popular. Any other strange occurrences?"

"Well, going back a while, there were that sailor what

ended up dead. Samuel Wright. He were here for nigh on a week, just stuffing his face and swilling, with a deep purse, if you see what I mean. Yet his boots were holey and his jacket none too thick. What do you think of that?''

"I think you're a very observant man, Mr. Satterley."

The innkeeper nodded, pleased. "I am that, My Lord. Innkeeping's a people-watching kind of business. There was someone asking about Sam after his body turned up down Poulton way, and I could tell them quite a bit.''

"I'm sure you could," said Justin, seeming only politely interested.

"Well, he made no secret of having a package from Ireland for Lord Stanforth, one that was to be given only into his hands. That was a rum setup too, when you think on it, but we all reckoned it was horse stuff. Ireland's the place for horses, and Mr. Stephen was always on the lookout for a good hunter. Took the duty very seriously, did Sam. I'll give him that. But he were growing impatient after a week. Heysham isn't the liveliest spot, after all, so he started to say he would go up to the Hall to find someone to speak to about it. I reckon he must have done that the night he left here, the night before the sad news came about Mr. Stephen.''

"Did he say what happened at the Hall?''

"Never saw him again," said Mr. Satterley succinctly. "It were next day his body washed up. It were high tide that evening. He must have slipped in somehow, though if he were off to Lancaster to find a ship, as I supposed, it were strange of him to go thataway.''

A weather-beaten sailor in a heavy jacket was sitting by the fire, puffing at a long clay pipe. Now he spoke. "I saw Sam Wright after you, I reckon.''

"After that, Tom?'' queried the innkeeper.

"That evening. He walked down near the boats. He would now and then. I were mending a net in the last of the light, watching the sunset like, and we talked of this and that. He let on as how he missed the sea. Said he'd been up to the Hall and got rid of his package at last.

Didn't say who he gave it to, though, if Lord Stanforth weren't there.''

"He surely weren't," said the innkeeper with a sideways glance at Chloe. He wouldn't say it but they all knew. By that evening Stephen was dead. "Did he have his stuff with him, Tom?''

"Nah." The man hawked and spat into the fire.

"Then he must have come back here after for it," said the innkeeper. "Funny thing that he never said good-bye. He'd paid his shot earlier, so there was no need. He must have just slipped in when we were busy, took his kit, and gone.''

"Probably just because you were busy," said Justin reassuringly. "Was there an enquiry into the death?''

"Well, it came under Sir Hambly Kellaway in Poulton, as that was where the body came in. He just identified him and put it down as drowning. What else was there to do? Sam lies in the graveyard down there. There was still enough coins in his pocket to pay for that.''

Justin and Chloe took their leave.

As they walked the horses down the cobbled street, Chloe was thoughtful. She remembered the drowning of the sailor, though she had heard nothing of this business of a message. Her mind had been on Stephen and his death. Now, knowing about the missing papers Samuel Wright carried, she had to look at the matter in a new light.

How did it fit in with other strange events? If Belinda had killed Frank, could there be any connection to this matter? Surely not. Belinda could have no interest in government papers. Chloe needed to know exactly what these papers were, but that would have to wait until later.

"The sailor would never have given the package to Belinda," she murmured, then stopped. "What am I thinking of? Belinda wasn't married to George then. She was just Farmer Massinger's daughter. He must have given it to George.''

Justin nodded. "So why did George deny any knowledge? It makes no sense. I'll never believe he was a foreign agent." He shook his head. "He was a greedy man. Perhaps he simply ate it."

"Ate a message?" said Chloe, astonished.

"Well," said Justin with a rueful smile, "that's why there's been such an interest in apples and potatoes. It's believed the message was sent in disguise—looking like an apple, everyone thought. Now you have us wondering if it should be a potato."

Before Chloe could ask one of the dozens of questions newly sprung into her mind, they encountered a new group of people—two widowed sisters, Mrs. Holyoak and Mrs. Grange, accompanied by Mrs. Williams, the doctor's wife, and her pretty daughter, Phelie. Phelie did her best, within the bounds of good manners, to attract the attention of the handsome viscount. Chloe was pleased to see her fail.

After escaping these enthusiastic ladies, there was no time for conversation, though Chloe's mind worked furiously when it could.

George had known something, or else why did he burst into silly laughter whenever anyone mentioned apples? No wonder someone had been searching the storage rooms from time to time. The first occurrences had been before Belinda married George. They had intensified during George's tenure, then ceased until the summer.

After a brief flurry, there had been no more such occurrences until recently. No one person had been at the Hall throughout, except herself, the Dowager, and Miss Forbes. For the first time Chloe wondered if she was suspect. It was painful and infuriating, but if Justin had any doubts about her honour, it could explain his reluctance to tell her facts she had a right to know.

They trotted past the Massingers' prosperous farm. Chloe saw the Delamere laundalette there, the horses loose in a paddock. Belinda was still safely at home. However, Belinda's affairs, even if they had led to a man's death, were not the issue at the moment.

They needed more local information. People talked

more easily with her along than they would have to Justin alone. Despite that, only the sailor at the inn had given them new knowledge. Who would be the best person to approach now?

Not far from the Massingers' gates, an old lady sat by a cottage door, knitting. Chloe smiled in satisfaction. She dismounted and went over. Justin followed.

"Hello, Granny Twitchell."

"Hello, my dear," said the old lady easily, broad smile producing two apple cheeks, despite the sunkenness of lost teeth.

"Catching the sun? I've brought the new Lord Stanforth to see you, Granny."

The old lady nodded amiably. "Pleasure, I'm sure," she said.

"Granny's an important person hereabout," said Chloe to Justin. "She was the midwife for the longest time. Delivered Stephen and Belinda, I've no doubt."

"Of course, of course," said the old lady. "And Frank Halliwell."

There was a wicked glint in the old woman's eye. Chloe knew her instinct had been right. Granny would have things to tell, but it was against her code to go gossiping. If someone were to ask, now . . .

"They were very close at one time, I hear," said Chloe.

The old woman nodded, and chuckled. "A lot closer than they ought to have been, I would say."

Chloe wasn't surprised. "I would have thought Mrs. Massinger would have kept Belinda close at home, seeing she had such ideas for her."

"Oh, she tried, did Nellie. But Belinda's always had a mind of her own. She's a good heart, I'll grant, but too much independence."

Chloe was rather surprised by this assessment, and yet, in her own way, Belinda was an individualist, if not quite in Chloe's own flamboyant style.

"Slipping up to the Hall grounds of an evening," mused

Granny, as if speaking to herself, "wasn't beyond Belinda."

"She must have loved Frank," said Chloe sincerely. "Belinda wouldn't act that way lightly. I suppose her parents would never have agreed to the match, though."

"No. Though that wouldn't have counted with Belinda when she came of age. He were a good man, Frank. God rest his soul. But ambitious. Ambition causes a deal of misery," the old woman added.

"I wonder why and how she married George," asked Chloe.

The old woman cackled. "I told you. Ambition. Now the how of it has interested me. She must have had something which appealed to Mr. George, I reckon."

"Youth and the good health to bear children, I suppose," said Chloe. "I cannot really understand why she would do it, though. Even for a title, George was a lot to swallow. Perhaps she felt, with her parents so set against Frank, she had little other choice."

"Nellie and Bob had nothing to do with her decisions, I'll warrant," said the old lady. "Belinda had stood against them all along. Swore blind she'd marry Frank in the end. She'd slip up to the Hall near every day, and he'd escort her back here, you see. I saw them arm in arm many a time, and the last time were not many days before her engagement to Mr. George was announced."

Chloe frowned as she tried to make sense of this. Though the picture Granny was painting of Belinda was a little different from the one Chloe was accustomed to, she could believe the girl to be spirited and independent in her own environment. Why then, within eighteen months of achieving her majority, would she throw it all away and marry George?

"Do you know when that was, Granny?" asked Justin, breaking into the conversation for the first time. "The last time you saw them together."

"Yes I do," said the old lady, eying him shrewdly. "It were the night before Lady Stephen here became widowed. That's a day as stands in the memory. After that, Belinda and Frank were never close the same way again.''

"That must have been when she encountered George, and he fell madly in love with her,'' said Justin dryly.

The night the sailor delivered his package, thought Chloe, trying to make the pieces fit.

"Happen,'' said the old lady, meeting his eyes. "But the only person I saw Belinda meet that night was that sailor as was hanging about.''

Chloe caught her breath and looked at Justin, who met her eyes alertly. "How do you know that, Granny?''

"They walked past here, the three of them together,'' said Granny cheerfully, and Chloe guessed she'd been wanting to tell this tale for a year now. "Belinda and Frank were on the way from the Hall to her home. The sailor was likely going back to the inn from the shore, where he went to talk to the fishermen. I'd seen him stroll this way before. Once or twice we'd pass the time of day. Belinda and Frank were arm in arm but proper like, not wrapped around each other as they often were.''

Granny finished a row and neatly switched the needles around. "The sailor walked alongside them, puffing on his pipe. I could hear a bit of what they said—sound often carries at night. It was warm for that time of year, and I had the casement open. I heard nowt interesting, though. Frank just said he'd walk down to the village with the sailor and have a beer.'' Granny Twitchell looked up, eyes wise in her wrinkled face. "Now Frank's dead, and the sailor's dead. Mr. George and young Stephen gone too. That were an unlucky night. An unlucky night.''

Chloe sensed the tale was now told, though she wasn't sure yet what to make of it. "Indeed it was, Granny. It's been good to talk with you again,'' she said. "I must come this way more often. And you be sure to send word to the Hall if you're ever in need of anything.'' She realised she might not be there herself and added, "Lord Stanforth will always assist you.''

"He knows his duty,'' said the old lady with a nod,

adding, "It's about time someone sorted things out around here."

As they walked back to the horses, Justin said, "I think I was just given my orders."

"And very good ones too," said Chloe. "It seems to me this has been a mismanaged business all along."

As they trotted back towards the Hall, Chloe considered. The linking of Frank, Belinda, and the sailor put a whole new focus on things. There were also an ominous number of deaths open to question. Not just Frank, after all.

She said, "Mr. Satterley didn't mention Frank being in the inn that night, and the sailor never returned."

"Suspicious, isn't it?" remarked Justin. "I really think we're going to have to have a talk with Belinda."

"We?"

"We," he said firmly. "I'm scared to be alone with her."

Chloe gave him a frowning look, but agreed to be part of what was bound to be a difficult interview.

When they had left their horses at the stable and were walking back to the house, Justin suddenly said, "I think we should have another look at the place where Frank fell."

Though puzzled, Chloe willingly turned in that direction. "Why?" she queried. "There can surely be nothing to see after all that rain."

He did not reply, but when they got there he looked around and smiled. "Just as everyone said. This spot can't be observed from the house."

"True," said Chloe. "Is that of significance?"

He looked down at her with a smile that melted her bones. "It depends how discreet you want to be," he said. Even his voice seemed to stroke her skin and set it quivering.

"Why?" she whispered, though she knew, and was frantically trying to decide what to do about it.

For answer, he took her in his arms and pulled her down to sit on the smooth grass. One arm around her, the other hand came up to cradle her face. His thumb brushed gently against her lower lip. She let out her breath in a trembling sigh, while the rational part of her mind commanded her to tear herself out of his arms.

Reason lost. She stayed quiescent as his lips came to hers, first to brush lightly as his thumb had done, then to play more firmly over hers. Before she could discipline her body as to what it should do, her lips opened like a flower to the sun, and her hand crept up to twine in his hair.

It felt, thought Chloe, nothing like a first kiss. It felt as if they had been lovers all their lives. She already knew the taste of him, the shape of him beneath her hand, and it was nothing to do with Stephen.

But, as with longtime lovers, it was going too fast. With desperate resolution, she pushed him from her. They gazed at each other, stunned and breathless.

"Chloe, marry me," he said harshly. "Preferably now."

She choked with laughter and turned away, hands to her burning cheeks. "Give me a little more time, Justin. A little more time. Please." Part of her was screaming. Why? Reason was saying this was no way to decide the rest of her life.

He rested his hands on her shoulders. "Of course, my darling. I'm just so afraid of losing you again."

Her heart gave a shudder at his admission. She turned to look at him. "You never said a word."

His smile was twisted. "How could I? What would you have done if I had?"

Chloe tried to imagine it. "I don't know.

He pulled her to him in a desperate hug. Her senses were overwhelmed by the feel of him all around her, the spicy scent of him. . . .

"Your wedding night," he whispered against her ear. "I thought I would die."

The anguish was horribly real in his voice. It seemed even more horrible that she had not felt that anguish at the time, merely puzzled disappointment. It made her doubt her feelings now. If she had loved him as he claimed to have loved her, would she not have felt something then? Would she not have distinguished between the cousins when first she met them?

"I need time, Justin," she repeated, as she pulled gently out of his embrace.

She glanced at him, frightened of what she might see there, but he was in control again, though his cheeks were tinged with colour and his eyes darker than usual. He even managed a laugh as he leapt to his feet and helped her to rise.

"All the time in the world," he said lightly. "But if you take too long, my darling, you'll find me huddled in insanity with the Dowager, I give you warning."

Oh, the temptation to surrender. But as with most temptation, it was much better avoided, she told herself as they walked side by side, not touching, back to the house.

They approached the conservatory and saw a job-coach turn away down the drive.

"Macy, I suppose," said Justin.

"He cannot have wasted much time," Chloe remarked. "You know, I find it difficult to imagine him as such an urgent suitor, and cannot see the attraction Belinda holds for him. I don't mean to be unkind, but she has no particular beauty, her portion as George's widow is not a fortune, and she'll never be rid of the taint of her background."

"Interesting, isn't it?" said Justin, and Chloe was alerted.

Did he think to mix Macy into the tangled web? Good heavens, he was probably a government man come to investigate the missing papers. Perhaps his interest in Belinda was not amorous at all. Interfering with government work was surely treason. What on earth would Chloe do if Belinda was dragged off for such a crime?

10

C HLOE HAD TO admit that Humphrey Macy appeared to be exactly as he claimed, and very unlike a spy-catcher. He was gushingly polite to her and doting towards Belinda, who had just arrived back at the Hall.

"My dear, dear Belinda," he said, retaining her hand. "I do hope you will permit me to address you so. I grew so accustomed to poor George talking of his lovely Belinda . . ." He sighed. "What a sad house this has been, but destined for happier days now, I'm sure."

Mr. Macy, man-about-town and intimate of royalty, was undeniably possessed of an air of elegant sophistication. His spindly legs, topped by an ample paunch, had been given a veneer of manliness by excellent tailoring and handsome, gleaming Hessian boots. His hair was an unlikely shade of chestnut, brushed up to give its sparsity a more youthful fullness. Chloe had long suspected he used rouge on his sallow skin, but if so, she had to confess, it was done with subtlety so one could never quite be sure.

He turned his easy smile on Justin and Chloe, and Belinda retrieved her hand. To Chloe, she did not seem overwhelmed by Mr. Macy's attentions. In fact, she looked worried, as well she might. If she had been responsible for the loss of the papers, then killed her colleague, the arrival of a government official must be terrifying. Once, Belinda glanced towards the door as if thinking of making an escape, but then she appeared to recollect herself and was composedly attentive to her suitor.

Chloe's suspicions immediately seemed ridiculous. What could account for the Massingers' well-educated daughter suddenly turning her hand to treason? Where was the advantage in it? Frank might dabble in something illegal if it promised a quick profit and escape from servitude, but would Belinda assist him? Love was a powerful persuader, but such strength of devotion did not mesh with Belinda's ambitious marriage to George.

The welcoming of Mr. Macy had to be cut short, as it was time for everyone to prepare for the dinner. Chloe took a moment to ensure that all the arrangements were going forward smoothly, and that an extra place would be laid at the table, then hurried to make her own *toilette*. For a great many reasons, she was determined to be at her best for this first formal entertainment in so long a time.

She had already chosen her gown, a spectacularly elegant silver grey satin, with an overdress of pink spidergauze woven with silver thread. The bodice was cut very low and wide, showing her shoulders to advantage. The gown was perhaps a little fine for a country dinner. Yet, the simplicity of its lines meant it would pass muster, and she would wear only the simplest jewels. The gown had never been worn before. She had found it a little too mature in style. Now, nearly two years after its making, it felt exactly right.

Agnes dressed her glossy dark hair high in a knot and circled it with a silver filigree *bandeau*. Into this were inserted a few deep pink rosebuds. For jewels, all Chloe wore were pink agates carved into roses—at her ears, around her slender throat, and set in a solid silver bangle on her wrist.

When she surveyed herself in the mirror, she was satisfied. She was a woman, one whose beauty was clothed in cool elegance. She hoped this appearance would persuade any and all gentlemen to keep their distance.

She hurried down to make a last-minute check of all the arrangements. Matthew was all pride and dignity in his

best uniform, with his hair powdered. He assured her the
wine was prepared exactly as it should be.

When Chloe entered the drawing-room, all the house
party except Mr. Macy were there. Everyone complimented
her on her appearance. Nonetheless, she saw Randal's eyebrows rise, and the Duchess looked cynical. Self-consciously,
Chloe took her place by Justin's side.

"You look wonderful," he murmured. "But just a little
untouchable."

"More than a little, I hope," she retorted with a warning look.

She could not prevent a betraying twitch of the lips,
however, and they shared a smile. Being by his side was
. . . completely as it should be, thought Chloe. She caught
Randal grinning at them, and blushed when he winked.

The Reverend Sotherby, and his sister, shy Mrs. Thornton, were the first guests. Chloe introduced them to Justin
and saw him instantly put them both at their ease. Randal,
however, made the mistake of paying the lady a gentle
compliment, which seemed almost to overset her.

"Is it my rank or my beauty?" he queried softly as
Justin took the blushing lady over to the Duchess.

"Well, she seems able to handle a few words with
Grandmama."

Randal crossed his eyes and pulled a hideous face.
"There. Is that better?"

Chloe choked on laughter. "Do behave yourself, for
heaven's sake."

She hurried over to welcome Doctor and Mrs. Williams. These sensible, kindly people handled introduction
to people of high rank with unpretentious good manners.
By the time she and Justin were ready to greet the next
arrivals, Chloe was pleased to see Randal and the doctor
involved in a lively discussion of sailing.

Herr van Maes, the young Dutch antiquarian, was all
geniality as he arrived, full of some recent discoveries
made at Cartmel, across the bay.

"But I cannot take time to tell you here, dear lady," he

said, bowing low over Chloe's hand, and retaining it longer than was proper. "Perhaps I can call on you one day?"

"I am afraid I will be leaving soon, Herr van Maes," said Chloe, noticing the severe study Justin made of the Dutchman, almost as if he suspected him of a crime. She remembered his jealousy over the pictures, and felt a tickle of guilty amusement. "Lord Stanforth, however," she said sweetly to Herr van Maes, "is very interested in historical matters."

Both gentlemen viewed this notion without enthusiasm, but Herr van Maes attempted to follow the lead.

"Indeed. How wonderful. What is your opinion, My Lord, of St. Patrick's Chapel?"

"It is in a very sad state of repair," said Justin.

The Dutchman blinked. "But it is over a thousand years old," he said, then shook his head and smiled. "Ah, I see. It is the English sense of humour. Lady Stanforth has also often caught me out like that." He moved off to talk to the vicar.

"There," said Justin. "Even he sees how much we have in common." After a moment, he added, "Is every man you come across in love with you?"

"Of course not," Chloe said.

As if to prove her wrong, the next arrivals were Sir Cedric and his stately sister Julia, who was just back from London. Chloe was sure her gown must be the latest style. She studied the pale green silk with genuine interest. It was still constructed after the Grecian style but had more embroidery and shaping in the bodice. What particularly caught Chloe's eye, however, was Julia's long silk scarf, worn draped over her elbows and trailing to the floor. She had heard of the new fashion and had to confess it looked very well indeed.

Julia lightly kissed Chloe's cheek. "How nice you look, my dear," Julia drawled. "How pleased you must be to finally be liberated from this benighted spot. Every time I go to London, I can scarce bear to return."

Chloe introduced her to Justin and Randal. She was

amused to see Julia study Randal with interest, then clearly decide he was above her touch. The woman focussed on Justin and had soon managed to move him a few steps away.

"I think you're about to be cut out," said Randal to Chloe, sotto voce.

"Should that concern me?" replied Chloe. Randal laughed and wandered off. Chloe turned her sweetest smile upon Sir Cedric. Meanwhile, she was aware of Julia and Justin with every nerve in her body.

"Why have we not seen that gown before, dear Lady Stanforth?" said Sir Cedric playfully. "It must be the most beautiful one you possess. It lends you such dignity."

Chloe looked at him. This approval was an unexpected, and undesired, effect. "Am I so short of dignity, Sir Cedric, that I must borrow?"

He laughed indulgently. "Well, my dear, if you borrow, it is we gentlemen who pay the interest. Is that not the way it always is? As for dignity," he added, blind to her irritation, "we all know you have been inclined to impetuousness from time to time."

He, she was sure, had never been rash in his life. "There are times in life, Sir Cedric," said Chloe sharply, "when impetuousness is called for. Or so much can pass you by."

His smile faded a little. "Have I offended you? I beg your pardon. You must surely know I do not hold you to blame. Your husband did not guide you as he ought, and you have been forced to bear burdens unsuitable for a female. If you have at times been obliged to be less than the perfect lady, I understand."

Had he always been so insufferable, Chloe wondered, or was it only in contrast with Justin he appeared so? The thought that she had been in danger of considering this man as tolerable horrified her.

"Sir Cedric," she said clearly. "Must I remind you I eloped from the schoolroom at seventeen?"

A faint hint of colour touched his smooth cheeks. "You were a mere child, and led astray."

Chloe looked him straight in the eyes in a most forward manner. "I would do it again today," she said firmly, "in the same situation."

"That isn't possible," he responded with steady good humour. "You are no longer seventeen."

Chloe was prevented from uttering a blistering comment on this dense reference by Justin joining them. He was perfectly amiable and maddeningly obscure in all he said, until Sir Cedric, clearly of the opinion that the most recent Lord Stanforth was mad, wandered away.

Justin looked down at her and shook his head. "You really cannot disembowel our guests before dinner, Chloe. It simply isn't done."

Chloe had recovered her sense of humour and laughed. This mischievous Justin delighted her. "Sometime during the third course, perhaps?"

"You'd only upset the servants." He surveyed the company. "All in hand, I think, as long as Randal is safe from the interesting and sharp-toothed Julia."

Chloe glanced up at him but could see he was not interested in the older lady. Not so Randal. From Julia's delighted reactions, Chloe guessed Randal was paying her his most skillfully risqué compliments. Chloe threw him a minatory look and received an unrepentant wink. She shrugged. She was quite confident of Julia Troughton's ability to keep a cool head on her bony shoulders.

Soon Colonel Sir Arthur and Lady Swayning arrived along with Sir Hambly and Lady Kellaway, the two couples in complete contrast. The Colonel and his lady were both tall, grey-haired, and elegant. They treated everyone with the same friendly courtesy, but Chloe noticed the Colonel take the first opportunity to buttonhole Justin, doubtless for a very professional discussion of the war. Sir Hambly and Lady Kellaway, on the other hand, were short, gaudy, and raucous.

The man had the bloated features and bulbous, red nose

of the hardened drinker, and his manner suggested he was already outside a few bottles. Lady Kellaway had unwisely dressed her bulky form in a low-necked, skimpy gown of silk which showed all the places her tight stays squeezed her flesh. It could be the stays which caused her ruddy face, or perhaps she too was a frequent imbiber.

Chloe thought those stays might pop when the lady discovered she was in the presence of the highest ranks of the ton. Not just such a lowly member of the peerage as a viscount, but the mother and son of a duke. No sooner had she been introduced than she plumped herself down by the Duchess and proceeded to tell her of all the other important people who were her intimate acquaintances. As the Duchess endured the woman's gushing, she sent her granddaughter a look which promised retribution.

Chloe surveyed the company. Apart from the Duchess, everyone seemed to be tolerably content. Mr. Macy, as she should have expected, was socially adroit and happy to entertain. It was difficult to know who was the most gratified—his audience to be the recipient of his anecdotes about his royal friend, or he to be the deliverer.

Justin too had all the social skills at his command. He possessed the Delamere charm, of course, but in Stephen that had always been an unpredictable benefit, quite likely to slip into overwarm flirtation or excessive high spirits. Justin, however, was perfectly controlled, handling Sir Hambly Kellaway's broad sense of humour and the Reverend Sotherby's dry anecdotes equally well.

Herr van Maes, seeing Chloe alone for a moment, took the opportunity to attempt a mild flirtation. She had no particular objection, for she had never believed he was seriously smitten by her charms. He was just the kind of man who liked to talk to pretty ladies. Despite his flirtatious intent, he always ended up talking about his obsession—Viking remains. As she expected, within minutes he was pouring out his latest research on the Battle of Brunanberh.

"Do you know, Lady Stanforth," he said, his blue eyes

ardent with enthusiasm, "I do believe Thorold may have died at that battle. . . ."

Chloe made suitable murmurs as he talked, but her eyes went to where Justin sat. She forced her lips to stay straight when she caught him glancing over at her. He looked so jealous. He doubtless thought the Dutchman's ardour was directed at her, not at people dead nearly a thousand years.

Chloe saw Belinda slip quietly into the room and sit by the Duchess. A cunning strategy. The Duchess welcomed escape from Lady Kellaway, and though that lady sneered, she would doubtless not cut Belinda in these circumstances.

Chloe waited anxiously to see whether the Dowager would take it into her head to join them. She was not expected, and no place was laid for her, but she might decide to come. However, by the time dinner was announced, she had not appeared.

Chloe took her seat at the end of the table, facing Justin. They shared a glance over the wavering light from the candles. Such events as these would be part of their lives, if they married. She found the idea surprisingly attractive, even if it meant having to listen to Sir Hambly's slurred yet vicious attacks on Luddites, Radicals, the Irish, Catholics, and women who did not know their place. She knew that boors and idiots were to be found everywhere. Better the ones you knew.

Perhaps it was the wine, perhaps it was the neighbourly atmosphere, both good and bad, but when she led the ladies away for their tea, Chloe was feeling mellow. She was even well-disposed towards Julia Troughton and pressed the woman to show off her skill on the little-used harp.

This had an unexpected benefit, as the instrument needed some tuning, and this happily occupied Julia during this period which had been known to bring out her less attractive features—until the gentlemen appeared. Julia was not much taken by the company of women, particularly women like Mrs. Thornton and Mrs. Williams. These two ladies began to compare notes on grandchildren and sewing patterns and were somewhat awed to find the Duchess joining them. It appeared that common interests—in grandchildren, at least—overcame rank, for soon the three ladies were chattering away.

Chloe was delighted to improve her acquaintance with Lady Swayning.

"How sad it is," said that lady, "that we have met so rarely, Lady Stanforth. Of course, as long as Sir Arthur was gazetted at the Horse Guards, we spent most of our time in London. Now he has retired, we will spend more time here, but you, I suppose, will be leaving."

"Yes," said Chloe, feeling a contrary urge to protest. "Next week, my grandmother and I travel south. We will spend Christmas at the Towers, my uncle's home."

"So soon?" said the lady in surprise. "And your cousin, Lord Randal? Does he go with you?"

"It is planned that he escort us, yes."

"Then Sir Arthur and I will have to take care of Lord Stanforth for you," said the lady with a smile. "We will invite him to our house for Christmas. Our son and his family always come to us for the celebration, so there will be some young faces. What of you, my dear? Will you miss this part of England?"

Chloe felt bereft at this practical discussion. It seemed so final, as if she was never to return. "Yes, I will," she said. "I will miss it very much. It may not be majestic, like the Lakes, or pastoral like the southern countries, but I find it very beautiful."

"So do I. I have often wished I were an artist, and able to record the scenery. Do you paint, Lady Stanforth?"

"I do," said Chloe, "but I claim no particular gift."

"Still," said the older lady, "I would like to see your pictures, if you would be so kind. It is always interesting to discover how others perceive familiar scenes."

By the time the gentlemen joined them, Julia had the harp tuned and began her first skillful trills. After a further request from Lady Swayning, Chloe left the room to find her portfolio of sketches and watercolours. She had taken them from the drawer in the library when she became aware of someone entering the room. She knew it would be Justin, and feelings warred within her.

When she turned, however, it was not Lord Stanforth she saw, but her other suitor, Sir Cedric.

"Should you not be admiring your sister's performance, Sir Cedric?" she said lightly, hoping to stave off what she feared was going to be a proposal.

"I have many opportunities to enjoy her playing," he said calmly, "and far too few opportunities to enjoy *your* company."

"At the moment, I am afraid, we should both return to the party."

"Julia will be happy to play for a little while yet," he said with the amiable firmness which infuriated her.

It had never been so clear to her before, but now she realised he spoke as if nothing she said had any real importance at all.

"I wanted to enquire," he carried on, "as to how you are, given the distressing events of Tuesday. It would not have been surprising if you had felt obliged to cancel an entertainment after such an ordeal."

Was that a criticism? If it was, Chloe had no patience for it. She knew she had at times been guilty of behaving as he expected, not as suited her nature, but she decided such times were past. "It is certainly unpleasant to be involved with sudden death, but not sufficiently to prostrate me, Sir Cedric."

"You are very brave," he said indulgently. "To find a corpse cannot but distress a lady. I noticed, however, how very unsympathetic and unsupportive your cousins both were. . . ."

"Justin is not my cousin, Sir Cedric."

"By marriage," he allowed with a smile.

"As you will," Chloe sighed. Cedric was impossible to irritate or excite, and it would be impolite to give vent to her exasperation. "We really should rejoin the company, Sir Cedric."

He merely smiled. "The word is out you will soon be leaving here, dear lady—"

"However did you hear that?" Chloe interrupted.

"You know the local gossips, my dear. In fact, your footman is meeting with my gardener's daughter. Kestwick's wife is dead so Sarah keeps house for him. I gather she walks over here frequently to speak to him."

"Matthew?" she queried in surprise.

"Yes. If you disapprove, you'll have to speak to him. As the girl is not in my employ, I have little say concerning how she spends her time, and Kestwick is too good an employee to disturb with such a matter."

"I don't disapprove," Chloe said. "Servants should be allowed some life of their own. I just had no idea. She must be a very frequent visitor, for I only decided to leave on Tuesday."

"I gather the girl was over twice that day. She came back in the morning full of the news of the accident."

"She was here at the time of Frank's death?" asked Chloe with interest.

"Yes, but she saw nothing. I did check. She and Matthew spoke briefly in the kitchen garden."

"With Budsworth nearby?"

"No," he said, looking irritated. "He had gone in for a cup of tea. My dear Lady Stanforth, I didn't come here to talk about the servants' courting. I came to talk of ours."

"Ours?"

He was obviously put out at having made such a blunt declaration of his purpose. "You know, surely, how I feel about you, my dear. I have waited impatiently until such time as you had a man to guide you. I thought of asking Lord Stanforth's permission to address you, but he is not, in fact, your guardian."

"No," said Chloe, biting back sharp words about his patriarchal attitude. He was only behaving in a manner the world would think correct. She could not help but add mischievously, "There is my cousin, however. He could be held to stand *in loco parentis.*"

Sir Cedric's lips tightened. "I hardly think Lord Randal . . . I understand he is a suitor himself for your hand."

Again, Chloe held back a comment. The local gossip was working overtime. This must explain Cedric's urgency. He feared rivals. The only thing was to allow him to make his prepared speech and then refuse him gently. She was aware of having, in a mild way, encouraged him.

"I have long hoped you would become my wife, Chloe," he began. "I can offer you much the same comfort as your first husband, and a home here, where you are loved . . ."

Next door to Justin, thought Chloe with a shudder.

"I admire you greatly, my dear, and not just for your beauty, which is fine but must surely fade with time. I desire nothing so much as to cherish you and remove all your cares. Your path will always be smooth and even with me by your side. No obstacle shall ever lie in your way."

"Cedric." Seeing he was well set into one of his perorations, and horrified by the picture he was painting, Chloe had been forced to interrupt. "Cedric, I am truly honoured and touched. We have been good friends, you and I, and you have been a great support to me during this trying time. But I cannot feel for you as a woman should towards a husband. I'm sorry." Chloe was very pleased by this speech. She had never had to refuse an offer before.

Cedric, however, was not accepting his dismissal. He took her hand and was about to attempt further persuasion when the door opened and Justin walked in. His brows rose, and Chloe felt like sinking through the carpet. What must he think, always coming in to find her in a man's clutches?

"Am I intruding?" he said politely, but with icy displeasure.

"No, of course not," said Chloe gratefully.

"I was just asking Chloe to be my wife," said Sir Cedric primly.

She heard the breath hiss pass Justin's teeth but he merely became as formal as his rival. "Am I to wish you happy, Chloe?"

They reminded Chloe of two dogs, curling their lips at each other, and walking stiff-legged about the edges of their territory.

"I have just told Sir Cedric it would not do," she said simply. "Please excuse me." With that she swept from the room and silently hoped the two of them enjoyed a pleasant conversation.

As she entered the drawing-room, Randal came over, grinning. "I knew I shouldn't have let you out of my sight," he said. "You've sliced up the pair of 'em. I admire your style with the lovelorn. I must copy it sometime."

Chloe looked over and saw Herr van Maes looking eager. She sighed. "I warn you, Randal, if you start to pay court to me, I'm likely to accept. It would serve you right."

Chloe found safe refuge with the older ladies for a while as they admired her art work. The watercolours were not impossible. She had a certain gift, and in some of them, she had caught the subtle mood of the sea.

She looked up to find Justin beside her admiring her work. He leant forward so his lips were by her ear.

"I didn't know you had such skill," he said softly. "How can you appear so perfect and yet constantly reveal new delights."

She flashed him a warning look. The ladies seemed absorbed by her art, thank goodness.

"Randal said you were threatening to accept the next proposal you received," he murmured. "I thought—"

Chloe stood and moved a little away from the group. "I said no such thing," she said. "I merely threatened to accept *him* if he proposed. I know nothing would be less to his taste."

"You're too harsh on yourself, my dear," said Justin, with a twinkle of amusement. "Mrs. Thornton, for example, would rank lower in his preferences, as would the sharp-edged Julia. . . ."

Chloe relaxed and chuckled. "Why not bring Lady Kellaway into the budget?"

Justin shook his head. "Even Randal, my dear, would not pursue a married lady."

"Of course not," said Chloe dryly. "They never run away."

She looked up to see Justin regarding her with fond good humour. She noticed how the lines of care she had noticed on his arrival seemed to be smoothing out.

"You look happy," she said.

"I am happy, just to be near you. I could, however, be happier," he added meaningfully.

At this moment, Chloe was rescued by the doctor and his wife taking their leave. They were soon followed by others. Eventually even Sir Hambly, who had fallen asleep, and his lady were eased out into their coach. Chloe couldn't help feeling relieved to have them all gone.

She found herself thinking wryly of the glittering social life she had been promising herself. She remembered now that it was not all delight. Yes, there were wonderful occasions where spirits were high and the wit flowed like champagne, but there were so many others—the fashionable crushes where one always met people one would rather avoid; the amateur *musicales* which threatened the ears; the dancing partners who smelt of garlic and less bearable things and trod on one's toes.

Peaceful domesticity at Delamere had a great deal to offer. Evenings by the fireside with Justin would be delightful. She no longer had the desire to be constantly in the company of strangers.

The Duchess and Belinda had retired, and the gentlemen had disappeared somewhere—doubtless to seek a restorative from the brandy bottle. Many of the candles were guttering, and Chloe extinguished them, leaving only two, and the firelight, to ease the darkness. She sat quietly at the piano and played simple music as she thought.

She had hardly had a moment to herself since the afternoon with Justin. Now she could consider that meeting, and all the secrets surrounding Delamere.

Who had received the missing papers, and where were they now?

Belinda and Frank were both under suspicion, though she failed to see the young woman's motive. George was the most likely person to have received the papers. To the sailor, the Honourable George Delamere might have appeared important enough to be trusted with them. If so, however, there was no reason for him not to have passed them on to the proper authorities.

Chloe suddenly realised Matthew also was a suspect. In the throes of refusing Sir Cedric, his words about Matthew had not fully sunk in. Now she realised Matthew had been in the garden at the time of Frank's death. If there was any connection between the death and the papers, the footman required close scrutiny. He had come to Delamere shortly after the papers went missing, recommended by Humphrey Macy. If Macy was a government man, perhaps Matthew was one too. It should be looked at, she thought.

She remembered then that Justin had promised an explanation tonight. Had he forgotten? She toyed with the idea of seeking him out but abandoned it. He was doubtless with Randal and Macy, and if she should find him alone, goodness knows what would happen. Her resolution to make decisions about her future with a cool head was being slowly eroded.

She returned her mind hastily to the mystery. Frank, she decided, was by far the most likely candidate for traitor and a safe one now he was dead and buried. Having survived one scandal, Chloe had a horror of being involved in another. If Frank had obtained these mysterious papers, however, he would have sold them to the Bonapartists, bought his livery stables, and been a prosperous man. Instead, he had lived on, poor and unhappy, at De-lamere. Why did this mystery always go in circles, never making sense?

She was interrupted by Justin, alone. She fumbled the notes and produced a discord.

"I persuaded Randal to play billiards with Macy," he said as he came over to the piano. "I'd like to keep that man under our eyes while we decide what to do. I think our conference will have to take place in the Duchess's bedroom later, after he's retired. She has part of the explanation to give and there's no danger of us being overheard there. We'll have to wait until tomorrow to try to drag the truth out of Belinda."

"You think Macy's a government investigator too," Chloe said. "We certainly don't want him to arrest Belinda."

"Don't we?" He seemed startled by her words.

"Surely not," she said anxiously. "If she has those papers, we can persuade her to return them. We wouldn't want the scandal of a trial for treason."

He frowned. "I suppose not, though it may not be in our power to prevent it if she is guilty."

"She is certainly nervous around Macy, and yet she implied at one point that she would consider marrying him."

"I appear to make *you* nervous," he said with a direct look, "and yet I hope you have every intention of marrying me."

"That's not the same—" she said and then broke off, red-faced. "I don't know my intentions."

He smiled slightly. "Well, mine are strictly honourable. Unfortunately."

They were feet apart, separated by the bulk of the instrument, and yet he could make her ache, dry her mouth, speed her pulse. . . . The crumbling fire flared up, tinting the shadowy room a hotter shade of red.

"Being with you like this is almost more than I can bear," he said, calmly, though she could sense the strain in his shadowed face. "I can see you respond to every word I say, and yet you deny me."

She leapt to her feet, prepared to flee him, prepared to flee her own wantonness. "Are you suggesting I should take you to my bed?" she demanded.

He moved slowly towards her. There was a slight smile on his lips, but his eyes were pure passion. "Would you? If I suggested it?"

"Of course not," she said in an unconvincing whisper, her traitorous body melting towards him.

So casually she did not think to resist, he took her into his arms. Being there, against his body, felt so right. She fit. She belonged. Helplessly, she relaxed and laid her head against his chest.

"Just think," he said softly as his warm hand rubbed comfortably on her back, and his breath stirred her hair. "We could do this every day, every night."

She raised her chin to stare at him. This was seduction of the most subtle kind. His hand traced gently along the side of her face.

"Do you know how dreadful it is, my darling, to lie in my bed at night and know you are so close? A few steps to heaven. It is sacrilegious to ignore what we have here."

To fight her desire to let him take her here, on the drawing room carpet, bathed in the crimson light of the dying fire, she said sharply, "That is a highly irreligious statement."

He kissed the tip of her nose. "You are my religion, my goddess."

Chloe used all her willpower. "Profanity too," she said, moving out of his arms.

He took the separation calmly, though the warmth in his eyes bridged the gap. "Not in my religion," he said lightly, leaning against the side of the piano. "There, the only sin is denial of love."

Chloe felt as if she should hug herself, do something to prevent herself from flying into pieces. "Not many years

ago," she retorted, struggling for a light tone, "you would
have been burnt at the stake, My Lord."

"And you are burning me now, my darling."

Surely it was only the reflection of the fire which made
his eyes smoulder so, but then why did her body feel
heated, consumed? Oh, this was terrifying, what he could
do to her. She must escape. She made as if to walk past
him to the door.

"I prescribe a course of sea-bathing," she said flip-
pantly, thinking it might do her good too. "The waters of
the bay are suitably cold—"

He caught her shoulders, almost bare in her fine silky
gown, and pulled her roughly against his body for a violent, burning kiss which bruised her lips and heated her
blood, leaving her trembling with shock and passion.

He pushed her slightly away and she stared at him.

"I will give you time, Chloe," he said. "I will let you
dance around this that we have—for a while at least. But
never convince yourself it is a flimsy thing, blown in the
wind. I will never let you go to another man. It is only a
question of time, and I'm sorry, I cannot give you endless
amounts of that and survive."

Chloe was speechless, adrift. Never in her life had she
known this kind of passion; the kind she saw clearly in
him and sensed in herself; a hunger which could wipe out
reason, discipline, breeding, and all the laws of society.

He must have read her thoughts in her face. He closed
his eyes briefly. "I never knew it would be like this,
Chloe," he said softly. "I thought I could woo you gently,
wait patiently. I have waited so long, after all. You push
me to the brink of insanity. Perhaps you are right when
you say you must leave here. . . ."

After a moment during which Chloe could count every
beat of her heart, he released her, then walked to the door.
"In the Duchess's bedroom, as soon as Macy retires," he
said curtly and left the room.

His last statement, coming so quickly after the passion,
conjured up the most peculiar vision in Chloe's mind and

she collapsed on the sofa in hysterical giggles. When she had collected herself, she paced the room, hugging herself. In the mirror she studied her huge, shocked eyes and reddened lips.

Stephen, her only real experience of men, had always been gentle. His lovemaking had been courteous and quiet, and though she had felt a vague dissatisfaction, she had never imagined it being any other way. Justin had revealed a whole other side to life, a side which both terrified and excited her. Earlier, walking through the gardens and the farm, she had been promised halcyon days of sunshine and laughter. Now she knew there would be stormy nights too.

She had hated the life of feckless unpredictability Stephen had given her, though it had once seemed what she wanted. Was the life of stormy passion Justin offered any more likely to bring contentment?

More than ever she needed to escape, to search her heart in peace and make decisions she could hold with all her life; but she could not leave just yet. She owed it to the people she still thought of as her own to unmask the evil which had invaded Delamere and restore peace.

In the meantime she should heed the warning. Justin was rapidly approaching his limit, and the sooner she left Delamere the better. She did not believe he would try to stop her if she decided she could not marry him, but her capacity to hurt him troubled her deeply. Until such time as she made up her mind, she should treat him with great circumspection for fear of unleashing a force she could not control.

In him.

In herself.

Right now, she could not bear her own company and did not dare to seek out Justin's, and so she went to watch Randal and Macy play. Randal glanced curiously and shrewdly at her, but said nothing. Macy exchanged only courtesies before returning his attention to the game.

It was an interlude of tranquility, with the click of the balls punctuating the crackling of the fire in the grate. The men spoke briefly and occasionally. The house around was quiet, as most of the staff were in their beds.

It was only four days since Justin had returned to Delamere, four days since her primary emotion had been boredom. It was impossible that he could gain such a hold on her mind and her body in four brief days. With honesty, she had to admit his hold had begun years before.

She watched Randal as he played. Both men had removed their jackets for ease of movement, and as he stretched to line his cue up on the ball, an artist could have made studies of him—long, lean, and beautiful, a thoroughbred, a god. Yet, she felt not the slightest desire to touch him. Her heart and pulse continued their steady, accustomed pace. He excited her no more than plump Humphrey Macy.

Justin, however, disordered her constantly. If he had come home from the war scarred or crippled, it would have been no different.

She sat staring at the flames and fell into a brown study of life, men, and marriage. By the time she was jerked back to reality by Macy declaring he was for his bed, she had not summoned one sensible thought.

After Macy had gone, Randal replaced the cues in the rack.

"Care to tell me what's got into you?" he asked.

"No," she said.

"I could try guessing, and I wouldn't need three."

"Randal . . . ," she warned.

"Pax!" he said, throwing up a hand. "I won't say a thing. But," he added with a grin, "you must put poor Justin out of his misery soon."

"And why, pray, should I have any kindness at all for a man who has been keeping secrets about events in my own home?"

"His home," Randal pointed out calmly.

"About which he doesn't care one jot!"

"Of course he cares. If he's been keeping mum there must be a reason."

Chloe calmed slightly. "Do you give me your word, Randal, that he hasn't already told *you* what's going on?"

"Ashby honour," said Randal firmly.

Chloe walked to the table and idly rolled a black ball down the baize. "I need to be sure, Randal," she said.

He took a red out of a pocket and accurately spun it down to cannon off hers. "How sure can we ever be in love, my dear?"

"It's such a terrible risk. He's been here for only a few days. I don't know him."

He just looked at her. "Don't you?"

Chloe turned away. Everyone seemed sure of her heart except herself. "It's all very well for you," she said bitterly. "You know nothing of commitment. Your idea of love is a physical thing, paid for with money, and got rid of the same way when it grows stale."

She caught a flash of dangerous anger in his eyes. Then he calmed, though his lips were still tight. Chloe found herself trembling slightly. She had never been afraid of Randal in her life. Was something at Delamere poisoning everyone's life?

"One thing's clear," he said at last. "My interference in your affairs, though well intentioned, does no good. I'll try to resist the temptation. But don't judge me like that, Chloe. I know the difference between lust and love."

"What is it then?" she asked simply and he laughed dryly.

She thought he wouldn't answer but then he said, "If you love someone, you will seek their happiness even if it means you will never touch their body again. If you lust after someone, you will seek their body, even if it destroys them."

He swept up the two balls and dropped them in a pocket, then put on his jacket.

Chloe realised Justin had sought her happiness by leaving, once she was married to Stephen. Unsure of his ability to control himself, he had put the greatest possible distance between them. Stephen, however, though she could not accuse him of lustful evil, had never really concerned himself with her happiness at all.

"Come along then," Randal said, cool and composed as ever. "Bedtime, I think. It will all work out, sweet coz."

Chloe hoped he was a better prophet than a matchmaker. She walked up with him to the bedrooms, but after he had entered his room, Chloe crept quietly along to her grandmother's. At last she was to discover all the Stanforth secrets.

Justin was already in her grandmother's room when Chloe arrived. He glanced briefly at her, then away again. She took a seat as far from him as possible, knowing the Duchess had noted the move. There was a strange, pungent odour in the room. Turpentine?

"I am going to tell you," said Justin, "all I know of events here at Delamere over the last year. Unfortunately, I don't yet have all the answers. I think I need help to find them, which is why I am going to disobey express orders."

He then recounted the story told to him in London. He told Chloe about the list of Napoleonic agents, its dispatch in the form of waxed fruits, the disastrous pursuit of d'Estrelles and the package's arrival in Heysham. So many puzzling incidents clicked into place. The disturbed storerooms, the soldiers, possibly even the increased number of strangers in the area could all be explained by this.

When Justin revealed the Duchess's role, Chloe gasped. "Grandmama! how could you have kept all this to yourself?"

"Didn't like it," said the old lady, "but I had my orders. If I'd realised there was such danger involved, though, I'd have said to hell with them."

"And Stephen was trying to serve his country too," said Chloe, feeling tears gather in her eyes. "He wasn't just on one of his crazy starts."

Justin was glad he'd edited that part of the story slightly, but he hoped some new-found hero worship wasn't going to drive a wedge between him and Chloe.

"And that was why," Chloe went on, "when I heard strange noises in the storeroom and the dining room, I found you there before me, Grandmama. You were searching."

"Yes," said the old lady bitterly. "For a damned apple! Incompetent nincompoops. I did wonder about potatoes, though, and had a poke around through what was left of last year's stock. Decided I was getting addled."

"And last night?" asked Chloe. "Was that you too?"

"Last night?" asked the Duchess in surprise.

"No," said Justin, with a rueful smile. "I was the guilty party. After you made your comment about *pommes* and *pommes de terre,* I decided to check the stores, though without much hope. I'll know next time not to be so messy in a well-run household!"

"Indeed," said Chloe, severely. "You show a great carelessness as to detail. I'll go odds it was you who tampered with my pictures."

Justin's face showed his guilt, and his chagrin at being detected. "Now how did you notice that foolishness? I made the cuts very neatly."

Chloe smirked. "And replaced the pictures in the wrong order," she said.

Justin groaned, but with a smile. There was almost ease between them again.

"I'm just a crude soldier," he said. "I'm not cut out for this kind of work."

Chloe dragged her mind back to business and frowned as she thought over the situation. "We still don't know whether the message was sent as a potato or an apple. Whichever it was, surely there's little chance it still exists."

"The only people who want it destroyed," replied Justin, "are the French. To the best of our people's knowledge they are still frantically searching. Let's consider the options. If George got it, he could have destroyed it for some insane reason no one would ever understand. As that would get us nowhere, we'll ignore the possibility. If he behaved half rationally, he would hand it over to the nearest authority. Did he?''

Chloe answered. "If he received it the night Stephen died, no. He didn't travel at all at that time and no one visited him until Humphrey Macy came. Would George have given it to him?''

"That was weeks later, surely," said the Duchess. "What did he do in the meantime?''

"Marry Belinda," said Chloe taking the question literally.

Everyone looked thoughtful and puzzled.

"There's something there," said Chloe at last. "But what? It's possible Belinda and Frank managed to inveigle the package from the sailor, or even steal it from George, but then why didn't they sell it, if profit was their motive, and marry?''

"They may not have known how to dispose of it," said Justin. "After all, it would be a chancy business, trying to trade with the French. Did either of them make a journey?''

"No. I'm certain they didn't," said Chloe. She sighed with exasperation. "This whole thing is like an out-of-focus eyeglass. It needs to be twisted. But how?''

Justin ran a hand over his face. "It is certainly a puzzle. The matter is urgent. Every day, doubtless, brave men die because of traitors still at large. On the other hand, the package has been mislaid for over a year. It is unlikely to be destroyed tomorrow.''

Chloe wondered. "You know," she said, "I have this unreasoning feeling that matters are coming to a crisis. I don't know whether Frank's death was a symptom of this or its cause, but things have changed.''

Justin nodded. "I can't speak for change exactly, but I am aware of something in the air. An interview with Belinda is even more important—first thing in the morning. If she had any contact with the package we must find out.''

"But Belinda could not possibly be a spy," pointed out

Chloe. "She has a brother in the army and worries about him constantly."

"I feel that way too, but she may know something, however innocently. Frank was quite likely the villain."

"And his death?" asked Chloe.

"I admit I don't see any reason for it. Perhaps it *was* an accident. If he had the package, however, his death makes it less likely we will find it."

"I think it must have been an accident," said Chloe, wish stronger than logic. "Belinda is not a murderess."

She trailed off, remembering Belinda's words. "I am not sorry for anything I've done." Said so fiercely. Thrown in the face of fate.

"I hope not," said Justin calmly, "for if she is, it's quite possible that she killed George as well."

"Good God!" exclaimed the Duchess. "She's a regular Lucrezia Borgia, and she brought me some medications today!"

Chloe defended Belinda. "She's very skilled, Grandmama. I've never known anyone to suffer from her remedies. George was ripe for a seizure," she said to Justin. "You should have seen him. His face was red, he was always wheezing for breath."

The Duchess reconsidered. "That embrocation did my hip a world of good," she said at last. "Have a look and see what you think. My woman put it back in the dressing room. Smelly stuff."

Chloe fetched the earthenware pot, and unscrewed the wide lid. Now she knew where the smell came from! Turpentine, camphor, goodness knows what else. It was the same mixture Belinda had given to the Dowager. She tilted the jar. The stuff was runny, like oil.

"The Dowager has been using this mixture for days, Grandmama. Besides, I'm sure something rubbed on you couldn't do harm."

Justin took the pot and shrugged. "I wouldn't know. But all Chloe's reasonings are good, Your Grace. I wouldn't worry. I think we'll have to think of a reason for a thorough search of the house, though. If those papers are here, we must find them. I don't know what Macy is up to, but I prefer to keep an eye on him, or to keep Randal's eye on him, in fact.''

"Do you not think he's a government man?" Chloe asked.

"I'm a government man," pointed out Justin. "They told me about the Duchess, but no one mentioned Macy. It's possible they're being extra cautious and I've written to enquire. He's probably just what he claims to be, but until I'm sure, I want him watched. Chloe, can you try to keep track of Belinda tomorrow?"

"Of course." She then mentioned Belinda's suspicious behavior, and her attempt to follow the young woman that morning.

"If there's a clue to Frank's death outside, I am not that concerned," said Justin. "It may seem heartless, but the lives of hundreds of men hang on these papers, not just one, already lost. But try to keep track of her. If she did kill Frank, it might have been to get the papers. She may panic and destroy them.''

With that, he left, and Chloe checked to make certain her grandmother had everything she needed.

"What have you and Justin been doing to yourselves now?" asked the old lady.

"Nothing," said Chloe firmly.

"Must be frustration eating at you both then," was the retort, making Chloe blush.

"I am not going to make any decision about Justin until all these alarums are over, and I have peace and quiet away from here to consider matters.''

"It'll do no harm," said the Duchess, "as long as you keep your mind straight. Good night, my dear," she said, kissing Chloe's cheek. "Have sweet, or at least interesting, dreams.''

Chloe left before her grandmother could say something even more outrageous.

11

CHLOE HALF HOPED her grandmother's words would come true. The unconscious mind, however, ever a trickster, served her instead with dreams of Stephen at his most delightful, engaging in a mad search for apples and potatoes through her old schoolroom at home. She awoke confused and unsettled and chose to breakfast in her room.

She couldn't hide forever, though. Justin sent a message asking her to go to the study. She knew it was time to confront Belinda.

Deliberately Chloe dressed in her least becoming half-mourning gown, a mushroom colour which achieved the nearly impossible and made her look sallow. She also dallied a little, hoping Belinda would be there ahead of her.

When Chloe saw Matthew going into the dining-room to clear the breakfast table, she thought of Cedric's revelations, and followed the footman.

"Matthew."

"Yes, Your Ladyship."

He was a well-enough-looking young man, she thought. His features were rather sharp, and he lacked the height for a footman in a great house, but she could see why Sally Kestwick might be enamoured.

"I understand you are seeing a young lady from Sir Cedric's estate," said Chloe.

The man coloured uncomfortably. "Yes, Your Ladyship."

"I have no objection," she reassured him, "though I

cannot speak for Lord Stanforth. I understand she was here on Tuesday morning at about the time of Frank's death.''

He looked slightly anxious, but surely he would appear more so if he had committed murder that day. ''Yes, Your Ladyship. But only to bring me a shirt,'' he assured her. ''I didn't take time from my duties. It was the time we normally all have a cup of tea.''

''So I understand. But it was about the time that Frank died, was it not?''

''Yes, Your Ladyship. I saw Lady Stanforth—Lady George—coming into the kitchen garden as we left. So it must have been just before.''

Perhaps, thought Chloe. ''Left?'' she queried. ''Where did you go?''

He reddened even more. ''I just walked with Sally aways down the drive. It was instead of the tea, Milady.''

Chloe felt rather guilty at upsetting him. Many employers felt the duty to regulate their servant's personal lives, but Chloe tried to avoid it. They were all part of large local families, after all . . . except Matthew, she remembered. He had fit in so well, she was inclined to forget. He had come from Preston way. Humphrey Macy had found him for George with excellent references from previous employers there, but she wondered if she should make enquiries all the same.

She assured him she would not interfere in his courtship as long as his duties were performed, and then made her way to the study, thoughtfully. In the matter of Frank's death, Chloe had been so obsessed by Belinda that she had forgotten the rumours of ill-feeling between Matthew and Frank. Matthew had been out of the house at the time of the groom's death. She'd go odds the staff had concealed that fact from Cedric and Justin. They always stuck together when necessary. His sweetheart would doubtless cover for him, but there was no guarantee they had been together all the time.

What possible reason, though, could Matthew have for killing Frank, and was he even capable of it? He was inches shorter and a stone lighter. He was hardly an active type either, more effete than anything.

Matthew, however, had been introduced to Delamere by Humphrey Macy. Perhaps he too was a government man, but that made no sense. If he had killed Frank to obtain the missing papers, they would now be safe in official hands.

What if Matthew and Macy were working for Napoleon, she wondered. Humphrey Macy? Impossible. Some French *émigrés* had switched allegiance to Napoleon, hoping to gain back lands and titles lost in the Revolution, but someone like Macy would have nothing to gain and everything to lose. He could not possibly support Napoleon's rampaging conquest of Europe.

Matthew alone? It seemed too great a coincidence that he would have been innocently brought to Delamere if he were a spy.

She sighed in frustration. It was like a *roman à clef* and she lacked the key. George was the most likely person to have been given the papers; Frank was the most likely to have stolen them. Belinda seemed the prime suspect for Frank's murder, if he had, in fact, been pushed, but no one had any clear motive for the deed unless it was to regain possession of those papers. If the papers had changed hands, no one had showed any sign of having done anything with them.

And, Chloe thought as she approached the study door, where on earth had the papers been for a year, and why had Frank, if he had stolen them, not used them to his own advantage? Perhaps the interview with Belinda would shed some light.

Belinda arrived just as Chloe opened the door and looked even more disturbed than during the last few days, with an air of distraction which was very unusual.

"Chloe. Justin. What can I do for you?" she said with a busy air. "I have many other duties."

"Please have a seat, Belinda," said Justin firmly. "I'm sure there's nothing so important it can't wait a little while."

She sat in a swirl of black. "Very well. What is it?" Her eyes were frightened.

Justin looked at Chloe briefly then said, "Belinda, on the night before George became the viscount, you were seen talking to a sailor near the village. The man's name was Samuel Wright. Do you recall this?"

"Talking to a sailor at night?" queried Belinda with heightened colour. "What in heaven's name are you implying?"

"No impropriety, with him at last. In fact you were with your lover, Frank Halliwell, at the time."

Chloe glanced at Justin. That was a bludgeoning tactic. Belinda had turned white.

"So?" the young woman asked faintly.

"So what passed between you and the sailor?"

Belinda made a gallant recovery. "I really couldn't say. It's over a year ago. If I spoke with a fisherman, it would doubtless be to talk of the weather and the tides."

"Not a fisherman, Belinda. A sailor. He wasn't from these parts. He was staying in the village with a package to deliver to Stephen. You must remember him."

Belinda had regained a superficial calm, but was looking down at her hands. "I do, now you mention it. We don't have so many strangers here. I don't recall a meeting with him, though."

"The package he had. He didn't mention it to you?"

Belinda looked up. "I said I don't recall the meeting. How could I recall what he said or didn't say?"

Justin looked stumped so Chloe spoke up. "This is very important, Belinda. Please try to remember. We think you came up to the Hall that evening to visit Frank, and then he walked you back down to your home. The sailor came up here that evening too. Did you see him?"

Belinda obvious felt less intimidated by Chloe. She visibly relaxed. "I don't remember the night even. I don't ever remember seeing a sailor up at the Hall. There, does that help?"

"Not really," said Chloe, wanting to shake the girl, who was clearly concealing something. "This was the night before George became the viscount. People seem to remember it. Don't you?''

"What was all that to me, then?" asked Belinda, rather pertly.

"But within four weeks," interrupted Justin, "you and George were married. How did that come about, then?"

Belinda paled again, and almost looked as if she would dash out of the room. She stared down at her hands. "How does any marriage come about?" she retorted in a thin voice.

Justin answered the rhetorical question. "People meet, spend time together, fall in love. The bans are called, the bride gathers her *trousseau*. Was that how it was with you?"

Chloe saw Belinda swallow. "George was in mourning," she muttered. "The ceremony was a quiet one." She looked up. "But we had bans. We did have bans."

Justin pressed her. "The first reading of the bans must have been the week after Stephen's death. The night before Stephen's death you were out with Frank. When did George propose to you?"

Belinda raised her chin. Chloe could see she had her nerve back. "The next day. He'd had his eye on me for a while. We'd talked now and then. When he came into the title he decided he should marry, and didn't want the fuss of looking afield. I think he reckoned I'd be content to stay here when he went back south, and he was right.'' It sounded like a rehearsed speech.

Her composure disconcerted Justin. "And what of Frank?"

"What of him?" retorted Belinda, though something flickered in her eyes. Chloe thought it could be loss.

"Didn't he mind?"

"Well of course he did," Belinda said, as if talking to a simpleton. "But a girl can't marry every man who woos her."

Justin stared at her. "You loved Frank—or that's what the gossips say. Why marry George?"

Belinda opened her blue eyes wide and stared at him. "Turn down a peer of the realm," she said, "for Frank Halliwell?"

Justin turned to Chloe helplessly. Chloe tried once more.

"And you know nothing of a package? The sailor lost it, you see, and it should be found."

"No, I don't," said Belinda. "What was this package anyway?"

The tone of the question caught Chloe's attention. Belinda desperately wanted to know. She shared a glance with Justin.

"Very important," he said briefly, then turned the full force of a charming smile on the young woman. "I'm sorry if we have distressed you, Belinda, but we have to get to the bottom of this. I had hopes you could help. Please don't be concerned that the matter of you and Frank will be talked of. It is nothing to do with all of this. But if you think of anything later, please let me know."

"Very well," said Belinda coolly and stood.

"Before you go," said Justin. "When I was in London the family solicitor said he had received an anonymous letter claiming George made out a later will, in his own hand, and hid it at Delamere."

"That's absurd," Belinda bristled, obviously wondering if her comfortable jointure was at risk.

"Quite possibly," said Justin easily. "You know of no such thing?"

"No. It is a piece of nonsense. George had a solicitor from Lancaster come and draw up his will after our marriage, and the man never came back again."

"But he wouldn't need a solicitor for a holograph will, Belinda. I just want to reassure you. If by any chance George altered his will to your detriment, I guarantee your current allowance."

"That's kind of you," said Belinda sincerely. The girl hesitated, looking at Justin with a slight frown. Chloe thought she might be overcoming her fear, might even tell the truth of whatever had gone on that night so long ago. But then the mask came back. "There was no reason for George to make any changes. He doted on me."

Chloe was startled by that word "doted." It was hardly accurate. George had always seemed uncomfortable about Belinda, and had once referred to her as "that farmer's daughter.'' As Belinda swept out, Chloe shrugged. Deceiving oneself as to the state of a marriage was hardly a crime, or unusual. She should know.

"I don't think we gained very much from that," said Justin.

"She's afraid of something," said Chloe.

"If she killed Frank, she is afraid of the hangman, and so she should be.''

"I'm sure she could not have killed him," Chloe said. "She loved him. When the funeral bell tolled she looked so . . . so desolate.''

Justin was unconvinced. "Even if he was threatening her in some way? Perhaps he swore to kill her and her child if she wouldn't marry him.''

Chloe stared at the fire and tried to imagine the scenario. Even if Belinda was attached to her position as a member of the aristocracy, was killing her lover better than marrying him? She tried to imagine killing Justin because he stood in the way of her marrying the Prince of Wales.

Chloe shook her head. "She wouldn't. And I don't think he would have threatened such a thing. He wasn't insane. He was just very unhappy. What of the package? If Frank stole the package, perhaps Belinda tried to get it back from him.''

"After a year?''

"She really wanted to know more about the message it contained, though,'' said Chloe.

"I noticed that. I wonder why? I hope you can keep her under your eye, my dear. If she knows anything, I don't want her to panic and destroy the package. After lunch we will search the house to look for the 'missing will.' I think I'll ask Randal and Matthew to search the ground floor. If she's willing, Belinda can assist them. You, I, and the upstairs maid can do the bedrooms and servants' quarters. I've spoken to the Duchess and she says she's able to supervise a search of the lower floor.''

"What of the stables and outhouses?''

Justin shrugged. "We will have to ignore them for now. I confess I think the most hopeful explanation for all this is that George got the package and for some reason hid it instead of passing it on. I've checked with the staff, and I'm sure you can verify that he never went into the kitchen region or up to the attic floor. He never went to the stables either. If he wanted his carriage he had it sent to the door, and he hardly ever left Delamere during his period as viscount.''

''That's true. He hated travelling in less than perfect weather. Belinda bullied him into taking her to a Christmas assembly in Lancaster, and he complained for days. I don't think he did more than take a turn in the garden his whole time as Lord Stanforth. He wasn't well, you know. Slight exertion made him wheeze, and brought on a dizzy spell.''

''So if he had it, it is almost certainly still in the house. I hope to God we find it. I don't relish digging up the county in search of it, and I want to get on with my life.''

Simultaneously, it seemed, they became aware that they were alone again. Chloe felt a stirring of panic, or lust, inside her.

''Don't, Chloe,'' Justin said softly, raising a hand to gently caress her cheek. ''Don't fear me. I'm sorry about last night. It won't happen again.''

Absurdly, Chloe wanted to protest that, and perhaps he caught some fleeting expression, for he smiled slightly. ''At least, not until you are more comfortable with the notion.''

''I'm sorry, Justin,'' she said, taking his hand in both of hers. ''Can you understand how I feel?''

''Yes,'' he replied. ''I am paying the price, I think, for that elopement. It was stupidly irresponsible of us to persuade you to it. You were a child. At our instigation, you threw your heart over a fence and came a cropper. Not surprisingly, you hesitate to leap blind a second time, particularly with the same persuader.''

She had to ask him. ''Why did *you* not want to marry me?''

He pulled his hand from hers and walked over to the fireplace. ''It honestly didn't occur to me at first. Stephen was simply quicker off the mark. When the idea began to stir, it was too late. I couldn't imagine you would want to exchange a rich viscount for a commoner with a mere competence.''

''Did I appear so mercenary?'' she asked, hurt.

He turned and smiled at her. She felt light-headed and wanton; she longed to throw herself into his arms. "No, of course not, but most women are, it would seem. We were both fresh from our first brush with London Society, where poor Stephen had been fairly hunted down. I think it was your lack of wiles which most attracted him." He flushed slightly. "I'm sorry. I didn't mean . . ."

She wanted desperately to smooth the concern from his sun-browned features. "We so lightly move onto dangerous paths, do we not?" she said quietly.

"And you are determined not to do so again," he said. "I do understand, my dear. But if you wait for total surety, you'll wait your life away."

Before she had a chance to comment he said, with a grin, "That gown is dreadful."

She laughed. "I know."

Warm brown eyes met sparkling grey. "I see," he said. Then the smile became heart-stoppingly sweet. "If you were to lose all your beauty tomorrow, Chloe, I would still adore you."

She longed then to kiss him, a simple kiss of friendship, because he had overcome his passion and understood her needs. It was agony to deny herself, and yet she knew such a gesture was the last thing she should do.

"Thank you," she said softly, and left.

As soon as she was outside the door, she remembered Belinda, who should be under supervision. Chloe hurried up to the youngest Lady Stanforth's suite and scratched. The door was promptly opened by the nursery maid.

"Is Lady George here, Rosie?"

"No, ma'am. She's out in the garden."

Chloe dashed off for her bonnet and shawl, then hurtled down the back stairs and out into the kitchen garden. It was as well, she thought, she had no desire to be a patterncard of decorum.

The only person around was Budsworth, digging over cleared ground with smooth economical movements. "Morning, ma'am," he said, leaning on his fork a moment.

"Good morning, Budsworth. Have you seen Lady George?"

"Ay. She passed through here, then went over to the rose garden. She won't find much there, though," he added morosely. "Pretty near cleaned it out yesterday."

Chloe knew Budsworth complained at people picking in "his" garden, but was not inclined to soothe his feelings now. Matthew came out of the house.

"Tea's up, Mr. Budsworth," he called, "and Mrs. Pickering asks if you have any of them Brownell's Beauty spuds. She says they mash a treat, and there's none in the stores." Belatedly, he noticed Chloe and touched his forelock.

"Right," said the gardener. "I wasn't going to dig them till next week but I'll get her a few."

Chloe was about to leave to track down Belinda when she saw a figure come around from the front of the house. A young woman. She walked forward, stopped when she saw Chloe, and turned and walked away.

Matthew had turned red. He hesitated, then went after the young woman. So that was Sally Kestwick. A pretty girl. Chloe wondered for a moment whether Frank and Matthew could have fought over her, but then reminded herself that whole business was of minor importance at this moment.

She cursed her dilatoriness when she rounded the sea side of the house to find it deserted. She checked down at the cliff edge where Frank had fallen. No Belinda, and no sign of the occurrence. The rain had washed it all away. With little hope, Chloe went towards the stables. She met the stableboy halfway, and he had not seen Belinda that day.

Heavy with a sense of failure, Chloe walked back to the house. She and Justin should not have stayed together to talk for so long, hard though it was to be apart. Oh, what a fool she was to fight this attraction. If she succumbed she could lie in his arms tonight, but that was the way of Stephen's friends, and she had never surrendered to it. Even if she pledged herself, they would wait. She remembered Justin's passion with a smile. Even if she agreed to marry him, she thought she would have to leave Delamere for a while if they were to observe the proprieties. Or a special licence . . .

Yet, she had set her heart, if she married again, on all due process and formality. But did it matter?

Her head was whirling with sensual longings, and plans of propriety, so the sound did not immediately register.

A scream. Shouting. All coming from the kitchen garden. She raced over there.

"Oh, Milady!" wailed Mrs. Pickering, who was kneeling in the dirt. "Someone's gone and killed Budsworth. What's the world coming to?"

A bunch of the staff stood around gawking at the body on the ground.

Heart pounding, Chloe ran forward. Justin and Randal appeared from the house. They all gathered around the body.

Chloe was immensely relieved to see that the man was breathing, though he was very pale. She made a pillow of her shawl and put it under his head. Justin loosened the man's clothing and instructed someone to fetch a blanket. Budsworth began to groan and his eyelids flickered.

Slowly the gardener came to consciousness, though he looked extremely ill. Glancing around, Chloe saw Belinda emerge from the house through the kitchen door, followed by the Duchess's maid, sent to find out the cause of the commotion.

Justin inspected the gardener's wound. There was already blood on Chloe's shawl, though not a great deal.

"It's not too bad, I think," he said after a moment. "But the doctor should be sent for." He sent Humphrey Macy's valet to the stables with the message.

"Can you talk, Budsworth?" Justin asked.

"Yes, Your Lordship," said Budsworth slowly. "But I feel right queer."

"We'll get you to your bed in a moment." Justin took the blanket a maid had brought and laid it over the gardener. "Can you tell us what happened."

The man tried to shake his head and groaned. "No, My

Lord. I can't. It seems strange, but I don't remember a thing. I were digging up taties. Then I were in the dirt . . . I don't know . . .''

''It's often that way,'' said Justin in a calm voice. ''Don't worry about it. Just rest quiet. I'm sure you'll be yourself in a day or two.''

His manner soothed the fretful man. Chloe looked at his strong, lean hand laid on the gardener's shoulder and thought for the first time that Justin must have been an excellent officer. She had somehow assumed he was a daredevil kind of hero, but now she suspected his commendations might have been for leadership and efficiency as well as bravery. Thus, another barrier in her mind tumbled. Justin Delamere was a man to trust when trouble was on the horizon.

Justin looked around ruefully. ''I'm afraid there's a shortage developing of able-bodied men. I wonder if Matthew could be called upon to help.''

Chloe realised then that there was no sign of Matthew. Where had he and his sweetheart been when this occurred?

''Oh, what the hell,'' Justin said. ''Randal, let's you and I carry him.''

The two gentlemen made a cradle of their hands and carried the protesting gardener, wrapped in a blanket, to his cottage, where they gave him over to the ministrations of his anxious wife. Chloe, who had followed, made sure the woman had all that was needed. She assured her the doctor would call as soon as possible and should be instructed to send his bill to the Hall.

As they walked back to the House, Randal said, ''This is all damned queer. Do you mind telling me what's going on?''

''No time,'' said Justin, ''Let's get back to the hall fast. I don't want Belinda out of our sight. And I confess to wondering about Macy. I was thinking of that poor man, or I'd never have left them alone so long.''

''Why?'' asked Chloe. ''Do you think . . .''

"I think the package was a potato and someone just got hold of it."

As they hurried back, Chloe told them Matthew had been out of the house. He was, after all, a new servant, and had come to Delamere after the package had gone astray.

In the Hall, Macy was found in the Sea Room drinking coffee and reading a days-old newspaper. Being on the far side of the house, he had apparently not heard the commotion and evinced only mild interest in the event.

"Servants," he drawled. "They have their own strange tribal life."

Which left Matthew and Belinda. Justin undertook to check on the footman and sent Chloe to Belinda, with instructions not to allow her the opportunity to destroy anything. Chloe hurried off, Randal's plaintive demands for an explanation floating after her.

What possible excuse could she think up this time? Belinda opened the door at her knock.

"I came to visit my little cousin," Chloe said brightly.

"I'm just about to feed her," said Belinda with surprise.

Chloe felt ridiculous, but she reminded herself this was all in the service of her country. "Would you mind terribly if I watched?" she said. "I have thought I would like to feed my own child, when I have one, but I know nothing about it."

She would have sworn the look Belinda flashed at her was amused, not frightened. Was she so obvious? Had the evidence already been destroyed? But if it was a solid wax potato, as supposed, it would not be so easily disposed of. An attempt to burn it on the fire would produce thick, acrid smoke.

Belinda said she would be happy to show Chloe how to nurse a child, and led the way into the nursery. Rosie was holding the freshly washed baby, who was sucking on her fist and giving restless little wails.

"Let Lady Stephen hold Dorinda a moment," said Belinda. "I must just fetch something."

Chloe received the delightful bundle with nervous delight. So soft and sweet. Big blue eyes gazed up at her. Meanwhile, Belinda had left the room. Chloe had been outmaneuvred!

Chloe hurried to the door. In the *boudoir,* Belinda was dribbling the last few petals through the grid into the Dowager's beautiful *potpourri* pot. She placed the lid on top and picked it up.

"I have just filled this with fresh mix. The poor lady frets so if she's without it, so I will return it now. I won't be a moment."

There was clearly nothing else in her hands and no obvious lump in her skirt which would denote a potato in her pocket. On what ground could Chloe protest? She could only watch her go.

The baby made a small squawk and Chloe glanced down. She felt a sudden pang. Because she could not grow fond of Belinda, she had virtually ignored Dorinda's presence at Delamere. Now, the infant kicked and chirruped in her arms.

"And that, my angel, isn't fair," Chloe murmured. Dorinda, under a misapprehension, turned her head and rooted anxiously at Chloe's breast.

"Oh no, poor dear," said Chloe. "I wish I did have food for you. I wish you were my own little one."

Once she thought she might have been with child, but if so, it had soon miscarried. A very strong reason for remarrying was to have children of her own, children who would be allowed to grow free, not as she had been brought up.

A quiet voice whispered, Justin's children. She imagined nursing babies as she looked out over the bay, watched by Justin—and saw her children free to explore the sands and rocks and tidal pools.

Dorinda, thwarted, set up an angry wail. Chloe looked around anxiously. Rosie too had disappeared.

Chloe began to walk and jiggle the child. "Hush, little

one. Mama will be here soon. Be good. Hush, my angel. Oh, do please stop.''

Desperate, she gave the child a finger to suck on, as she had seen the village women do. Dorinda quieted, sucking steadily with amazing force.

After a little while, however, when no milk appeared she pulled back and began to wail in earnest. Chloe was about to go seeking Belinda when she suddenly reappeared, unflustered, and took the child.

''Hush a minute, Dorinda. It's coming,'' she said, lapsing into a broader accent than was her norm, perhaps in an echo of her own childhood.

She sat in an armless rocker by the window and undid the front of her bodice, which fell down to reveal her loose shift, easily moved aside to give the baby access to the nipple. With expertise, Dorinda fastened onto the source of food, her small body relaxing with satisfaction.

Chloe realised Belinda's gowns must be specially designed for easy feeding. Could that, not some strange notions of status, be why she had stuck to mourning? It would appear she had often misjudged the young woman. What an ordeal it must have been, coming to this house and facing so much hostility. Her own choice, of course, but still one which demanded courage.

Since Belinda seemed unselfconscious, Chloe watched this most natural process with delight and longing. Her excuse to stay with Belinda had been fabricated. She had never considered how she would feed a child. Some Society women fed their own babies, at least for a little while; others sought out wet nurses. Good wet nurses, healthy and not given to strong drink, were hard to find, however. Surely this was a better way.

Belinda looked up from her babe. ''It's a pleasure, feeding her,'' she said with a gentle smile, ''and not hard. It's as if they're born knowing how.''

''Thank you for letting me see,'' said Chloe sincerely. ''I wish you hadn't left me with her, though,'' she said mildly, still anxious about Belinda's disappearance. "I know nothing of babies."

"I'm sorry," Belinda said, and sounded honest. "I forgot. There's not many ordinary folk don't get used to them. It's either brothers and sisters, or nieces and nephews. I felt it better to return the Dowager's jar. She's a bit fidgety today. You know how changes upset her."

"Yes, you're right," said Chloe.

"How's Budsworth?" asked Belinda with only casual interest.

"Justin seems to think he'll recover, and I should imagine he's seen plenty of wounds."

"Good," said Belinda, and looked straight at Chloe. "If he died, you'd doubtless be trying to put that one on me too."

Chloe could feel herself colour under this attack. "Now what possible reason could you have to hurt Budsworth?"

"None," said Belinda. "He's never done me any harm." Dorinda slipped off the nipple and waited while her mother switched her to the other side, where the babe settled again to the ecstasy of warm milk.

"The question is," said Chloe, "what reason could anyone have to attack the man? For it was an attack. Unlike Frank's death, there is no chance of it being an accident."

"True enough," said Belinda. "People don't get hit on the head by rocks by accident. Not unless they're under a cliff."

"Perhaps he saw something he shouldn't have," mused Chloe.

"What?" asked Belinda. "Are you thinking of the papers which were lost? Surely no one would attack a man for those."

She waited for an answer. Again, Chloe thought Belinda wanted to know what the papers were. She made no reply, however.

Belinda shrugged. "The only secret I know of around

here is Matthew and Sally Kestwick, and that's hardly a secret when everyone knows, and you too, I gather.''

"Are they really in love?'' Chloe asked, thinking the attachment might be some Machiavellian plot by the footman to conceal his true activities.

"Lord, yes. They practically swoon whenever they meet and Sally's up at the house every day, sometimes twice, with embroidered handkerchiefs and cakes, books and pomatum. The presents he's given her in return must have cost near all his wages.''

Still, thought Chloe, it could be all an act. If Matthew was in French pay, his presents would be an investment against greater gain. What use was Sally to him though? An alibi. She would always cover for him.

Just to keep the talk going, on the chance of learning something, Chloe said, "Will the local people accept Matthew?''

"I would think,'' said Belinda as Dorinda finished her feeding. Belinda sat the sleepy child up, and rubbed her back. "He's not got on the wrong side of anyone, except Frank.''

"Matthew and Frank were at odds?''

"Yes. There's no harm in speaking now. Frank had begun to pay attention to Sally. I don't suppose she was interested exactly, but Frank's always been seen as the catch of the young men, if you see what I mean, and she might have been flattered. He and Matthew were squaring off about it.''

Was Belinda just speaking the truth or was she laying down a false trail about Frank's death? "Didn't it bother you? Having Frank interested in someone else?''

"No, of course not,'' said Belinda, but she looked down at Dorinda and Chloe could not see her expression. "I think maybe he hoped it would, but I would have welcomed him setting his sights elsewhere.'' She sounded honest, and her words made sense.

This situation might have given Matthew a motive for

murder, however. "Do you think Matthew pushed Frank off the Head?"

Belinda settled her sleepy babe in one arm and began to rearrange her clothing. "I think he could have, if Matthew caught Frank off guard. In a straight fight Frank would have made mincemeat of him but . . . I'm not accusing, mind. It could just as well have been an accident, and I don't suppose Matthew had the opportunity. Didn't Sir Cedric check and say the staff were all together?"

Chloe saw no point in confusing the matter. "That's correct."

She walked into the nursery with Belinda and watched as she settled the baby on her tummy in the cradle, and drew up the cotton blankets.

"You are very lucky to have such a beautiful child," Chloe said, wondering again if Dorinda was Frank's daughter, not George's.

Belinda looked down at her daughter, and Chloe could swear she sighed. "Yes, I know," said Belinda solemnly. "But luck is just a chance well taken. You should marry Justin."

Chloe looked at her. "Should I?"

"Yes," said Belinda, looking up. "Chances like that rarely come around twice in a lifetime. It'd be pushing your luck to expect a third."

Before Chloe could think of a reply, the luncheon bell rang. Belinda tidied her hair, and Chloe took a moment to do the same. All the world thought she should marry Justin. Perhaps all the world was right.

12

EVERYONE IN THE house party assembled for luncheon that day. As the meal drew to a close, Justin explained the plan.

"Any notion of another will is ridiculous," said Belinda, "but I am willing to help with a search." She seemed completely undisturbed by the notion. Either she had nothing to hide, thought Chloe, or it was hidden very well.

"That is good of you," said Justin. "As you say, it is doubtless a piece of nonsense, but if we do a thorough search we can put the matter to rest."

"Sounds damned strange," said Mr. Macy, as if the matter was a personal affront to him. "I was here with my old friend. I was a witness to the will you have. He'd have called upon me to witness any other."

"Not, perhaps, if he wanted you to be a beneficiary," said Justin, smoothly. "After all, when you were so kind as to spend so much time here with him, he might well have felt a desire to reward you with a keepsake."

"Could be, could be," said Macy, apparently pacified. "But if he hit it, it could be anywhere. Sounds like a waste of time."

Justin appeared relaxed now. "Well, the letter said specifically that the will had been hidden in a small box, so at least we do not have to look between the pages of every book in the library. I think we will assume something about the size of a deck of cards. That should make the business easier. Anyway,'' he added with a smile, "Randal's been complaining of boredom, so we'll regard this as a treasure hunt.''

"Oh, one of Ashby's mad starts," said Macy offhandedly. "Well, perhaps I'll join in the game.''

"I think we'll work in teams,'' said Justin. "Perhaps, Macy and Randal, you could do the ground floor, with Belinda to assist, since she is familiar with the house. The Duchess has agreed to descend to the nether regions and supervise the search there. Mrs. Pickering and the kitchen maid will do most of the searching, with Matthew to help in any heavy work. I feel there is little likelihood of Uncle George having hidden anything there, however.''

"Who's to do the bedrooms?'' asked Randal.

"Chloe and I,'' said Justin smoothly. Randal flashed a look which made her blush. "With Margaret, the upstairs maid, of course,'' Justin added.

Miss Forbes made so bold as to speak. "I wonder if perhaps *I* could search dear Sophronia's rooms,'' she said anxiously. "She is so easily upset.''

"No, I am not,'' said the Dowager clearly. "I am never upset. You shouldn't say such things, Lady Hertford.''

Miss Forbes looked flustered. "Of course, my dear—''

The Dowager was paying no attention. "You!'' she said explosively, pointing at Belinda. "Miss Massinger. Thank you for the *potpourri*. Very kind to put the jar back. I like that jar. Clever . . . I would like some brandy.''

Miss Forbes rose quickly to her feet. "Oh dear. Perhaps up in your room, Sophronia. I could make you a posset. Come along.''

The Dowager allowed herself to be raised from her chair. "Yes, that would be nice,'' she said dreamily.

"Perhaps, Miss Forbes,'' said Justin, "Chloe could come up now and search the rooms with you. There would be no need to disturb you again.''

"Yes, that would be best,'' said the lady distractedly, concentrating on her charge. Chloe went with them.

The Dowager hummed a little tune as they walked up

the stairs, and once she curtsied to the wall. Chloe hoped she wasn't going to deteriorate.

"She heard about the attack on the gardener," Miss Forbes whispered. "Belinda mentioned it to me, and she overheard. Her hearing gets better some days, worse on others. It has upset her."

Once in the room, the Dowager said, "Show the queen that lovely *potpourri* jar. All fresh today. All fresh."

As the companion was busy settling her charge into her chair, Chloe went herself to the mantelpiece and obediently admired the pot again. She lifted the lid, and fresh fragrance wafted out—a touch of pine and lemon this time, she thought. The business of *potpourri* was beginning to interest her. The straight sides of the white jar were smooth and cool beneath her hand. The delicate glazed design was slightly raised. When she looked over to comment, she saw the Dowager was humming and had obviously drifted off into a world of her own.

"Let us do the search," she said.

"Of course," agreed the companion. "How shall we go about it?"

Chloe looked around, daunted. The Dowager had surrounded herself with all sorts of furniture and knick-knacks. "We have to be systematic," she said at last. "If we're looking for something the size of a deck of cards, we don't have to search every inch. If we start at his corner, and work our way around, it will not take long." She reminded herself that they were really looking for an object secreted since the morning.

"Has anyone visited you this morning, Miss Forbes?"

"Just Lady George when she collected the jar, then returned with it freshened."

"And she just came and put the jar down?"

Miss Forbes looked puzzled at these questions, as well she might, but she was not the kind to protest. "Yes. Sophronia and I were on the balcony in the sun. Well wrapped up, of course, against the wind."

Chloe didn't feel able to pursue the questions, but Belinda had been gone this morning long enough to hide something if she had been unobserved. She had to assume the girl had some time here alone. They would have to search the whole place. She had hoped to eliminate the bedrooms, at least.

Chloe sighed. If there was to be any purpose to the search, it must be thorough. It was remotely possible, after all, that the companion was their evil spy. If Miss Forbes had left the Dowager alone on the balcony, the odds were the lady would never have noticed.

Chloe looked at her. "Did you go outside this morning, Miss Forbes?"

"On the balcony, yes."

"No, in the garden. I wondered if you were there when we had all the excitement with Budsworth."

"Good heavens, no. And if we were to be nearby, I would hurry Sophronia away. Disturbances are *very* bad for her." This was said with a slightly reproving air.

Chloe told herself she really couldn't suspect everyone. She decided to get the search over with as soon as possible, which proved not as difficult as it had first seemed. Surfaces were covered by vases and pictures, snuffboxes and shells; but a sweep of the eye assured her there were few boxes large enough to conceal a potato. What ones there were Chloe opened and found to be full of pins or beads, powder or dried flowers. The drawers, presumably because of Miss Forbes' attentions, were orderly. They were quickly riffled through. For appearances' sake, Chloe took care always to look in small boxes, but she was actually alert for a firm, rounded shape.

The Dowager's dressing table presented the worst task. As usual, it was covered by bottles, jars, and pots. With a grimace, Chloe set herself to check each one. After all, the potato could have been pushed into the large ancient box of hair powder. She had only to lift it, however, to tell it was too light. Or it could possibly be in a jar of face cream. She poked her finger in to be sure, then wrinkled her nose. The stuff was old and rancid.

She came to the heavy earthenware jar which contained the lumbago embrocation, and sighed. The things one did for one's country. The wide neck was certainly large enough to drop in a potato. She peered inside, but could only see the oily dark stuff. She shook the jar gently, but could not tell if there was a hard object inside. Still, she refused to put her hand in and grope.

Chloe looked around and found a shallow bowl. She poured the liquid out, almost gasping as the fumes assailed her. Her eyes began to tear. There was no solid object in the pot. Then she and Miss Forbes, who was regarding her very strangely, had the job of pouring the stuff back in. Some missed and slithered down the side. Chloe grabbed a towel and mopped it up.

"Dear Lady Stanforth, it is good of you to be so thorough," said Miss Forbes, "but have you considered? The late Lord Stanforth's will could not have been in there. That jar was only brought here three days ago, by Belinda."

"Of course," said Chloe, wondering how she would ever get rid of the smell from her hands. "How silly of me."

She sighed, and brushed an errant lock of hair away from her eyes. She let out a cry.

"Lady Stanforth! What is it?"

"My eye! Oh! Water!"

Miss Forbes quickly brought a wet cloth, and Chloe dabbed at her smarting eye. That blasted stuff had been on her hands. After a moment, the eye stopped tearing and she looked in the mirror at the inflammation. Wonderful. Now not only did she stink, she looked dreadful too.

Chloe looked around once more. Was there anywhere in this room unsearched? The mantelshelf. It held two narrow vases, two candlesticks, a clock, and the *potpourri*. She conscientiously opened the back of the clock, just in case. The rest were clearly impossible.

She moved briskly to the bedroom, trailed by Miss

Forbes. They checked through all the gowns, pressing lightly to be sure nothing was concealed. Chloe ignored the companion's obvious amazement at the thoroughness of the search.

She couldn't help lingering over some of the gowns—rich creations of an earlier age, and exquisitely beautiful. Heavy, embroidered satin and silk, froths of gilded lace. She had heard the Dowager had been a Toast at one time, and these gown recalled those glorious days.

Chloe checked inside shoes and under the bed. She felt the pillows and the mattress, a soft feather one. Surely a potato would be obvious inside it. Besides, she told herself, having once encountered a feather mattress with a small rip in the ticking, any opening and the feathers started to seep all over the place. It would have been impossible for Belinda to slip a potato in there, particularly if she were in a hurry. Moreover, Chloe thought rebelliously, she refused to be part of a search which involved ripping open a dozen feather beds. She must also stop assuming that Belinda was the culprit. Who else might have been hiding the package?

"Has Matthew been up here recently?" Chloe asked Miss Forbes.

"Certainly not," said that lady firmly. "We do not allow men into the rooms, except in extraordinary circumstances. I am so glad you have done this search, Lady Stanforth. I really did not like the thought of a gentleman, even Lord Stanforth, looking through our property."

That reminded Chloe. "I will have to look through your room too, Miss Forbes. Just to be able to say I have been thorough."

"Of course, Lady Stanforth."

Miss Forbes had a very small room for her own. It was neat and sparsely furnished. It did not take long for Chloe to assure herself there was no potato there.

She gave the rooms a final glance. Had she overlooked anything?

The coal scuttles. Oh good Lord, she'd be black.

As she went over and tipped the sitting-room scuttle out onto the hearth, Miss Forbes gave a squeak. "Lady Stanforth. That was empty this morning, and has only been filled again just before lunch. The will cannot possible be there!"

Chloe feared she'd have a reputation to match the Dowager's soon, but resolutely made her search of two scuttles, grateful for her own sake that the companion did not have a fireplace. When she had finished and neatly swept up all the coal dust, she had found nothing. She went to wash her hands in the bowl on the washstand.

"There," she said. "You can vouch for the fact that I have searched these rooms most thoroughly, Miss Forbes."

"I certainly can," said the lady, wide-eyed. "Why, I half expected you to climb the chimney, Lady Stanforth."

With horror, Chloe looked at the wide chimney. Then she relaxed. If anyone had put the potato here, it had been Belinda, when she brought the *potpourri*. There had been no trace of dirt on her when she returned. It was possible she had sneaked something in here, and even that she had dropped it in the coalscuttle, but not that she had poked in the chimney with a fire lit below.

Chloe went back downstairs to report.

The dining-room was deserted, as was the drawing-room. Mr. Macy, the Duchess, and Belinda were conversing in the Sea Room. They enquired when the search was to begin.

Chloe finally ran the two younger gentlemen to earth in the study.

"Nothing. I'm sure of it," she reported. "Belinda was the only person to visit there this morning, and she just dropped off a pot of *potpourri*. The poor Dowager is in a bad way, though. We should avoid disturbing her further."

"I'm sure we can manage that," said Justin. "I checked on Matthew. Unless something very tricky occurred, he can't be the one who attacked Budsworth. He was in the kitchen. He went out to call the gardener, and that was when you saw him. Then he went to speak to his young lady, but being nervous because you'd seen him, he only stayed a moment before returning to the kitchen. It was a good ten minutes, with him sitting at the table drinking tea, before Mrs. Pickering poked her head out to remind Budsworth and discovered the body. I don't think he would have been lying unconscious that long.''

"But where was he afterwards? When you looked around for someone to help carry Budsworth, he was nowhere to be seen."

"He went to the stables with the message. That fancy valet of Macy's claimed not to know the way to the stables. He probably thought the task beneath him. Matthew went to do it and the valet made himself scarce.''

"Could the valet have been the attacker?''

"No. He was in the kitchen at the crucial time just like the rest of the staff.'' Justin ran a hand over his face. "I must stop thinking of this as a puzzle. It's too damn seductive. The only important thing is to get those papers.'' He turned to Chloe. "I've just told Randal the entire story.''

"And I don't appreciate having been kept in the dark,'' said the young man in mock outrage. "Think what it implies about my reputation!''

"And mine,'' said Chloe, looking at Justin. She hadn't quite thought of it this way before. "Did you really think I was involved in treason?''

"Of course not,'' he protested, looking uncomfortable. "But . . .''

"But what?'' asked Chloe, frowning.

"The Duke of York and Lord Liverpool don't have much opinion of women. In York's case, he's probably still smarting over the Clarke affair.''

Chloe considered that point of view and dismissed it. "Then explain why the Duchess was sent here.''

Justin glanced at Randal for help but received no assistance. Instead he got a teasing grin. "Go on. Explain. I'd like to hear it. My honour's on the line too. It can't be the *family* they don't like.''

"They said nothing about you," Justin said with irritation to Randal. "I invited you here, didn't I? I must have been mad. And I had orders not to trust anyone.''

Chloe cleared her throat to get attention. "And me?"

Justin sighed. Randal stood and went to the door. "Excuse me. I'll just go ready the troops for the search.'' Before either could protest, if they wanted to, he was gone. For her part, Chloe was too angry to be concerned about being alone with Justin.

He spoke resignedly. "Your reputation, of course. They thought you'd had the opportunity to meet and be influenced by some disreputable people.''

"They were right," Chloe said, trying not to show just how hurt she was. Stephen had, after all, often filled the house with shifty individuals. "What I want to know, Justin, is did *you* have doubts of me?''

"Never.''

"Then why didn't you tell me?" It was a cry of betrayal.

He took her in his arms. "Oh, my love. Believe me, I never doubted you for a moment. But I'm a soldier, or was. I obey orders.'' He tilted her chin up and saw the tears in her eyes. He kissed one away. "It's a habit I'll try to lose," he said softly.

Chloe hid her face against his warm, firm chest, fighting tears. "Oh Justin. I want to be respectable. I want to be respected!''

His hand was in the curls at her nape, fingers working away the tension. "You will be. You are. Don't think of those doddering old men.''

She looked up with an attempt at a smile. "Hardly that.''

"They must be," he said with a twinkling smile. "Their wits are going. They're no better than Aunt Sophronia.''

"They're ruling the country," she protested, genuine humour beginning to chase away her fit of the dismals.

"God help us all."

"God helps those who help themselves, they say."

His hand moved around to cradle her cheek. His thumb tantalised the corner of her mouth. "Back to religion again, are we? Well, I take it as my godly duty to help myself, then."

He lowered his lips to hers. Chloe sighed as she drank in the taste of him. The soft spicy scent of his skin swam into her brain like brandy, and the feel of him beneath her fingertips spread through her body until she ached.

Desperately resolute, she ended the kiss. "The search," she said, staring up at his shining, warm dark eyes.

He grinned. "Bedrooms. Yes."

"Justin!"

He flicked out his tongue and licked her upper lip. "You have beautiful lips."

"The search."

He ignored her words, his hands cradling her face. His fingers threaded into her curls and raised them, then let them drift softly back onto her neck. She shivered. "The problem, my treasure, my diamond, my heart, is you are too beautiful. I'm tempted to waste time telling you that."

Eye to eye, a suspended moment passed. He sighed, long and soft.

"The search," he said, and let his hands slip away.

"Yes," whispered Chloe, thinking, Bedrooms.

Oh dear Lord.

13

CHAPERONED BY MARGARET, the middle-aged upstairs maid, their search was completely proper.

They started with the most likely place, Belinda's rooms. She had a bedroom, a *boudoir,* and a nursery in the south wing over the kitchen area. Rosie let them in, then retreated to the nursery.

Chloe saw Justin experience the same moment of panic she had felt when first faced with making a search.

"If we work around the room in opposite directions," she said, "it is not so bad. Perhaps, Margaret, you can feel the chairs for lumps and look under and behind them. Then check around the windows, and remember the pelmets."

The woman gave her a disbelieving look, but set to her tasks. Chloe and Justin turned to theirs.

Belinda was a tidy person and had few knickknacks, so the going was easy. Chloe looked in all the *potpourri* jars, empty and full, feeling through the dried petals carefully. She even remembered to check the basket of limp herbs cut the day before. She looked at the dying plants. Was this the way to handle them? She would have thought they should be hung up to dry or something.

Justin searched quickly through Belinda's small desk. Was he tempted to look at her letters, Chloe wondered, in search of treason? How distasteful this all was.

"Justin," Chloe asked. "Shall I do the bedroom?"

"Yes, why not," he replied.

"Don't forget the coal scuttle," she called back, as she went through the door, smiling at his groan.

Belinda's bedroom was simply furnished. These rooms had been little used until she moved into them. She would have been within her rights to bring in more elegant furniture from elsewhere in the house, and perhaps some ornaments. Chloe wondered if Belinda had been reluctant to ask. Chloe felt rather guilty. She would never have hesitated to ask for improvements, even if she were only a guest. It had not occurred to her that Belinda might feel less sure of herself.

At least the simplicity of the decor made the search easy. The plain bed had only light hangings and concealed nothing. An oak washstand offered no hiding place. The old-fashioned armoire held a sparse selection of gowns— a few new and fashionable ones bought at the beginning of Belinda's marriage, and a number of black ones. Chloe felt through them all and checked the slippers.

There were three hatboxes, containing only hats. One, following fashion, was decorated with a bunch of cherries. Chloe looked at it. There was absolutely nothing to indicate the message had been sent as cherries, though one part of the information had been. Still, she carefully investigated one of the glossy red fruits. It was lacquered plaster and contained nothing strange.

The drawers held beautiful underclothes. Chloe had seen Belinda doing elegant needlework on clothes for her child. She had obviously been assembling a *trousseau* for years before her marriage—but not for her marriage to George. The cutwork on the linen chemise, the lace on the stays, all this had been for Frank.

Feeling to the back of the drawers, she came upon a tissue-wrapped package. It was obviously not the package they sought. Vulgar curiosity and perhaps a more worthy need to understand her relative-by-marriage made Chloe pull it out and glance at it anyway.

Inside were six handkerchiefs, beautifully made of the best Madras cotton, each monogrammed, white on white—FH.

Chloe carefully restored the wrapping and replaced the package where she'd found it.

She went into the baby's room. Dorinda was awake and Rosie had the child on her knee. A rack in front of the fire held clothes warming for the next change. Chloe glanced quickly through the piles of snowy napkins, the stacks of pressed, white dresses, and tiny camisoles. There were lavender bags in the drawers and a *potpourri* bowl open on the windowsill. The room was warm and sweet. Dorinda made gurgling noises as Rosie bounced her.

Determined not to let maternal longings keep her from her duty, Chloe felt under the cradle mattress, and even did a thorough check of Rosie's narrow bed, conscious of the maid's surprised gaze.

"That bed only came there, ma'am," said the maid, "after Mr. George died."

"Of course," said Chloe. "How silly."

She looked around, then went over to check in the *potpourri*. Just petals. She looked in the jug of water keeping warm by the fire, ignoring the maid's wondering gaze.

Satisfied at last, Chloe relaxed and touched the perfect skin of the baby's cheek.

"Dear child," she murmured. "Is she a good baby, Rosie?"

"Oh yes, ma'am. She's no trouble. And she's going to be a beauty one day."

Chloe took the child for a moment. Dorinda swatted a hand towards the locket hanging around Chloe's neck. "She already is a beauty," said Chloe with a smile.

At that moment, Justin came in. He stopped at the sight. They gazed at each other over the baby's head, and Chloe trembled. She couldn't help imagining an infant with brown eyes and darker curls.

She handed the baby back to Rosie. "There is nothing here," she said.

"On the contrary," Justin said softly. "Everything of importance is here." Then added more briskly, "Except that damned—except the will." He smiled. "Dare I hope you checked the coal scuttle?"

Chloe looked down at her white muslin and raised a brow. He sighed and tipped out the shiny black lumps onto the hearth. Satisfied, he used the tongs to put them back again.

"There, finished," he said. "On to Mr. Macy's room."

As she followed him out, Chloe glanced back. Rosie was looking with dismay at the coal dust scattered all over the tiles of the hearth.

"Men," Chloe said softly to the maid. Rosie bit her lip on a smile.

Margaret, finishing the cleaning of the hearth in the *boudoir,* did not look amused at all. She was muttering to herself.

"Justin," said Chloe softly, "everyone will think us run mad if we go through the house checking the coal scuttles. They are filled every day."

"What else can we do?" he asked. "It would be a good place to hide the damned thing."

"Well, try at least to be a little tidier," she said, "or there is likely to be a mutiny."

He looked in surprise at the grumbling maid and grinned. "I see what you mean."

They went on to the next likely place, Humphrey Macy's room. It was difficult, to be sure, to imagine a top-of-the-trees dandy like Macy in French pay, and he hadn't even been in Lancashire when the package first went missing, but it was possible he had attacked Busdworth and taken the potato this morning. Chloe tried to visualize him, corsets squeaking, running through the house.

His corner room looked out over the carriage drive and the front of the house. It was smartly decorated in straw-coloured *chinoiserie.* Randal had been offered this room but had claimed an aversion to dragons, and taken the simpler room next door.

Mr. Macy's stick-thin valet watched them like a hawk. He ventured an objection when Justin opened one of the drawers. "With respect, My Lord, Mr. Macy said you were looking for a box hidden in the house nearly a year ago. All the drawers and presses were empty when we arrived, I can assure you."

Chloe wondered how Justin would handle that.

"They have to be searched, however, for the legal men to be satisfied," he said in a crisp, authoritative voice.

The valet did not raise any further objection in the face of the power of command.

Chloe left the inspection of the intimate items to Justin. She checked such places as inside vases and clocks, while the maid looked under the bed and felt down the sides of the upholstered chair.

This coal scuttle was half-full. Justin carefully removed some top pieces so as to be able to check without creating mess. When he was finished he looked quizzically at Chloe, and she gave him a smile of approval.

Next, they moved on into Randal's room. They had exhausted their likely suspects but went through the motions. Randal had travelled light, without a valet, so it was an easy search.

The Duchess's two rooms were a direct contrast. She never travelled without a coachload of possessions. Still, after going through dozens of gowns and pairs of shoes, ten hatboxes and all the room fixtures, they had, as expected, found nothing. Looking at the cluttered dressing table, Chloe was relieved the Duchess's expensive lotions and cosmetics all came in tiny or narrow-necked containers.

There were two small empty bedrooms and they were quickly finished. Chloe, Justin, and Margaret stood in the corridor.

"Do we search our own rooms?" asked Chloe.

"Of course," he said with a grin. Chloe realized, with a flicker of embarrassment, that he had never been inside a bedroom of hers. How silly to be so conscious of such a thing.

Justin surveyed Chloe's room like a man studying a work of art, a beauty of nature. It was a large room with two windows looking out over the bay. The corner by the windows was given over to a sitting area, with a writing desk, a small table and chair, and a chaise. He could imagine her spending many hours here, reading or writing letters, as she watched the water come and go. Surely it should work to his advantage that she loved this place.

The pink and gold arabesques of the carpet were matched in the pink brocade hangings and bed-cover. Now, when he dreamt of her lying in her bed, he could imagine the exact surroundings. On her bedside table sat two dolls. One was a rag doll with an unpleasant kind of leer. The other was an exquisite French bisque doll in fine, lacy clothes. He remembered them. She had taken them in her scanty baggage on that elopement journey.

God, they must all have been out of their minds.

"Margaret," he said roughly. "Check the furnishings. Chloe, help me to search the drawers. It must be done."

Chloe wondered why he had suddenly become so brusque. Had it been the sight of Jenny and Lisbet? She supposed it was silly to still have dolls at her age, but she had taken so little from her home and never cared to ask her parents for more.

She opened the doors of her matching japanned armoires, and almost giggled at his expression when he saw the masses of gowns and spencers, pelisses and cloaks.

"I sent for all my belongings from London when Stephen died," she explained. "I expected George to be living in Clarges Street, of course. There are some boxes in the attics as well, which, incidentally, we should hunt through too."

"Not," he muttered, "unless there is any evidence someone has been there this morning. I don't have to look through this. I know you didn't hide anything here."

Chloe looked at him. Despite obstacles and incredulous servants, he had been resolutely thorough in the search thus far. "I appreciate the vote of confidence, Justin, but think. Belinda, if it is she who hid it, was not under observation for every second. She would have to be a fool to hide the thing in her own quarters. There's nothing to say she didn't slip in here."

He groaned slightly and began a thorough search, while Chloe took down all her hatboxes and checked them.

Justin's groan had not been from the work involved. He wasn't sure he could handle riffling through Chloe's garments. Her soft spicy perfume wafted round him. The shimmer of silk, the sheen of satin, even the simple softness of her creamy muslins all made him think of her skin.

He turned to find her checking her shoes and upturning her boots. A glance showed him Margaret shaking her head. He fled the thought of searching through Chloe's underthings. That task he left to the maid, taking the safer one of checking the vases on the marble mantelpiece and looking in her writing desk.

Only personal correspondence, of course, he thought, looking at the neat piles of her embossed stationery. The business of the estate had been conducted from the study. He opened the drawer to find sealing wax, sand, pen-wipers, and such like.

There was a small wooden box.

Because he saw Margaret was watching him, he opened it. It contained a folded letter. He was about to close the box when Margaret exclaimed, "Lawks, sir! Don't say you've found it!"

Chloe hurried over. "What?" She looked at the box. "What is it? Why, it's George's little treasure box. He would keep odd buttons, broken studs, and such in there. How strange."

"It's the will," declared Margaret, hands clasped. "You could knock me down with a feather!"

"Me too," muttered Justin, as he took the paper out of the box. It was a single sheet, not new and crisp, and not the treasure they were hunting for. Below it was a carefully folded handkerchief. *Had* George made another will?

He unfolded the paper, aware of Chloe leaning over his shoulder and Margaret doing the same thing, a little more discreetly.

Ma chère Chloe,
Je suis désolé sans toi. Je me souviens de tes baisers brûlants, la douceur de ta peau sur mes lèvres . . .

I am desolate without you. I remember constantly your burning kisses, the flavour of your skin upon my lips. . .

Chilled with shock, Justin glanced at the bottom of the brief but torrid missive.

ton amant, ton esclave,
Claude

His first thought was of relief that the maid could not read French. The letter was undated. When had this been written?

He remembered the Duke of York. Women will do anything for a certain kind of man. . . .

He looked up as Chloe said, "I've never seen that letter before in my life!" He saw the genuine amazement in her eyes change to shock, then anger as she read the doubt in his.

"I have never seen that letter before in my life," she repeated, coldly and precisely. She reached for the handkerchief.

He got there before her. He turned it so the embroidered design was clearly visible. The Ashby coat of arms and the monogram RA. The only person who possessed such handkerchiefs was Randal.

Justin looked at the piece of linen. He trusted Chloe. Of course he did. But she had been playing hot and cold with him, welcoming his kisses, refusing to commit herself. Could it all have been a game, designed to distract him until she could get away from Delamere, away with the message for her French lover? Was she Randal's lover? Surely not both.

He couldn't think. Not now. Not here. It was hard enough to stop his hands from shaking, to keep choked back the words he must not say. He put the letter and the handkerchief into his pocket.

"Of course," he said, not looking at her. "It certainly isn't what we're looking for."

Chloe watched as he walked across the room. She felt chilled from head to toe. In fact, she feared she might be shivering. One letter, and he would believe it? Did he too think her without morals and sense? And *what* did he believe? Adultery? A lover since her widowhood? Many lovers?

Treason?

Anger began to replace anguish. Anger at Justin for harbouring a moment's doubt. Anger against whoever had put that letter there. It had not been there the day before. It had been secreted in her desk since word was given of the search, intended to do just the damage it had.

"Are we finished?" asked Justin in a strained voice. He sounded lost.

"Hardly," Chloe said crisply. "There is the master bedroom."

"My room?"

"Of course." She could feel her words come out hard and cold. "We are looking for George's will, remember? Where more likely for him to hide it than in the room which was his?"

He gained control of himself. "I had forgotten," he said flatly. "By all means, let us be thorough to the end."

The master bedroom was at the center of the house, with wide windows looking down the drive towards the Lancaster road. After his marriage, in a thankfully brief nesting urge, Stephen had refurnished the room in the Egyptian style, modified by Chloe's reluctance to have mummies and sphinxes looking down from the walls. All the furniture, however, had been commissioned new from Waring and Gillow in Lancaster and sat upon long thin legs formed of Egyptian figures—except the bed, that is, which had short, fat crocodile ones. Chloe always made sure to hide them under a long coverlet.

The suite had stood empty from George's death until Justin's arrival, and thus far Justin had spent little time there. A few garments in the press and the drawers, his brushes and shaving kit, some books. He had not yet hired a valet and used Matthew for his simple needs. She supposed his other possessions, coming by cart, would arrive one of these days and make more of a mark.

The search was rather cursory. Margaret was out of patience with the whole business, Justin was abstracted, and Chloe was convinced nothing would be found here. She was also fighting the turmoil caused by silly things such as his shaving equipment on the stand, his slippers by the bed. The man didn't trust her. He thought she was working for the French. How could she allow herself to turn weak at the knees at the smell of his soap?

Eventually, in silence, they left the room and closed the door, to stand in the wide, carpeted corridor. It was as if a yawning gulf lay between them, rather than a foot of crimson Axminster.

"I think I will see how they're doing downstairs," said Justin abruptly.

"They would have sent us word if they had found anything," Chloe pointed out.

He ignored that and ran his fingers through the soft curls on his forehead as if confused. "Perhaps we should look quickly through the maids' rooms and the attics, unless they're full of junk?"

"No," said Chloe coolly, staring at an insipid hunting scene on the wall. "This is a very orderly household. There are only a few trunks and suchlike."

"Why don't you and Margaret start up there, then. I'll join you in a minute."

With that, he walked briskly off and down the stairs. Full retreat, thought Chloe, watching him coldly. She discovered her jaw was tight, her teeth pressed painfully together. If he had escaped to think, good luck to him. She marched off towards the narrow stairs which led to the upper floor.

"Milady," said Margaret plaintively. "There's no chance at all Mr. George would have come up here!"

"Once it's done, it's over with," said Chloe tightly.

There were two maids' rooms. Margaret, Agnes, and Susan, the Duchess's maid, shared one. Rosie and the kitchen maid had the other. Each room contained three beds, hooks on the walls, and a chest of drawers. Each room had a single basin and ewer on a pine washstand. There was nothing in evidence except the servants' simple belongings.

Margaret and Chloe moved on to the storage rooms. The attic space had dust, a few cobwebs, and a dozen boxes and trunks. The dust on the floor, and on the boxes, was undisturbed.

"Do you care to go through these, ma'am?" asked the maid dispiritedly.

Chloe sighed. Her anger had seeped away, leaving only bitter dregs. In Justin she had thought to find a man to depend on, a man who would also trust and depend on her. She had foolishly allowed him to wear down her defences, work his way into her heart. Now, at the first, shallow suspicion of possible unworthiness in her, his regard had evaporated. Would she never learn?

"No," she replied. "There is no need to search them. But when all this fuss is over, Margaret, have them taken down to my room. I must go through them anyway, to see what I wish to take when . . . when I leave. So many things are out of fashion now."

She smiled for the woman. "Thank you. You have been a great help. It was a useless project, I know, but it had to be done. You may have the rest of the afternoon to yourself."

The woman flushed. "Thank you, ma'am."

There was no sign of Justin when Chloe came down the stairs. She was about to find refuge in her room, when she became aware of raised voices below. It sounded like an argument. Had something been found?

A flicker of excitement chased back the depths of her depression. If that list had been found, it would be something to place in the balance against her shattered dreams.

She hurried down.

Chloe found Justin, Randal, and Macy facing an angry Belinda in the library. She was waving a piece of paper.

"George never wrote this!" she shouted.

Mr. Macy pursed his lips. "I must confess, it looks like his hand."

"Illegible and illiterate," murmured Randal, giving Chloe a humorous look.

"What is it?" she asked of no one in particular.

"A charming scrawl from old George," drawled Randal, "to person or persons unknown, saying, in effect, I don't like Belinda, she scares me, and I never wanted to marry her in the first place."

"It's a lie," Belinda said fiercely, tears in her eyes, but whether of pain or anger was difficult to tell. Chloe could sympathise. The two emotions were easy to confuse.

"May I see?" she asked. "I know George's writing reasonably well, though he did little enough of it."

Belinda handed over the grubby, scrunched piece of paper.

"Where was it found?" Chloe asked, as she smoothed it out.

"In the Meissen vase," said Randal, "by yours truly."

Uncle George had only been marginally literate, and his writing was appalling, but the gist of the letter was still clear and exactly as Randal had succinctly put it: "... *fule to let her. Stand up and tak it. Honner of Delamere. Help me to eskap this wiced trap ...*"

Chloe remembered the letter upstairs. Had someone been seeding the house with scandalous correspondence? For what purpose? There was every indication, however, that this letter had been written by George. Such childishness would be almost impossible to reproduce.

"It is his writing," Chloe said slowly, and looked at Belinda.

"He didn't write that," the young woman declared. "I know he didn't. Someone made it up and put it there!"

"True or not," said Justin wearily, "it has little to do with anything. It is not the . . . the will. No one here will spread what is in the letter, Belinda, or think the worse of you. Uncle George was given to strange mental processes."

Belinda looked as if she would protest further, but shut her lips tight. With a sudden movement, she took the letter and hurled it into the fire. It blackened, flamed, and was gone.

Chloe wished she had possessed the forethought to do that with another piece of paper.

"Have you finished here?" asked Justin of the men.

"Pretty well," said Randal, "and no luck. The only place we haven't touched is the study. Thought you and Chloe should be there, or we'll doubtless make a pig's dinner of it for you."

Chloe saw him look at the two of them with puzzlement. She hoped he wouldn't take it into his head to tease them. It was four days until Tuesday, the day she and the Duchess planned to leave. She could not bear the thought of being in the same house as Justin for four days. Could she persuade the old lady to move faster? Her grandmother didn't like to travel on the sabbath, but surely if Chloe explained.

She trailed after the men. Belinda stayed behind.

Chloe turned. "Are you coming?"

"Why should I?" Belinda replied angrily. "I can go to my room now, can't I?"

"Yes, I suppose you can," said Chloe on a sigh. "You're right. Why should we bother?"

Chloe saw Belinda's anger fade as she looked at her. "Has something upset you, Chloe?" she asked.

"Everything is upset these days," Chloe said, as much to herself as Belinda.

"Yes," said Belinda quietly. "This was a happy house once." She took the lid off a pot of *potpourri* on a small piecrust table and touched the petals. "You and Justin didn't find anything upstairs then?"

Chloe thought of that disgusting letter. "No," she said.

"We weren't looking for a will, were we? We were looking for that mysterious package the sailor lost."

Chloe was too heartsore to fabricate. "Yes."

"What is it? Government papers being smuggled out to the French?"

"No," said Chloe. "French papers being smuggled in to the British. If you have them, Belinda, please just give them to Justin so we can forget all this, and get on with our lives."

Chloe saw Belinda's face set. A sign she had something to hide. "Why are you always harping on about *me* having them?" she demanded angrily. "That would be treason, wouldn't it? Do you want me to hang?"

"I don't think you have them," argued Chloe, trying to find the key to Belinda's cooperation. "But I think you may know something. What if Frank had them?"

Belinda stiffened. "So now you think Frank was a traitor, do you?" she spat. "That would be nice for you all, wouldn't it? Having a convenient member of the lower orders to take the blame."

Chloe felt some guilt, for in a way Belinda was correct. It would be simpler if Frank could be blamed for everything. "Who then?" she demanded in exasperation.

Belinda looked away. "How would I know?" she said quietly. "But neither Frank nor I would have served the French."

Chloe believed her. "I'm sorry," she said, not exactly sure which of a myriad things she was sorry about.

"I'm sorry too," said Belinda. "You have been kind to me."

"Not as kind as I might have been," said Chloe. She added, "Unless you intend to go back to live with your parents, Belinda, you'd do best to go away from here."

Belinda looked out of the window. It was not a pretty day, for the sun was hidden behind a cloudy sky. Wind tossed the trees and flicked up rough waves on the water.

"I suppose I would," Belinda said. "For Dorinda's sake." She looked at Chloe and smiled, perhaps the most open, friendly smile she had ever directed at her. "I must feed her now. That's the way it is with a child. One thing after another."

Chloe watched her go, then went to the window and stared at the rough, grey sea. It looked cold and unforgiving. Like a bad name once earned.

14

AFTER THE STUDY had been searched, and Randal and Macy had gone away, Justin took out the letter and forced himself to read it again. It disgusted him.

It was the sort of letter he might write himself to Chloe, if they were apart.

He wanted to tear Claude limb from limb. He wanted to destroy all Randal's cool, seductive beauty. He wanted to strangle Chloe with his bare hands. . . .

She had denied all knowledge of it.

Who would put such a thing in her desk, though, and for what reason?

He knew he should be thinking about the missing list, making further plans to find it, but all he could think of was Chloe. If he did not go to her soon and apologise, wipe out all trace of doubt and suspicion, he would lose her.

He couldn't lose her. Yet he couldn't eradicate all doubt either.

Perhaps there had been lovers. It would not be so surprising with Stephen such a neglectful husband. With bitter humour, Justin allowed that in some circles, only two lovers would be considered moderate. He could surely forgive her that. After all, it must all be in the past.

He remembered her in Randal's arms. Perhaps she *had* treasured that disgusting letter. No, she had simply forgotten about it.

The thought could not be strangled. Perhaps her current

lover, Claude, was a French spy. Chloe could have struck
Budsworth this morning, then secreted the potato somewhere. Soon she would be away with it to join him.

Justin discovered he had the letter compressed into a
pellet in his hand, and smoothed it out again. For no good
reason, he felt he should preserve it.

He groaned and pounded the desk with his fist. The
truth was, he didn't care how many lovers she had taken
to her bed, or if she was a traitor. He didn't care if her
work led to a thousand deaths. He wanted her with a flaming passion all the greater for having been smothered so
many years.

With heavy effort, duty rose to take control. If she had
the package, he must find a way to get it from her. Then
he would do his best to save her from the consequences of
her actions. Perhaps then he could begin again to try to
win her love.

He struggled to make intelligent plans but found his
brain unable to cooperate. With a sigh, he tucked the letter
and the handkerchief back in his pocket and went to change
for dinner, steeling himself to act as if none of these revelations had ever occurred.

He met Randal coming away from the library.

"I assume, by the way," said his friend lightly, "that I
am off Macy-guarding duty?"

"Of course," said Justin. The effort to speak normally
was excruciating. "I don't know what to do next."

He must not be a very good actor. He could see Randal,
as if through glass, looking at him with a frown.

"You could talk it over with Chloe," suggested Randal
meaningfully.

They said Randal tired rapidly of his conquests. Was he
trying to palm off his unwanted mistress on his friend?
Justin knew one of his hands was a fist, and kept it out of
sight.

"I don't think so."

Randal studied him with apparent concern. "I'm doubtless meddling again, but you didn't do anything silly, like try to drag her to your bed, did you?''

Justin felt sick. Was he going to receive a lesson on how to handle his beloved? "Under the watchful eyes of Margaret?'' he queried.

Randal shrugged. "Oh well." With that, he ran lightly upstairs.

Justin watched coldly. Such easy charm. Such a perfect body. If Justin had a pistol in his hand, he might very well have fired it—destroyed the man and removed him from Chloe's orbit forever.

In a moment, the madness passed, leaving a sour miasma to disgust him. It was only a handkerchief. Anyone could have put it there. Anyone could have written that letter. He had to trust them both. It was that or go mad. It occurred to him that next time he saw *Othello* performed, he would have much more sympathy for the vengeful Moor.

Justin climbed the stairs slowly, feeling old and unbearably tired.

Chloe was tidying her hair in a dispirited fashion when there was a knock at her door. She opened it to find Randal. He was inside before she could object.

"Randal. The last thing I need now is for anyone to find *you* here!''

"Anyone being Justin?'' he queried lightly, picking up a spray of pink silk roses from her dressing table and turning them in his fingers.

"Anyone,'' she repeated stonily.

Oh God, if Justin finds you here, she thought, it will confirm all his suspicions. And I mustn't let you know what he suspects, or you'll probably blow his head off.

Randal eyed her thoughtfully. "You never used to be so missish. What did he find? Love letters?''

Chloe could feel her face burn. Randal's eyes opened wide with surprise. "Don't tell me you *did* have a lover? God Almighty. I never suspected a thing.''

"Of course I didn't," she said sharply. "And keep your voice down, for heaven's sake."

"But he found letters?" He read the answer on her face. "Even if it wasn't a full-blown affair, it was damned indiscreet to leave letters lying around, coz."

"I did *not* have an affair," said Chloe precisely. "I did *not* have any love letters. When I come to think of it, I have never had any love letters." It suddenly seemed a matter worthy of tears. "There was no time to receive any from Stephen before we eloped," she mused sadly, "and he was hardly one for writing them when we were apart." She dragged herself back from the brink of being maudlin. "Be that as it may, someone planted a disgusting epistle in my drawer, and Justin Delamere believed every oozing French word of it!"

"French?"

"Very. Some little worm named Claude."

"Spicy, I gather," said Randal, eyes bright with amused interest.

Chloe turned away. "If you like that sort of thing," she said.

"Well I do, as it happens. Writing them is one of my *fortés.*" When she spun around suspiciously, he said quickly, "But I didn't write this one. Honour of an Ashby."

Chloe blinked back tears. "Who did, Randal? I can never forgive Justin for his suspicions—you realise he thinks I'm a spy now, working for the despicable Claude—but if I find out who did it, there would be some satisfaction."

Randal had sobered. "Shall I kill him for you?"

"No!"

"One less Frenchman. What's the difference?"

"I thought you meant Justin," Chloe said. "Claude is surely an invention."

"Then perhaps I should remove the inventor from this earth."

Chloe found the notion surprisingly acceptable and told

him so. "First, however, we have to find out who he, or she, is."

"Who can write in French?" Randal asked practically.

Chloe considered the matter. "Myself. You and Justin, I suppose. The Duchess is very fluent, having spent a lot of time in Paris before the Revolution. Macy will be able to, I'm sure, but I don't know about the Dowager, Miss Forbes, or Belinda."

"Belinda went to a good school, I understand. They'd teach her French, wouldn't they?"

"I would think so. The same thing doubtless applies to the other two." Despite that, she knew where her suspicions had landed. "Why would Belinda do such a thing?" she asked, hurt to think the girl should be so malicious.

"If she's up to her neck in treason, she'd do anything to escape the consequences. Perhaps *she* has a French lover named Claude."

Chloe shook her head. "No. She truly loved Frank, for all she wouldn't marry him, I think because it would injure Dorinda's chances. I believe she sacrificed herself for the sake of the child."

Randal was unmoved. "Sacrificed Frank as well, by the looks of it. Even if she didn't push him off the cliff, there has to be a connection between their love affair and his death."

"You're doubtless correct. And I think there has to be a connection between that dratted list and Belinda." Chloe had a sudden thought. "Randal, did anyone find out exactly how Budsworth was injured?"

"He was hit on the head with a rock, I think. There was one there with blood on it. Large enough to fit into a hand. Quite smooth."

"But he could have been hit with a stick, a frying pan, anything."

Randal looked at her with a puzzled frown. "What are you saying? The cook went demented and clonked him?"

"No," said Chloe, feeling the excitement of clarity. "But it could have been anything, yet Belinda specifically talked about him being hit on the head with a rock. She never came close enough to see the rock you saw.''

"So she must have done it? You'd better tell Justin.''

Chloe felt the heavy misery fall back upon her. "You tell him if you want.''

"And what about Belinda?''

"We've searched the place. If she's hidden the potato, she's been careful. I don't know if it was wise or not, but I told her what the package we're looking for is, how important it is. I'm sure, if she knows anything, she will come forward with the information.''

"Very well." He went towards the door. "Any chance of me making you see sense?'' he asked gently. "You can't exactly blame a man for being upset at finding erotic letters in his lady's possession.''

Chloe raised her chin. "I see everything all too well," she said. Randal just shook his head.

As Randal walked out of the door, Justin was in the corridor. It was as if a flame burned in his eyes. Randal felt the hair rise on his neck in response to the challenge, but Justin said nothing, just turned to go downstairs.

Randal whistled quietly and went off to change. Justin's suspicions had obviously spilled over onto all mankind. He'd be lucky to leave here with his skin, much less his friendship, intact.

Chloe was dismayed to find the whole household down to dinner that evening. She felt unable to handle the Dowager at the moment and raised her eyebrows at Miss Forbes, who slipped over.

"She would come, Lady Stephen. I tried to dissuade her, for she is a little disturbed, but she became most upset. I will see to her.''

Chloe nodded. Her mother-in-law was wearing one of her more recent gowns in grey and blue cambric. With a small, lacy cap on her greying curls, she looked quite decorous. She was staring into the fire and muttering to herself.

Chloe went to sit safely by her grandmother.

"Well," said that old lady. "Fascinating business, watching a kitchen being turned out. You'd be amazed at what they have there, my dear. Thank the Lord no one has ever asked me to cook anything, for I wouldn't know where to start."

"But no unusual potatoes."

"Not a one. I had a most interesting lecture, however, on the types of potato. Never realised there were so many, and all used for different things. Fascinating."

Chloe smiled. The Duchess had that effect on her. "I daresay you'll be poking around in the kitchens at the Towers when we go there."

"What?" exclaimed the Duchess. "Invade Monsieur Fraquette's preserve? He'd resign on the spot. He's had offers from most of the people in England rich enough to afford him." She looked at her granddaughter shrewdly. "Now that I've got you to smile, tell me what occurred this afternoon."

"Belinda's letter?" said Chloe, deliberately evading the issue.

"No. I got all that from Randal. Probably perfectly true. George wouldn't be the only man in England to be tricked into marriage. In fact, you'd think just about anyone could do it, once that bumpkin was worth the effort."

"But I still don't see why Belinda would think it worth the effort. I don't believe she's so mercenary."

The old lady's eyes were shrewd. "No, but perhaps Frank was."

Chloe looked at her with sudden understanding. "Frank *made* her? And she did it because she loved him." She thought it through and it began to make sense. "It was clear George would not live very long, and once she had her jointure . . . But by then she had Dorinda, and as she said, she couldn't give Dorinda a father like Frank Halliwell. Do you know, I think Dorinda must be George's daughter, after all."

Chloe looked over at Belinda with understanding and tremendous sympathy.

"Now," said her grandmother. "About that other letter."

Chloe was mutinously silent.

"The upstairs maid has it Justin found a letter in your desk and, so the story goes, 'came over all queer.' "

"I am not going to talk about it," said Chloe with icy clarity. "Not here. Not now. But it is even more urgent that we leave. I want to leave tomorrow."

"I'll get the rheumatics again," said the old lady calmly.

"What?" Chloe stared at her. "It was all a put-on?"

"Well, at my age, a twinge or two is unavoidable, but I thought I'd better make an excuse in case you panicked. I gave that foul-smelling embrocation to the Dowager. Now she has two pots of it. No wonder Belinda has such a reputation as a healer if she always makes stuff like that. Anyone'd get better to avoid it."

"Grandmama," said Chloe forcefully, "did you hear what I said? I want to leave tomorrow!"

"Tuesday," said the Duchess implacably. "Randal!" she called, summoning her grandson. He came over and the old lady said, "Save me from this blasted wench. *You* don't want to leave tomorrow, do you?"

"Well," he said, with a glance at Justin. "It depends a bit upon the temperature. But assuming it warms a little, I wouldn't mind staying another week or two."

"Getting delicate, are you?" said the Duchess with surprise. "You young people. No stamina."

Chloe's gaze had followed Randal's to Justin. He looked up. She saw the pain in his eyes, and the unwilling suspicion.

She couldn't endure it. The lighthearted banter of the Duchess and Randal was like an abrasion on her nerves. Chloe stood and walked over to the window, drawing the velvet curtains back a little to look out at the bay. The moon rode high, nearly full, and the rippling waves were silver against the deep.

Someone walked up beside her, and she knew by a shiver of awareness it was Justin. They stood in silence, and a great urge came over her to lean her head upon his shoulder and weep.

"I don't *want* to believe it," he said at last, softly.

What could she say to that? A cloud passed over the moon, and all the dancing lights on the tips of the waves were extinguished. She dropped the curtain and turned to him.

"But do you?"

He looked at her, his brown eyes full of pain. "You are so beautiful, and Stephen neglected you. It would not be surprising if you had lovers."

"I have no morals?"

"Some people would not consider it immoral."

Chloe fought a shocking urge to violence. She found she would like to score his sun-browned cheek with her nails, like a cat. "I have no loyalty, then, to my country and my king?" she asked desperately.

He hesitated just a moment too long, then said, "I know you would never intentionally do anything against your country."

Chloe felt a bitterness well up which threatened to choke her. "You think I am merely a fool then," she said with brittle flippancy. "You are well rid of me, aren't you? And look, there's Matthew, come to announce the meal. By all means, let us go and feast!"

Justin watched her walk away, sweetly beautiful in soft creamy white sprigged with pink roses, dark curls nestled at the nape of her long, slender neck. Above the neckline of her gown he could see the beginning of the delicate hollow of her spine.

Why, he wondered with despair, could he not simply have said the words he had intended to say. "That letter is nonsense. It has nothing to do with you. And as for Randal, you are close but not lovers." Instead, he had found himself unable to lie to her, and now he had surely lost her forever.

And worse still, he had hurt her terribly.

Chloe was suffering the beginnings of a headache by the time she sat down to dinner. She longed only to retreat to her room at the earliest opportunity, and not emerge until Tuesday. Perhaps *she* would develop the rheumatics.

The conversation was desultory. Only Macy and Randal made any real effort to do their social duty.

"Well," said Mr. Macy at one point. "Treasure hunt enliven your stay, Ashby?"

Randal smiled slightly. "Turned up a thing or two, I'd say."

"But no missing will. Knew it all along. Legal men satisfied, Stanforth?"

"I'm sure they will be," Justin said flatly.

"When I was a girl, at Musterleigh," said the Dowager Lady Stanforth in stately tones, "we often had treasure hunts. My brother Arnold was very ingenious."

She sounded so normal, Chloe ventured a question. "In what way, Mama?"

The Dowager seemed to be looking back through the years. "He hid my new satin slippers in the curtains. Pinned them in the middle. I didn't find them for three days."

This was such a rational conversation, Chloe really thought she should continue it, but with her headache and general malaise, she simply couldn't. She looked urgently at Miss Forbes, and that lady began to chat amiably to her charge, not minding if the Dowager suddenly wandered off the subject, or forgot entirely what was going on.

"King's in a very bad way," said Mr. Macy, seemingly out of the blue, but everyone could follow his train of thought. The King was reputed to be slipping back into madness. The company discussed the likelihood of the Regency finally coming into effect, and the desirability of it. Macy, a friend of the Prince's, was all for it. The Duchess was far less so.

"George III has been a good king," she said firmly. "God willing, his doctors may still bring him back."

Macy shook his head. "Not this time, Your Grace. Not this time. His daughter's illness had been the final blow. When the poor Princess Amelia dies—and it cannot be long now—the worst is feared."

"I must thank you for the *potpourri*, Miss Massinger," said the Dowager, as if unaware of any other conversation.

"It is no trouble, Lady Stanforth," said Belinda comfortably.

"Oh, but it must be a great deal of work," said the older lady as she pushed pork and boiled potatoes around her plate. She seemed to have forgotten what to do with them. "So clever the way you mix it. I only ever used to use roses. . . . What was the name of that rose? Oh dear, my poor memory. Dear Henry planted it, especially for me. . . ."

She sat, frowning, wandering through the wasteland of her memory.

The Duchess spoke up to fill the silence. "I have a lovely wall of red roses at the Towers. When we were married, the Duke had his gardener create a new one for me called Lady Beth. It took years to produce just the bloom he wanted, and dear Clarence did not want it ever to grow anywhere other than at the Towers. He was, I'm afraid, a very possessive man. Since he died, I have given cuttings away quite frequently, whenever I encounter another Elizabeth whom I like. You should plant something, Chloe. There is a satisfaction in seeing a growing thing for which you are responsible."

"Surely that is what children are, Grandmama," said Chloe dully. She would doubtless never have children now. Having lost Justin, she would never marry.

"Plants are a great deal more reliable," said the old lady tartly, and Belinda laughed.

"They are also more controllable," the young woman said with unusual dryness.

"Devoniensis!" exploded the Dowager triumphantly. "A beautiful perfume, and quite unmistakable. You have it in the *potpourri* you brought to my room today, girl. Devoniensis. So clever. The blend you use is most unusual. You must tell me sometime why you include what you do. . . ." Her voice trailed into uncertainty and she looked around. "Vegetables," she said.

Chloe wondered if the Dowager thought she was sitting at table with a group of elegantly dressed cabbages. She looked meaningfully at Miss Forbes.

"Did you want more beans, Sophronia?" asked that lady anxiously.

"Beans?" The Dowager studied the long slivers of scarlet runners. "You wouldn't think they'd have a perfume, now would you?"

"They taste very good," said the companion desperately.

The Dowager looked at Miss Forbes. "What has that to do with it?" The old lady peered around the table. Chloe saw, with a pang, the remnants of the Dowager's normal self realise she wasn't being rational, that she was talking nonsense. Her mother-in-law stood with a sigh. "I am afraid I feel very tired," she said with dignity. "I will take dessert in my room."

It was a creditable exit, except for her voice floating back. "Did the King leave, Amy? I didn't notice. . . ."

Randal moved adroitly to fill the silence. "Did you hear about the time old Grivenham fell asleep in front of the Prince. . . ."

When the ladies retired, Chloe thought to escape, but the Duchess took hold of her arm. "Oh no you don't," she said. "Ashbys never run."

"Grandmama, I have a headache."

"Play some Bach. It'll do you more good than a powder."

So Chloe sat at the pianoforte and desperately played

Bach, while the Duchess and Belinda sipped tea and conversed. Since discovering Belinda's ability at cards, the Duchess had been more kindly disposed to the young woman.

Playing familiar pieces gave Chloe time to think. She shied away from thinking about Justin. She knew she should work on the puzzle of the missing papers, but it all seemed unimportant now.

She let her fingers trail to a stop, and no one seemed to notice. She found she was resting her aching head on her hand. This was ridiculous. Then she heard the approach of the gentlemen. No. She wouldn't. Her grandmother could go to hell.

She stood sharply. "You must excuse me," she said. "I am not well."

She reached the door just as Justin opened it. She sailed through without a word, the gentlemen parting before her. She thought she might have heard his voice saying her name, but if so, she ignored it.

15

IN HER BED, the headache was no better, but she had a feeling of security, and time for thought.

It would appear she could never hope to gain a reputation for integrity. Even the man who claimed to love her thought her either wicked or foolish. She found she had the sheets clenched tight in her hands. God damn him for not having faith in her.

Now, however, with a cooler head she could see it was jealousy which tormented him. She knew there could have been a profusion of evidence of treason all around her room, and he would have laughed it off. It was the evidence of her having loved other men which had driven him insane. "Jealousy is the greatest of all evils." Who had said that? La Rochefoucauld. But then the local people had a saying, "There's no love without jealousy."

How would she have felt if she had found a perfumed letter treasured in his room? She imagined it. *"I long for you, my darling Justin, for your kisses and the murmur of your beloved voice in the night, for your hand in mine and the feel of you . . ."* She broke off what she realised was a letter composed from her own desires.

How would she have felt if she had found him in Belinda's arms, no matter how innocent it all appeared?

Chloe suddenly realised how much she loved Justin. How right he had been to be irritated with her for pretending it was all academic—a matter to be considered and contemplated—when such a flame was burning between them. With disgust at her own stupidity and complacency, she realised she had been playing like a child secure in the knowledge of a parent's love. Now that his love had gone, she realised how much she valued it.

Had it gone? Not completely, but it was dreadfully strained. What should she do?

The only thing which would mend matters would be to find those papers and discover who had put the letter and the handkerchief in her room. Their only purpose, she now saw, was to distract herself and Justin so the villain would have time to find the papers without competition. Her headache fled, and her mind felt clear as crystal.

Probably the culprit hoped Justin would actually fight Randal over the handkerchief. That whole brouhaha would have kept everyone busy for days. Even now, she knew, Justin wasn't putting his mind to the problem.

Who could have authored such a plan? Belinda? Matthew? Could he write French? Macy? Miss Forbes?

Chloe was suddenly distracted by curiosity as to what was going on right now. She had heard Belinda come up a little while ago. It was likely that the Duchess had retired. If the men were still downstairs, would Randal and Justin end up in a fight? Justin was mad with jealousy, and, though Randal had a cool head, if he realised just how deep and unpleasant Justin's suspicions were, he might well lose control of himself. She imagined them even now in the garden, facing each other over long lethal pistols. Randal was a dead shot. She'd seen him shoot the flame off a candle without touching the wax.

She was out of bed, struggling into her robe, and halfway down the stairs before she thought how peculiar this was going to look. She froze at the sound of voices. Then relaxed.

Laughter from the billiard room. She heard Randal's voice and Macy's. They sounded on the go.

". . . her garter round the statue's neck!"

Laughter. "Reminds me of the time the Duchess of Glenatherton fell off her horse . . ."

Chloe retreated rapidly. Was Justin taking part in that

carouse? She doubted it, but had no intention of going in search of him. As long as he wasn't baiting Randal, it could wait until the morning.

Compared to her precipitate travels down the stairs, she crept back up them like the most cautious thief. She was terrified that at any moment Justin might appear and put the worst possible interpretation to her midnight wanderings.

Once safe again in her room, she sighed with relief. Why had she ever thought she wanted an adventurous life? This business was likely to drive her mad. The thought of tranquil, predictable days was as sweet as cool water in the summer.

She slipped with a sigh back into her bed, still pleasantly warm from before. Her mind seemed less tangled now. She tried to consider again who might be the French agent in the house and how to catch him, or her. Gradually, however, tiredness began to drift over her. She wasn't sure whether she had slept or not, when a sudden notion popped into her head and jerked her fully awake.

Vegetables? In *potpourri?*

The Dowager's wanderings often made sense. Had the older lady discovered a vegetable in her *potpourri?* She tried to recollect exactly what the Dowager had said. She'd talked of Belinda's unusual mix, then mentioned vegetables . . . then something about perfumed beans. . . .

Sitting straight up in bed, Chloe thought furiously. No one could get a potato in the *potpourri* jar. On the other hand, it was a very strange design. Perhaps there was a way of removing that wire grid, after all. Would anyone else be made curious by the Dowager's words?

She would be unable to sleep until she had investigated the possibility. She leapt out of bed.

Her fire was out, and the room pitch dark. Chloe drew the curtains back, but the moon was clouded over and only the faintest light entered. Her eyes were accustomed to the gloom, however, and she could make out shapes. There was no need to light a candle. She knew the house perfectly and there was always a night lamp in the corridor.

After the day's events, Chloe did not want to be discovered creeping around the house so late.

Carefully, she eased open her door and slipped out into the passage.

Justin heard a noise. It was faint, possibly the natural sound of an old house settling in the cool of the night.

He had been unable to sleep. The disastrous outcome of the search haunted his mind. He had considered a hundred alternative ways of handling it, from laughing the whole thing off, to murdering both Randal and Chloe.

He had undressed, but made no attempt to go to bed. In his loose banjan, he sat by the window and suffered. Beneath his conscious attempts to think through the situation, he was aware of lurking suspicion. Why had Randal been in Chloe's room? Had they been plotting together? Would they attempt a tryst tonight? It would hardly be discreet, but desire could overwhelm common sense. Justin knew that only too well.

Almost against his will, he was on his feet and moving quietly to the door. In his hand, he held the pistol he had prepared and laid on his dressing table. The click as he cocked it seemed to echo through the house.

If anyone was creeping around Delamere tonight, surely it was his duty to investigate.

As Chloe opened her door, she stopped, disconcerted. It was pitch dark. The corridor lamp had gone out.

Still, she knew the place well. It was only a matter of going down the passage to the end, where the Dowager's rooms were located. There were two right-angled bends as the passage worked around the stairs opposite the master suite, but she would expect those. She knew the placement of each of the four chairs and two tables which lined the passage.

She began to walk forward. It was disconcerting to step into the black even when she knew what to expect.

She heard a noise and froze. A mouse? No. A sharp sound,

as if someone had knocked against one of the chairs. She almost called out, then realised the other person could be the villain, on exactly the same mission as herself.

What should she do?

She should get help. Justin's door was to her left, not very far ahead.

No. Impossible. With things as they were, she simply couldn't creep into Justin's room at night.

Randal's room was a little farther down. She shuddered. That option was even worse.

Curse the events of the day which had led to her being unable to call upon help without scurrilous doubts. Nonetheless, she would press on. It was not so large a house, after all. If she found there really was evil afoot, she would scream and all her gallant swains could come running.

There had been no other sound, but now she found herself stretching her senses for any hint of movement. Had she imagined it? Could she herself be heard? Her soft leather slippers made no sound on the carpet, but her silk robe brushed against the floor. She gathered it up around her.

At the head of the stairs there was the faintest trace of light from windows on the lower floor. It only illuminated shades of grey but was a relief. Chloe thought of going back to her room for a candle after all, but she hoped the other person, if there was one, was unaware of her presence. She wanted to catch the villain red-handed.

She came to the place where the corridor turned back. Randal's door must be to her left. She again considered seeking his help. But, apart from other considerations, if she opened the door and spoke to him, she would surely be heard by anyone else around.

She wasn't, however, looking forward to rounding the corner into the stygian dark again.

Resolutely she crept around.

Something touched her, fumbled. A hand grabbed her arm.

"A sound and you're dead." The voice was a murmur.

Shocked, Chloe hesitated for a fatal moment. An arm came around her throat and something cold touched her there. She felt as if she'd stopped breathing, then a small squeal escaped her as the edge of a knife scraped against her skin.

The arm jerked her. "Quiet! I have a blade at your throat and I will use it if I have to."

The voice was still a murmur, but Chloe recognised it and the portly body pressed against her back. Macy! Though she had put him on her list of suspects, she could hardly believe it. Humphrey Macy, man about town, intimate of the Prince of Wales, a spy? A desperate spy, she realised with terror.

He must know she would recognise him. Her life was not worth a farthing. She could not help but tremble as she waited for the cut of the knife which would end everything.

"Don't be afraid," he said softly by her ear. "I won't hurt you." She didn't believe him. "I need those papers and we both know where they are, don't we?"

Terror was threatening to deprive her of her wits, but she fought against it. If he did not kill her here and now, there was a chance. Strangely, it was the thought of Justin's grief at her death which was her strongest motivation to survive.

"Yes," she choked out.

She had hoped to make the sound louder, in the hope someone might hear, but fear tightened her vocal cords. Had she heard a sound somewhere in the corridor? Was help at hand? Macy's breathing in her ear and the terrified pounding of her own heart shut off all other sound.

"Sensible, my beauty." Macy spoke directly into her ear. "Are you not a little disappointed at your lover? I expected more from that letter and that handkerchief. If he really cared he would have killed Ashby."

She had been correct in her suspicions. The thought of the pain he had caused strengthened Chloe's nerve. She remained very still, waiting for a chance to escape.

"Ah well," said Macy, when she wouldn't react to his tauntings, "let us go forward slowly. You will take me straight to the Dowager's *potpourri*. Once I have destroyed what is there, you have nothing to fear.''

Does he believe I am stupid? Chloe thought as they inched awkwardly forward. He cannot let me live.

He also had no intention of letting her escape. He was half a foot taller than she, and he kept one hand tight on her upper arm. The other held the knife pressed to her throat. She felt it at every move, scraping against her skin. When she stopped so as not to collide with a heavy oak chair which stood near the Dowager's door, she felt a sting and then blood running down her skin. She couldn't hold back the gasp of fright.

''Did I nick you?'' he said without concern. ''Don't worry. It's no worse than a man cutting himself when shaving. That's what you've got against your delicate throat, my pretty. My razor. If I cut your throat, you'll know the difference.''

They had arrived at th Dowager's rooms. Surely, Chloe thought, she heard voices somewhere behind them. Who was still awake? How could she alert them?

''Why?'' she whispered, as loud as she dared. ''Why are you a traitor?''

''No noise!'' he said sharply, but always in that quiet murmur which would not carry. ''I am no traitor,'' he added, and Chloe could hear the desperate need to excuse what he had done. ''The petty information I give the French makes no difference to anything, but it pays me well. It's not cheap, being the Prince's friend. What is the layout of the Dowager's rooms?''

Chloe thought of lying, but could see no benefit in it. ''The door on the left opens into her *boudoir*. The door on the right into her bedroom. There is an adjoining door.''

''What about the companion?''

''She has a small room off the Dowager's bedroom.''

''Where is the *potpourri?*''

''I don't know—'' Chloe gasped as his hand tightened viciously on her arm.

"Don't lie. I'm no fool."

"She moves it around," Chloe lied. Then she had an idea. "It is usually on her dressing table."

He pushed her forward. "Open the *boudoir* door, quietly."

Chloe wished Delamere were less well maintained, for Miss Forbes had often complained of being a light sleeper. Chloe longed for a creaking floorboard or a squealing hinge. The turning of the knob caused only the faintest click, however, and the door swung wide without the tiniest squeak.

They walked forward a few steps, and he turned her back. "Now close it," he said.

When she had done so, she felt him relax slightly. "Good girl. If I'd known you were so sweet and docile, my dear, I'd have courted you myself." Something in his voice made Chloe feel sick. She gave thanks that he was too involved in saving his neck to pursue any other matters.

"I think we'll open the curtains," he said, allowing his voice to grow a little louder now that they were in a room. "There may be a trace of light."

He gave her no chance to escape, however. They accomplished the maneuvre without the blade ever leaving her throat. The heavy brocade curtains made a noticeable swish when she drew them back, but surely not enough to waken someone two rooms away.

Dawn was approaching and grey light trickled into the room, still giving only the hint of detail. For Chloe, who knew the room well, it was enough. For Macy, she hoped it would not be.

"Find the jar," he said curtly, and she felt a tremor in his hand. He too must be terrified, she realised. His name and his life were on the line, and she hardly thought he was accustomed to this sort of brutality. She hoped it would confuse him a little. To assist the process she affected even more terror than she felt.

"I will. I will. Please don't hurt me!"

"Keep your voice down! Behave yourself, and I won't hurt you."

"The dressing table. It will be on the dressing table."
She pulled him forward and felt the blade move a little
away from her skin. He didn't want to kill her. Yet.

"You'll have to let go of my arm," she said, "if I'm to
search. I have to do it by feel."

He released his bruising grip, but before she could move,
his hand twisted in her hair. "No tricks," he snarled.

Chloe heard the desperation. At any moment he could
decide she had served her purpose, and the blade would
bite. . . .

She groped with trembling hands among the half-seen
shapes. She wondered what he would do if she sent one crash-
ing to the floor—kill her? She really thought he would.

Oh God, she didn't want to die before she had told
Justin she loved him.

Was that a sound? Was it Miss Forbes?

Chloe had found the two identical jars. She needed only
the slightest distraction . . .

"Hurry up," he said, giving her hair a vicious tug.
Chloe gasped and tears came to her eyes. Fear fled before
blinding fury.

"There are dozens of bottles here," she snapped, hardly
bothering to lower her voice. "Do *you* want to try to find it?"

He pressed the knife back hard against her throat, so
she had to retreat before it, retreat against his portly body.
"Watch your tongue! You certainly are hot to handle,
aren't you, pretty Chloe? It's time someone taught you
manners. Find the *potpourri,* and fast."

This time he kept the razor at her throat. She felt it cold
and sharp as she leant forward and she couldn't stop herself from shaking. She couldn't delay much longer either.
If no one came, she would have to act alone. She grasped
a tall, smooth jar. "This, I think . . . ," she said and
flipped the metal catches which held the stopper.

With a hasty prayer, she raised the jar and hurled the
contents over her right shoulder. The reek of camphor and
turpentine filled the air. Macy howled. The knife jerked.
Chloe twisted out of his slackened grasp.

Still, she felt the blade and the flow of blood.

The door burst open and light flooded the room. None of the lumbago embrocation had got in her eyes, but the fumes surrounded her. They made her eyes smart and burned at her throat. Chloe sank choking onto the carpet and pressed her hand to her neck, feeling the warm stickiness of blood. Was she going to die?

Macy was cursing. There was a thump and crash. Someone tripped over her and she rolled and gasped. The light, in someone's hand, wavered as gigantic shadows leapt around the room.

Perhaps she fainted. The next she knew, she was in powerful male arms—Justin's arms—remembering there was something important she had to tell him. She looked up at him, so handsome, with the strong bones of his face thrown into relief by the now-steady light. All his love and caring shone in his eyes. She really didn't want to die.

"I love you," she said hoarsely and coughed. "I'm sorry I wasted so much time."

He held her closer. "It was I who was in a rush, love. We have the rest of our lives."

Chloe was surprised he hadn't noticed. "Macy cut my throat," she said.

He grinned. She couldn't believe it.

"Believe me, darling," he said, "people with cut throats don't give deathbed speeches. Let me see." He took a cloth and gently dabbed at her neck. His lips tightened, but his voice was even as he said, "A nasty little cut but the bleeding's stopped. I've had as bad from a clumsy barber."

Feeling ridiculous, Chloe sat up straight and scowled at him. "That's what Macy said. How is he?"

Justin moved aside and she saw Humphrey Macy, under Randal's untender care, cursing as he tried to wash the Dowager's lumbago embrocation off his face. It was thick on his hair and dripping down, but little had got into his eyes.

More light entered the room, brought somewhat gingerly by Miss Forbes, in a voluminous grey robe and a plain, encompassing cap.

"Whatever has occurred?" she asked in a wavering voice. "I do hope you won't wake poor Sophronia."

Chloe looked at Justin. What could he say?

"Mr. Macy was sleepwalking," he explained with a perfectly straight face. "He had an accident with the lumbago mix."

Miss Forbes looked around at the four invaders in their nightwear, the razor on the floor, the spilled embrocation, and the blood on Chloe's robe.

"I do hope he won't be staying," she said faintly.

"I can assure you he won't," said Justin.

"Thank you," said Miss Forbes, and retreated with the air of a nun fleeing an orgy.

Justin helped Chloe to her feet and held her close. She rested against him in great contentment. "What will you do about him?" she asked.

"I don't know. Do I gather from this that you know where those papers are?"

Chloe nodded. "Don't you? It was the Dowager's rambling on about unusual *potpourri* mixes and vegetables."

She walked over to the mantelpiece and took down the *japonaise* jar. She shook it hard and heard a thunk which did not come from dried petals. "I confess, I still don't see how Belinda got it in here," she said, inspecting the wire cover again. It was completely immovable.

"I suggest we go and ask her," said Justin formidably. "Randal, can you guard Macy?"

"Of course," said Randal, who had a pistol in his hand. He grasped the man, whose eyes still teared badly, and pulled him up. "I will await further revelations in his room."

Justin and Chloe went out to Belinda's room and knocked at the door.

After a delay, it was opened carefully. "Chloe? Justin? What has happened?"

Chloe held up the jar. Belinda went very still, then

opened the door wider. "Come in. But please try not to wake Dorinda."

"The first thing," said Justin, "is for you to show us how to get the potato out of the *potpourri*."

Without protest, Belinda took the jar and set it on the table. She put her hands on either side and lifted, with a turning motion. The whole outside of the jar came off, wire top and all, showing a straight-sided, plain white inner container. Justin reached in and retrieved the potato. He passed it to Chloe.

She studied the cause of all the trouble. It was a wonderfully accurate representation, even down to the eyes, but her fingernail raised a thin curl of brown wax. Real earth still clung to it from its time underground.

"Why?" she asked Belinda.

The young woman turned away. "I haven't slept tonight, wondering what to do. I never knew that thing was important to the British. You must believe me. I thought whatever it was, it was on its way to the French. When you told me the truth, I knew I had to get it to someone. Tomorrow, I was going to retrieve it and send it to London, anonymously. I hoped that would be the end of it all."

Justin took the wax vegetable and studied it. "What was the *start* of it all, Belinda?" he asked quietly.

Belinda sat down with a sigh in the rocking chair where she had nursed her child. Chloe sat down too.

"The start?" asked Belinda. "When do things ever start? When Frank and I played on the sands together?" She sighed. "He was growing so impatient because we couldn't marry and I wouldn't . . ." Her hands fluttered and she looked down in embarrassment. "We heard the sailor give the package to George. The sailor said it was clear Lord Stanforth wasn't coming for it, and it was someone's idea of a joke. He said George was the only man at Delamere, he could handle the matter. Supposedly, he said, it was important to the French. When the sailor left, George just stood there, looking befuddled. Frank— he was very quick—went forward and sort of took over.

He took the potato and said he'd handle everything. I don't think he had a plan, but he saw a chance to make some money.''

"Then you caught up with the sailor on the way back," said Chloe.

"Yes. That wasn't planned, though. We spent a fair bit of time in our secret part of the stables, talking about things. I didn't want Frank to interfere in gentry matters, but he wouldn't be stopped. I was afraid we were dabbling in treason, but he persuaded me we were stopping something from getting to the French. That didn't seem too bad.''

Belinda sighed, doubtless reflecting on the results of that night's work. "We came upon the sailor near my home. He had been down sharing a pipe with the fishermen. Frank tried to get more information from the man, but couldn't.''

Chloe wondered if she realised Frank had probably killed Samuel Wright.

"I came up to the Hall the next afternoon," went on Belinda. "I wanted to talk to Frank. I was worried about what he had planned. I needed to be sure he had no notion of passing those papers to the French. His main idea seemed to be to get money from Mr. Stephen not to tell what he was up to. He was sure he was a spy. I was here when the news came about Mr. Stephen being dead, and Frank flew into a rage over it. He thought we'd lost our chance. Then he started to think of ways to get something out of George now he was the viscount. Frank was walking me down the drive when we came upon George in a state of confusion. He was upset by Stephen's death, but excited at the thought of being the viscount, and rich. He was just like a child. He got to worrying about the potato. He seemed to think he should have inherited the knowledge of what to do with it now he was Lord Stanforth. He wanted it back.''

Belinda leapt to her feet and twisted her hands. "I honestly don't know how it came about. Frank was talking about George paying for the potato, and George was saying he didn't see why he should. He could be very stubborn if he took an idea into his head. Then Frank said if George didn't pay, he'd tell the justice George was selling secrets to the French, and the sailor would back him up. It was all so stupid, but George believed it. Next, Frank was saying George should marry me and the potato would be my dowry. He sold me like a heifer on the hoof!'' All the pain of that betrayal echoed in her voice.

"Why didn't you refuse?" asked Justin quietly.

"I did at first," said Belinda dully. "But he sweet-talked me. He always could. He said George wouldn't live long, which was doubtless true. He said George wouldn't be . . . be able to perform his marital duties, which was not true." She looked fiercely at Chloe. "I was a virgin when I married, and Dorinda is George's true child."

Chloe nodded. "I know." The look in Belinda's eyes thanked her.

"Frank just terrified George into it, plain and simple. If George balked, Frank would paint an even more lurid picture of what would happen once he told his tale to the authorities. Drawing and quartering, beheading . . . George was like a child in many ways and he believed it . . .''

Justin spoke again. "What happened to the potato?"

"I kept it in a jar of *potpourri,*" said Belinda. "I wouldn't let Frank have it because I wasn't sure what he'd do. If George became rebellious, I'd show it to him. It terrified him." She covered her face with her hands. "Oh, I have felt so badly about what we did to that poor man."

"How did he die?" asked Justin quietly.

Belinda looked up. "Not by my hand!" she declared. "He wasn't well and he suffered a seizure."

"With Macy by his side," said Chloe thoughtfully.

"Yes," said Belinda.

"Macy is the spy who has been trying to retrieve those papers," said Chloe and Belinda gasped.

"I did wonder," she said. "It seemed so impossible but . . . George was really pleased and flattered when he first came to stay. I don't think they'd been the kind of friends Mr. Macy always made out, but George thought he was wonderful. After a while, though, he grew frightened of him. I think Mr. Macy was after George about the papers, but George was too terrified to tell him. He thought, you see, that Mr. Macy was a government man, and was sure he was going to drag him off to the gallows. He tried to get rid of him but Macy just stayed on and on.''

"I never realised," said Chloe with surprise.

"Mr. Macy acted well. He kept saying what good friends they were, what jolly times they were having, and as George didn't deny it outright, it seemed so. I think he frightened him to death."

Chloe imagined poor George, terrified of Frank and Belinda, and then harangued daily by a desperate Macy. How could she have been so unaware of what was going on beneath her nose? She had been mourning Stephen, in grief and guilt.

"When George died," said Justin, "why didn't you just destroy the potato?"

"Everything was so topsy-turvy," Belinda said, a faraway look in her eyes. "I was supposed to be free, then, with a rich widow's portion, ready to marry Frank. Instead, I was pregnant and might be carrying the next Lord Stanforth. I couldn't decide what to do, so I buried the potato along with the seed potatoes Budsworth was putting in. I wouldn't have minded that much if he'd found it. I just left it to fate."

"Why then did you attack him when he did find it?" asked Justin.

Belinda gasped and stared at him with wide, frightened eyes. "I can't deny it, can I? I wish I could, the poor man. The feel as that rock hit his head '. . ." She shuddered."Thank the Lord he's no worse for it. It was you, Chloe, saying how the smell of *potpourri* lingered. I wondered if the potato would smell of it. Everything was going worse and worse. There was Frank dead, and you suspecting me. Then Budsworth was digging the Brownell's Beauties.''

She looked at Chloe. "I'd been trying to get out to retrieve that potato for days. I knew where I'd put it—right at the edge near the path. I came upon Budsworth digging there, right at the spot. I prayed he wouldn't dig it up, but he did and something about it must have struck him as strange. He picked it up and looked at it. I panicked. I couldn't seem to think straight at all. I could only think that if the potato smelled of *potpourri* everyone would know I had put it there. They would think I was in league with the French. The smell did linger too.''

She looked down at her hands, clasped tight in her lap. "I couldn't get a moment to myself to throw it into the sea as I'd intended. I went towards the sea and there you were, Chloe. I had to go back to the house and then the alarm was raised. I knew about the search. The potato mustn't be found in my room. If it was found smelling of *potpourri* it still would point to me unless I could make that seem reasonable. The only thing I could think of was to put it in the Dowager's *potpourri*. I hoped by the time it was discovered, anyone could have put it there, and that would account for the smell. It's all been so horrible, though, that I *wanted* you to find it this afternoon.''

Justin looked up at Belinda, and Chloe wondered what he was thinking. Surely he wouldn't hand her over to the authorities.

"How did Frank die, Belinda?" he asked.

Belinda's face tightened and aged. "He fell off the Head," she said, almost dreamily. "He still wanted to marry me, you see, but I couldn't. It wouldn't have been fair to Dorinda. I let him . . . I let him love me once. It seemed a terrible thing that we never had, but it was a mistake. It made him more desperate. He wasn't a bad man, Frank, but he didn't like to be thwarted. He went after Sally Kestwick, thinking I'd be jealous, but it didn't work. Next, he reckoned if he made me pregnant, I'd have to marry him, because he'd be the only one who would have me. He tried to force me. I pushed him away. He fell . . ."

The calm voice suddenly broke, and the girl bowed forward, shaken by racking sobs. Chloe went over and held her.

"The look in his eyes!" Belinda gasped and fell to weeping again.

Chloe looked over to Justin with appeal. He nodded slightly.

"Don't, Belinda," Chloe said softly after a little while. "Frank's gone now, and nothing will bring him back. You have to think of Dorinda."

Belinda fought her tears under control. "Yes."

"Justin will manage things so you are not blamed for any of this," she said. "Your greatest crime has always been to love too well."

Belinda looked up, red-eyed but somehow relieved of a burden. "I will leave here," she said.

"There is no need," said Justin, and Chloe loved him for it.

"Yes. I must leave if I'm to make a proper life for Dorinda, perhaps find her a worthy father. I kept thinking, you know, these past days, that if I were taken for treason, she would never live down the shame of it, Delamere or no Delamere."

Chloe threw open the curtains. The first dusky pink of dawn was lightening the sky. A few late birds were beginning to sing.

Justin stood and said, "You are a Delamere and so is Dorinda. You must never forget that." He went over and very gently kissed Belinda's cheek. A faint wail notified the world that Dorinda was awake and wanting attention. The sweet tyranny of child.

Belinda sadly smoothed her robe. "Thank you," she said.

16

CHLOE AND JUSTIN left the room and walked down the corridor. They needed to talk, and yet were still in their nightclothes. For the first time she looked at him, and admired his brown velvet banjan. She strongly suspected he was naked beneath it. Oh my.

"I will invite you into my room," she said at last, "if you promise to behave."

He grinned. "Would you care to define that more particularly?"

Chloe was blushing. She grasped her robe more tightly. "You know perfectly well what I mean."

He sighed. "Unfortunately, yes. You have my word. I will be a perfect gentleman."

They stood in her bedroom, separated by a yard or two. "Thank you for being so kind to Belinda," Chloe said.

He shook his head. "I may regret it later. It was a most affecting performance, but she did terrify poor George for the sake of her lover, and she pushed Frank off the Head, even under provocation. Not to mention poor Budsworth and the sailor."

"You never asked about Samuel Wright."

"I doubt she knew anything of that, though she may have some well-buried suspicions. I'd lay odds Frank killed him to protect the secret. I don't think I would have liked Frank Halliwell. I can't imagine why an intelligent young woman like Belinda allowed him to manipulate her."

"Some women love too well," Chloe said. "I would do as much for you."

He smiled and took a step closer. "And I would sell my soul to the devil for you," he responded quietly. "Have you forgiven me my stupid doubts?"

Chloe felt she would melt under the warmth of his gaze. At the same time, however, she was not disposed to succumb too easily with Belinda's example before her. "Well," she teased, "if you work very hard at it for the next forty years or more, I may forgive you in the end."

His eyes were passionate, his smiling mouth beautiful in the candlelight. "It really isn't fair, you know," he said softly, "to torment me when you have my word."

Heart trembling, Chloe smiled and released the tight grasp she had kept on her robe. It fell open at the front to show her demure cotton nightgown. She perched on the edge of her mattress, and leaned against the corner post at the foot of the bed. "One of the advantages of being a woman," she said softly. "One of the few advantages, I might point out, is that we don't have to play fair."

He came over to lean against the post and look down at her. "Would you care to tell me what game we're playing, my heart's desire, and what the rules are?"

She looked up, just a little nervously. The truth was, she wasn't sure. All the excitement seemed to have driven common sense out of her head. "A very inflammatory game?" she queried.

She could sense the passion in him, only barely under control, and her heart began a wild tempo. Was she really seeking to destroy his control? She realised she was. Having tasted the danger of losing him, she wanted to assure herself of her power over him . . .

He slowly reached down a hand, but it was only to grasp hers and pull her to her feet. She saw laughter spring to his eyes as he said, "You would be justly served if I were to let *my* garment fall open. Come."

With that he hauled her out of her room and down the corridor to Macy's.

Randal was sitting relaxed in a chair, with pistol in hand. Macy was still bathing his eyes.

"You could have blinded me," he spat at Chloe.

Then he sneered, and looked at her and Justin in so disgusting a way that she instinctively gathered her robe together again. "Excitement takes some women that way," he said with a nasty smirk.

Chloe felt Justin stiffen. Randal calmly raised his pistol, and Macy shut up.

"What do we do with him?" asked Randal, as one might talk of dirty laundry.

"An excellent question," said Justin, leading Chloe to a chair and seating her. "We should haul him before the authorities and let him hang. The trouble is, that would doubtless lead to a close scrutiny of events here, and that doesn't suit me."

Macy looked cautiously optimistic.

"You can't let him return to his activities," said Randal firmly.

Chloe realised with slight surprise that her cousin had for once taken a moral stance.

"Of course not. But once this list reaches London, I don't think Mr. Macy will want to be in England anyway."

The older man looked stunned. "But where can I go?" he bleated.

"To the devil if you wish," said Justin coldly. "I am going to put you on a boat to Ireland. After that it is up to you—Italy, perhaps, or the Americas."

A crafty look flickered in Macy's eyes and Chloe said, "He will try to convince the Prince of his innocence."

Justin shrugged. "Nothing we could say of events here would affect that. Even if he manages that feat, those in power will make sure he never has access to information of significance again."

Randal glanced down at his pistol. "Do you know," he said, "I have a marked disinclination to letting a man go free after he's betrayed his country and tried to carve up a member of my family.''

Chloe put a hand up to the wound on her neck. It still smarted. Justin laid a hand on her shoulder, promising love, and security, and tenderness.

"I like it even less than you," he said to Randal, "but I don't want his death here to raise too many questions." He looked at Macy, his eyes hard. "You might want to consider that aspect of the situation, however, if you are tempted to return to England. An excuse for a duel can always be found."

Humphrey Macy looked at the two young men and paled. "I never did any harm" he whined. "Useless, silly information. That's all I gave them."

He was still protesting when the three young people left the room and Justin locked the door.

Randal carefully uncocked his pistol. "You have the documents?"

Justin nodded. His arm had come around Chloe as if that were the only natural place for it to be.

"Should they go to London?" Chloe asked.

Justin frowned. "There is still some danger, you know. The French will have their eye on this place. I think Randal and I should ride to Lancaster and put the papers in the hands of the military."

Randal accepted this with enthusiasm. Justin looked down at Chloe. "If we are to make rational plans, we really must change. I don't know how it is, but the sight of you in the most diaphanous evening gown does not play havoc with my brain like you in two sturdy layers of nightwear."

Chloe knew she was pink again. She could say the same for his effect upon her, except that his daytime clothes were always solid and concealing, and it was constantly obvious to her that the silk lining of his long garment rested only on his skin.

"You have never seen me," she said lightly, "in my most diaphanous evening gown."

He smiled brilliantly. "Something I await with breathless anticipation."

Randal cleared his throat and, having got their attention, glanced down at his elegant robe of black brocade. "I am not so used to being ignored," he said.

Chloe smiled. "You look very nice, Randal," she said and he snorted. Justin burst out laughing.

"At any moment," he said, "Margaret will be up to light the fires. What she will think, I don't know."

"It will merely confirm her belief that we are run mad," said Chloe. "I just need to know how you two came so conveniently on the scene."

To her surprise, Justin did not immediately answer. "I will tell you, I think," he said cautiously, "when we are safely ensconced behind the breakfast table."

He dropped a quick kiss on her lips and disappeared into his room with amazing speed. Chloe looked at Randal with a raised brow. He kissed her too and slipped away, before she even had time to protest. Shaking her head, but feeling ridiculously happy, Chloe went off to dress.

Even though she'd had to wash blood and splashes of embrocation off her skin, she was downstairs too early. Matthew was only beginning to lay the places for breakfast. He looked at her in surprise and she realised the staff would not yet know of the night's events.

Matthew. She had forgotten all about him.

Taking the direct approach, Chloe said, "Did Mr. Macy pay you to keep an eye on Delamere, Matthew?"

He dropped a spoon and bent to retrieve it. When he emerged, he was still red-faced. "I don't know what you mean, Milady."

"He got you this place, didn't he? Why?"

"He knew I wanted a change, Milday."

"And why was that?"

Chloe decided she must be growing skilled as an interrogator for Matthew crumbled. "He knew I'd been dismissed from a place in London for stealing, Milady. I only ever did it once. He threatened to tell the Banhams, to set it up so I'd be caught again so as I'd hang for it. Said he wouldn't if I came here and kept an eye out. I was to send word if anything unusual occurred, and if a false apple were to turn up, I was to get hold of it if I could. It all sounded stupid to me, but I was in a state to begin with. Then it looked as if nothing would happen, and I came to like this place. I began to think he'd not done me such a bad turn.''

The thin-faced young man fiddled with the cutlery in his hand. ''Then people started poking around apples and I was worried. But again, nothing came of it. When Mr. Macy turned up again, I was in a fret because I didn't want to lose this place, especially not after meeting Sally. I suppose I'll have to go now you've found out what I've been up to.''

Chloe wondered if she should wait and consult with Justin, but poor Matthew was such small fry. ''No,'' she said, ''not if you've done no wrong. You've proved to be a good worker, and we can't break Sally Kestwick's heart, now can we?''

He looked up, blindingly grateful.

''Thank you, Milady. You'll never regret it.''

Chloe turned to wait for the meal in the Sea Room and then had a thought. ''You were to report to whom? Surely not all the way to London?''

''No, ma'am. To that Herr van Maes.''

Justin was right. The place was watched, and by the genial Dutchman. She waited anxiously to tell Justin what she had learned . . . and to be with him again.

She passed the time looking out at the birds flocking over the exposed mud, calling and squabbling over worms and crabs. Her thoughts, however, were turned inwards, on the matters interesting to lovers. The warmth of his smile, the scent of his skin, the feel of his hair . . .

The hall clock chimed the hour. People always said women took a long time to dress, and here she was while the gentlemen dallied. She realised they'd have to shave.

Randal's fairness had not shown a lot of beard, but Justin's chin had been decidedly dark. It was a warm intimacy to think of him, waking beside her, with the slight roughness of a beard on his chin. . . .

She thought of razors, and her hand went to the soreness of her neck. The skin was reddened where the blade had rubbed, but the cut was very shallow and healing well. Still, she had chosen to wear a high-necked gown. She did not want to remind Justin of how close she had been to death. A quarter inch, perhaps, to the jugular. That sort of notion could cloud a man's judgment.

He appeared in the room, shaved, groomed, and wonderful.

"Breakfast is ready," he said.

She walked over to him and placed her hand on his arm. They walked across the hall together but took seats opposite each other. Randal sauntered jauntily in, piled a plate high with food, and sat beside her.

Matthew was hovering, still looking pale. Justin told him to make himself scarce, and he looked relieved to do so.

Chloe informed them of what Matthew had said. "I told him he could stay," she admitted.

"Your word is law here, my love," said Justin with a smile which melted her bones. "Since we are letting two true villains go, it hardly seems right to wreak our vengeance on the little fish."

"What about the Dutchman?" Chloe asked.

Justin shrugged. "The same thing. Once he realises the game is up, he'll disappear. Just as long as he doesn't get wind of our success soon enough to make an attempt on the papers. Can we trust Matthew? There may be other French agents about."

Chloe looked at him, chilled by fear. Was it not over? "I am sure we can trust Matthew. He doesn't even know yet what was really going on, or that Macy has been caught."

Justin smiled reassuringly. "It is best if we move fast,

though. Macy can wait locked in his room. By the way, I put his man in there with him, with a tray of food. I suspect the valet is innocent, but there is no way to be sure. I don't want him raising an alarm just yet. Randal and I will ride to Lancaster after breakfast, then it will be over."

"I will come too," said Chloe decisively.

"No," responded Justin calmly.

"I will go mad sitting here worrying," she protested.

" 'They also serve who only stand and wait,' " he quoted. "I don't want to have to worry about you as well as the papers."

Chloe saw Randall was looking at the ceiling, pursing his lips as if silently whistling.

"You said," she pointed out to Justin, "that my word was law."

"Within the house," he reminded her, amiably firm. "Our little journey will take us out of it. I am not going to be a dictatorial husband, Chloe, but I can't let your whims interfere with the safety of the nation."

He was like a brick wall. Chloe stared, not sure if she liked this at all. "I haven't said yet that I'll marry you."

He grinned. "I'll tell the world you entertained me in your bedroom. Randal will force me to marry you."

Randal ceased his perusal of the plasterwork. "True enough."

Chloe looked at both of them with disfavour. "You still haven't told me how you came to interrupt Macy at his work."

Randal grinned. Justin looked less than comfortable, and didn't immediately answer.

Chloe looked at Randal, much easier to handle than Justin. "Well?" she demanded.

"He crept into my room," said Randal, "ready to murder me and . . . well, I'm not sure what he intended to do with you."

"With me? In your room?"

"In my bed."

Chloe turned stern eyes on Justin. He had a most uneasy expression.

"I heard someone in the corridor," he explained. "I opened my door, and I could smell your perfume. Then I heard a voice somewhere ahead. I just leapt to a conclusion. You and Randal. The only reason I didn't charge into Randal's room howling like a banshee was that I had some notion of preserving your reputation. As soon as I was in the room it was clear you weren't there. Randal woke and I had to confess the whole bloody stupidity. After he'd torn a strip or two off me, and I'd wallowed in guilt, we got around to thinking about where you had been going, and who you had been speaking to. When we got to the Dowager's room, we heard Macy howl. We burst in, and there you were."

Chloe looked at him thoughtfully. He was so uncomfortable about his suspicions that she wanted to hold him and tell him it didn't matter in the slightest. However, she was not sure it would be wise to let him off so easily, when he showed every sign of becoming a tyrant.

"I do hope you are not claiming to have rescued me," she said sweetly.

Justin looked taken aback, and then grinned. "I suppose you did rescue yourself, and fixed Macy nicely. I am sorry for doubting you for a moment, my dear. When we return from Lancaster, I'll spend the rest of my life proving just how highly I regard you."

"But you won't let me come with you," she said.

"No."

He and Randal rose to go. Chloe maintained an implacable silence until Justin turned at the door.

"God go with you," she said softly.

17

CHLOE SAT IN her sitting-room at Tyne Towers in Shropshire, and reread her latest love letter. Randal must have told him. Nearly every day of the four weeks since they'd parted, a letter had come for her. Some she had been able to share with her grandmother. Most she had not.

Today was her wedding day, and this was not a letter to show to anyone: *"The memory of your beauty is with me day and night, especially at night. I dream you are beside me and my hand is on your silken thigh . . ."*

She wished she had been able to write to him in the same vein, but it wasn't in her to do so. For a Scandalous Lady, she was rather shy. Her letters had been sweet and loving. She thought of the night ahead. Would her sweet loving be enough for the passion built over six long years?

He had wanted a quick wedding, but had accepted her need for a formal one. He had also wanted her to stay at Delamere, but had accepted the necessity of separation. Some kind of control in him had snapped and could not be made completely whole again.

The Duchess came in.

"Another one?" she queried. "Lord above, girl. I'm in favour of letter-writing but you two will wear out the mails."

"Not after today," said Chloe with a smile.

"True enough," said the Duchess. "Though it's no bad thing to write love letters even after you're married." A gently reminiscent smile made Chloe think the Duchess's correspondence would make interesting reading.

"Well," said the Duchess. "It's time you were preparing, unless you've changed your mind. You've done me out of seeing you take London by storm, so I'd be happy enough if you'd jilt the man and start again."

Chloe looked at the Duchess. "Truly?"

The Duchess laughed. "No, of course not. He's the man for you, my dear. Perhaps I'll live to see your daughter wreak havoc."

"I do hope so," said Chloe. "Meanwhile, however, I would point out that Randal does enough damage for three."

Chloe rose and rang her bell. Agnes came, accompanied by Chloe's two attendants—her only unmarried sister, shy Cressida, and pretty, vivacious Lady Sophie Kyle, whose flaming auburn hair and blue eyes seemed to sparkle as she darted about. She was the sister of Lord Wraybourne, one of the Duke of Tyne's closest aristocratic neighbours. Lady Sophie was sixteen to Cressida's twenty, and yet she seemed to have far more aplomb.

Soon Chloe was dressed in the pale pink gown she had chosen for her wedding. It was high at the neck, and long sleeved but made of layers of finest diaphanous silk gauze which floated gently as she moved. In her unbound hair, Agnes arranged matching silk roses as a tiara. A delicate necklace of rubies and diamonds glittered around her throat. Matching drops dangled from her earlobes. Justin's gift, matching the betrothal ring she wore on her hand.

She went down the stairs with her attendants and put on the warm cloak lined with chinchilla, which was Randal's outrageous bride-gift to her, especially outrageous in view of the note accompanying it: *"I recommend, sweet coz, that sometime you wear this, and nothing else, to bed."* Even now, Chloe knew she was blushing at the thought, and that part of the heat was anticipation, not embarrassment.

Accompanied by her dignified father and the two bridesmaids, she went out to the coach and off to her wedding.

It was a quiet affair, attended only by family and friends,
both by choice and because of the expected death of Princess Amelia. The latter had, as expected, plunged the King
into terminal madness.

Justin smiled as she walked down the aisle towards him.
He held out his hand and she placed hers within it. There
was no awkwardness or nervousness in either of them.
Everything was so completely right, she thought. Even
Stephen was doubtless approving.

Afterwards they rode back together to the Towers, but
not alone. The bridesmaids rode in the coach. Cressida
was tongue-tied as usual, but not Lady Sophie.

"A wedding, and to be out of school two weeks early
for Christmas! I can't believe what luck." She smiled at
Chloe. "I can't wait to be married myself. Sometimes it
seems I will be looked upon as a child forever. I intend
to have a Season as soon as may be, because then gentlemen will *have* to take me seriously."

Chloe saw Justin's lips twitch, and leant against his
shoulder. Sophie reminded her of herself six years ago,
but happier. The girl's father was dead, and Chloe had not
met her mother. Sophie's brother, however, the new Lord
Wraybourne, seemed to be an excellent guardian, loving
but firm. She doubted Lady Sophie would be tempted to
a runaway match. She would doubtless be a handful,
though, for some man some day.

"Do you have admirers yet, Lady Sophie?" asked Chloe
idly.

"Dozens," said the minx, probably truthfully. She was
very pretty. "But I have set my sights high. When I marry,
it will be to the most handsome, most marvellous man in
the world."

Chloe looked up at Justin. "He's already taken, Lady
Sophie," she said softly.

They had arrived at the Towers, and they climbed down.
Chloe was glad of her cloak, for a cold wind whipped

across the courtyard. She didn't care, however, about the season for her wedding. It was done, that was all.

She looked up at Justin and he smiled. His hands slid around her beneath the fur, and he drew her into his arms for a kiss of total passion. She felt his body against hers, and the warmth of his skin was a foil for the cold air. Knowing there were watching eyes, however, Chloe struggled free.

Justin released her and kissed her hand. "Tonight," he said meaningfully.

"In the Duchess's bedroom after dinner?" retorted Chloe with a wicked smile.

He laughed out loud and kissed her again, but quickly.

"Inflammatory games being the order of the day . . . or night," he added, then tore his gaze away. More carriages were pulling up to the Towers.

He looked around for their attendants, who were tactfully studying a stone griffin. Cressida's face was flaming red. Lady Sophie was merely amused. For a moment she looked older and wiser than she should be, but then she was all child again.

"Come along, do. It's freezing out here, and there's Monsieur Fraquette's special lemon tarts, Devonshire syllabub, and *puits d'amour* as well!"

Laughing, Chloe and Justin followed the young ladies into the warmth of the great house.

Author's Note

$\mathcal{T}$HE STANFORTH SECRETS is set in my corner of England—North Lancashire. I was born at home in a room overlooking Morecambe Bay, and grew up in the same house. Like Chloe in this book, I spent many hours watching the sea, the birds, and the ever-changing sky. This wasn't exactly the same view, however, for this book is set in the ancient village of Heysham (pronounced Heesham—the natives insist on it), a few miles down the coast from my hometown of Morecambe (pronounced Morcome).

In fact, Morecambe didn't exist in 1810. It was still the village of Poulton. It only grew, and received its name, during the holiday-making boom of the Victorian era. It is now a typical English seaside town, but a block from my old home there is Poulton Square, the old center of the village, which has on one side the New Inn dating back to the eighteenth century.

The historical details of Heysham are correct. There is a ruined chapel, said to have been built by St. Patrick, and a 1,200-year-old church—St. Peter's—which is still in use. The church is surrounded by a beautiful graveyard that overlooks the sea and a hogback stone was dug up there in 1800. When I was a child the stone was in the churchyard, and we children, knowing no reverence for antiquity, would sometimes climb on it. It was moved not long ago into the church for protection from the elements—and perhaps from little monsters.

Heysham is a charming and fascinating place. If you

find yourself in North Lancashire, perhaps on your way to the Lake District, do try to visit there.

Apart from Lord Liverpool and the Duke of York, the people who appear in the book, and the homes they live in, are totally my own invention. There never was a Delamere Hall or a Troughton House. Chloe and Justin, Randal and the Duchess and all the other characters live only in my imagination.

And now, I hope, in yours.

Jo Beverley
Ottawa, Canada

I hope you have enjoyed this book, and *Lord Wraybourne's Betrothed*, which preceded it. I welcome letters from my readers. Please write care of the publisher, Avon Books, and please enclose a self addressed stamped envelope is you would like to hear back from me.

Avon Romances—
the best in exceptional authors and unforgettable novels!

DEVIL'S MOON   Suzannah Davis
76127-0/$3.95 US/$4.95 Can

ROUGH AND TENDER   Selina MacPherson
76322-2/$3.95 US/$4.95 Can

CAPTIVE ROSE   Miriam Minger
76311-7/$3.95 US/$4.95 Can

RUGGED SPLENDOR   Robin Leigh
76318-4/$3.95 US/$4.95 Can

CHEROKEE NIGHTS   Genell Dellin
76014-2/$4.50 US/$5.50 Can

SCANDAL'S DARLING   Anne Caldwell
76110-6/$4.50 US/$5.50 Can

LAVENDER FLAME   Karen Stratford
76267-6/$4.50 US/$5.50 Can

FOOL FOR LOVE   DeLoras Scott
76342-7/$4.50 US/$5.50 Can

OUTLAW BRIDE   Katherine Compton
76411-3/$4.50 US/$5.50 Can

DEFIANT ANGEL   Stephanie Stevens
76449-0/$4.50 US/$5.50 Can